MW00440584

Turmoil

Descent into Madness

Chapter 1

Porth

     Stillness. His once flawless armor, now scratched and dented. Beautifully decorated silver that lined his armor now tarnished, the breastplate that once showed a fierce lion's head now covered with vicious claw marks. His fading brown hair blew gently in the wind, his right hand steadily gripped the hilt of his sheathed lightblade. He looked to his left, there stood Kionta. The struggles that led her to become a paladin are legendary, her voice was always calm and did not carry the rage that laid inside her. She held her halberd with an outstretched arm, the head matching the shape of a crescent moon. The length of the weapon was almost as tall as her but she wielded it with great ease. Porth held his breath and looked to his right, letting out hot air at the sight of his longtime friend, Zeraph. He looked almost like a statue, standing still while his thin black hair danced with the wind. He carried a giant rectangular tower shield on his back. Watching him stand still without tipping over was a feat in itself. His face was stalwart, filled with determination but don't let that fool you, his name compliments kindness.

Porth looked behind, standing before thousands of knights who answered the call to fight against the hordes of demons, the servants of evil wanting to cast the world of Terrazel into darkness. There were only a handful of paladins among the knights but each paladin could match the strength of a hundred demons easily. However, training a paladin took years, time they did not have. Finally, he looked forward where matching his sight were hundreds of thousands of demons that mimicked an ocean of blackness. A thin layer of grass covered the vast land where they stood. Above were vampires standing on the ledges of the cliffs, their eyes alone stood out like pearls.

Ryell

He wore no crown, yet a few hundred lycans stood behind their warrior-king who waged countless battles against the vampires in the blood wars. His orange eyes looked around, seeing the mass of humans to his right and elves to the left. Ryell didn't consider elves or humans to be equals but in dire times of need they formed a hasty alliance to fight a common enemy. He was a direct descendent of their god, Volcanous, a fiery lycan with unmatched fighting ferocity. A lycan walked up towards Ryell, put her paw on his right shoulder and gave a firm squeeze.

"Lead us to his arms," she whispered, leaning in. His ears perked up as he looked over and saw a familiar face; it was one of his generals, Trilla.

He nodded and replied, "For Volcanous." She pulled back her paw, rubbing her snout before crossing her arms while standing tall, her tail lowered, looking forward into the vast sea of demons and vampires. Ryell stepped forward, wrapping his claws around the hilts of his two fiery swords and quickly pulling them up from their sheaths, then slowly lowering his arms until the points of the swords touched the ground, catching the grass on fire.

Porth

He noticed a taller figure standing among the vampires on the edge of the cliff. Instead of the shiny white eyes that vampires normally displayed, this one had bright red eyes. It was a demon known as Tern'natha, able to spawn obsidian spears at will, deadly both in close and at long distance. He turned his attention to the demons on the ground as they stepped to the side as best they could. A slender demon with similar red glowing eyes approached. When she reached the front, all of the demons stepped back in place. She held out her delicate hand for a moment as a black blade shaped like a crescent moon appeared in her hands. She held the weapon by the handle in the middle as two large curved blades extended from each side of the handle. She dropped it, the blades sinking into the ground as if it weighed a few hundred pounds, while her eyes remained looking forward with a hint of sorrow.

The ground next to the demoness began to split as the earth pulled apart, creating a pit. A giant demon leaped from it, landing on the ground with its massive hooves. Its head was shaped similar to a ram with giant twisted horns upon a human's body. Its red glowing eyes glanced at the demoness then towards the humans. Another demon appeared from the abyss of the pit. At first glance, this particular demon had an owl's face but not red glowing eyes like the few others, instead it had hollow black ones similar to the rest of the demons. He turned to the demoness and gave a slight bow.

"Your Tormentress, Zary'Zadendra. Always a treasure," he whispered, walking by and standing next to her.

"Ker'es," she whispered back in the same manner, her eyes following him momentarily before looking back at the line of humans. A vampire leaped off the edge of the cliff and almost at the moment of impact, it opened its wings and flapped once, allowing it to land safely on its feet. The wings folded up behind its back and it turned to the ram-headed demon.

"We are ready, Gor'eck Kal," the vampire spoke, keeping its white eyes on the demon. "Together, Lord Volten, we shall cast this world into darkness." They both turned, looking outward, watching the humans unsheathe their swords and equip their shields. Two of the knights turned to each other, each with sword in hand.

"Are you ready for this, Luther?"

"Yes, a bit nervous, but yes."

"You know, I never mentioned it before but you've been more than a dear friend, a brother. I don't think I could have ever become a knight without your help." He reached out, placed his free hand on his brother's shoulder, and smiled.

"We are here for each-" He couldn't finish his sentence before an obsidian spear impaled into the head of the knight, blood erupting from the wound, spraying onto Luther's armor as the

5

knight fell to the ground. A loud demonic, infernal laughter filled the air as Luther turned his head to see the demon standing amongst the vampires on top of the cliff with another spear in hand.

"For absolute justice!" Porth yelled, pulling out his lightblade and pointing it towards the demons. Almost immediately, after all of the humans yelled out, they charged forward with sword and shields drawn. All of the knights near Luther ran towards the demons, thousands of footsteps beating into the earth and armor clanking into each other. He turned his head once more to see his fallen brother before charging forward.

"Forward! Crush the humans!" Gor'eck Kal bellowed, pointing his large hand into the approaching humans. The demons obeyed, charging with swords in hand, causing the earth to rumble below. Lord Volten looked up to his vampires and nodded, signaling the vampires to engage. They leaped from the ledges of the cliffs in unison, almost looking like a giant wave crashing down into the ground.

Ryell

Ryell let out a loud roar before sprinting towards the demons, his twin fiery swords dragged against the ground leaving a trail of fire behind him as the rest of the lycans followed suit. The elves followed closely behind the lycans, quickly pulling arrows out of their quivers and loading them into their bows. They released their arrows in unison and a volley of arrows rained down upon the first wave of demons. Ryell continued to sprint forward with demons falling to the ground to his left and right. At the peak of his sprint he leaped at a demon, raising his swords high before sinking them into both shoulders of the demon. The sound of the demon's chthonic howl, mixed with the sound of searing flesh, echoed as the two groups collided with swords smashing into armor. Ryell pulled down the swords with all his might, slicing the demon's arm off before changing his grip so the blades were facing up. He swung his arm, knocking the armless demon down then began to hack his way into the incoming waves of demons.

A giant vampire stood in front of Ryell, behind him a blood mage was channeling blood to the vampire, giving it increased strength and vigor far more than regular vampires who are more agile but less powerful. The vamperic juggernaut held a massive sword with both arms, raising it up and quickly swinging it down at the lycan. Ryell blocked the attack, raising both his swords into a cross, catching the blade in the middle. He grit his teeth, holding his swords up, and after a moment of struggling, Ryell quickly shifted the conflict to his right, throwing the juggernaut off balance. Using both swords, he slashed diagonally up, slicing the juggernaut's torso. It roared in pain, releasing a hand from its sword to hold its bleeding torso as it tried to swing wildly with one arm. The motion was too slow and uncontrolled as Ryell did a quick parry before completely slicing the juggernaut's arm off. After killing the juggernaut, he kept moving forward, slashing and hacking the waves of demons who all got in his way.

Luther

Bodies of demons, vampires and humans were piled high both left and right as Luther paced forward. Almost all of the ground was no longer green but covered in blood. The knight swung his sword, splitting a demon in half while he kept running. A vampire flew out, swinging its sword downward at him but Luther blocked it quickly before jumping up and stabbing the vampire, raining blood down on him. The vampire fell to the ground with a thud, clutching its bleeding chest. The knight lifted his heavy boot and stomped the vampire's face in, feeling the skull start to cave under his foot.

Another demon leaped out in front of him, knocking him down to the ground. He saw the demon raise its arms with a crude axe in hand, that moment giving him enough time to pull his sword with both hands to his face and thrust it into the abdomen of the demon. It let out a hellish roar as he quickly pulled the sword out and stabbed again, thick black blood gushing out from the wound. The demon hunched over, allowing Luther to push the demon off of him. As he got up breathing furiously, he noticed a considerably larger demon with a ram's head start to sprint towards him with no weapon in hand. He couldn't catch his breath in time but there was just enough time for him to adjust his hand on his sword. He knew he couldn't kill the demon at the top of the cliff, the climb was too high, so this giant demon would suffice for his fallen brother's honor.

They were just a few steps away when Luther raised his blade, readying for a strike when he noticed the demon move its massive arms to its side as if he were to swing. Not even a second later, the demon's hands were covered by purple fire and a giant obsidian hammer appeared. Luther took his final step, pulling down his blade for a downward slash but it was too slow. The demon swung his massive hammer, its head crushed into the chest of the knight, sending him tumbling backwards. He placed his free hand on his chest, feeling the impact. His plate armor was badly dented; his rib cage was crushed, collapsing his lungs, making him unable to breathe. He saw the ram-headed demon stand over him with the hammer in one hand. Luther used his last strength to yell, raising his blade in defiance, but it was no use. The demon knelt down, picking the knight up by his neck, tossing him aside. The sharp fall was numbing as he started to asphyxiate, the sounds of voices and metal beginning to hush. His eyes locked on the demon walking away and his vison started to blur, the sky becoming darker while everyone started to meld together into blackness.

Kionta

Eight bodies dropped around her as she finished swinging her halberd. A handful of demons who watched their own fall right before their eyes hesitated for a moment before daring to step forward towards the paladin. She glanced at the demons surrounding her but before they could raise their weapons, Kionta quickly swung her halberd in a full circle, the first swing slicing their torsos. Immediately after, a ghostly second halberd trailed behind the first swing, cutting the demons' heads clean off. Black blood flowed from their wounds as their lifeless bodies fell to the ground almost in unison. Kionta breathed heavily, turning around and meeting eyes with a tall vampire. It slowly moved its pale hand on the hilt of the rapier then quickly pulled it out from the sheath.

Kionta held up her halberd and sprinted towards the vampire, running past lifeless corpses and broken weapons scattered on the battlefield. When she was mere steps away from the vampire, she reared back the halberd, swinging forward as hard as she could with a loud grunt. Lord Volten barely moved his rapier in front of him, holding it vertically, blocking the attack with the very blade of his rapier. He was caught off guard by the halberd's second ghostly attack, struggling to hold his blade still. Kionta used his block to boomerang a second swing, this time swinging horizontally with full force. Lord Volten leaped backwards, avoiding the attack completely, watching the head of the halberd glide by his neck, followed by a ghostly white halberd trailing behind the initial swing.

Kionta did not slow down, her attacks were relentless, forcing the vampire to move around, evading her halberd. In a moment between attacks, Lord Volten tried to prepare himself for the next attack. She swung her halberd fiercely as he parried the attack, struggling with the sheer amount of force of each swing. He quickly swung his blade, going on the offensive as she moved her halberd to block the incoming attacks. His attacks were quick in succession, making his ghastly grey blade a blur. Kionta swung her halberd wildly, blocking the attacks with sheer numbers of swings.

He lunged with his rapier, thrusting it but it was quickly parried by the steel end of her halberd. Kionta swung her halberd left, aiming at the vampire's torso. Lord Volten pulled his rapier back and blocked the first strike and steadied his blade for the second. As soon as her first strike hit his rapier, she jerked her arms, swinging in the opposite direction with all her might, aiming at his head. Lord Volten blocked the second strike, turning his head as he caught sight of the incoming halberd blade and closed his eyes. The first strike dug into his neck but stopped halfway through, then the second ghostly blade cut Lord Volten's head clean off. His head tumbled to the ground with a thud as blood poured from his neck. His body fell to the ground with a heavy thud. Kionta breathed furiously, catching her breath while holding herself up with the halberd. The vampires that were left witnessed their leader, their father, die.

"Retreat!" Dolamar yelled as he and his fellow vampires took flight away from the battlefield.

Her short break was over as she heard the cry of a person's last breath. She quickly pulled her halberd and turned around to answer the cry when suddenly, she felt a sharp pain enter from her back. She let out a dry gasp as she fell forward from the force. She looked down to see the end of a spear protruding out from her torso, blood quickly gushing from the wound. She took her hand and wrapped it around the bloodied spear and tried pulling it out. She let out a muffled groan but it hurt too much trying to pull it out. She released her hand from the spear and pressed it against the ground, holding herself up. Kionta heard more screams of people dying and couldn't take it anymore. *My pain is only a fraction of theirs*, she thought to herself, taking her bloodied hand and curling it into a fist. She slammed her fist into the ground and pulled herself up, holding her halberd in both hands as she stood up. Quickly looking around, she could see the humans were getting overrun by the sheer amount of demons. She couldn't waste any more time if she wanted to even the odds.

Kionta took a step forward and felt another sharp pain entering her body from her back, knocking her forward but she caught herself with the pole end of her halberd. Her head dangled, looking downward she saw another spear end protruding from her

13

body. She coughed up blood and could see blood flowing from her wound, small red drops falling to the ground. Shaking her head and looking up, her vison started to blur and the sounds around her slowly faded.

She closed her eyes and could feel the darkness slowly swallowing her up. Her fingers began to turn cold, but suddenly she felt a familiar light, a warm light that glowed throughout her body. Light poured from her closed eyes and the blood that covered her chest and hand turned into a bright glowing fluid. She opened her eyes and everything was clear; she could see swords clashing into each other but the sound was almost nonexistent. No longer did she feel the pain from her chest but light glowing strongly instead. She pushed herself off using her halberd then swung it in a full circular motion, killing a handful of demons. She felt unencumbered by her armor as she sprinted across the battlefield, swinging her halberd wildly, leaving a trail of dead demons behind her. Bright light wings spread from her back allowing her to become highly mobile. Continuing her rampage as a red mist of blood followed her, demons were hacked into chunks of flesh and vampires sliced to pieces.

She could feel the light slowly fading away and with it her vison started to worsen. Her halberd felt heavier with each swing, the liquid light started to turn back into blood and the pain from the two spears steadily returned. Kionta laid eyes upon a vamperic juggernaut whose body was surrounded by a moving circular shield of blood. The juggernaut was knocking back humans, lycans, demons or anything in its path. She ran towards the ball of blood with her halberd raised up high, each step becoming heavier and each breath she took, shorter. She leaped into the flowing ball of blood as it painted her whole body red. With the last strength she had she swung diagonally, slicing the juggernaut into two as it let out a horrific wail. She fell forward to the ground as her wings disappeared and the light escaped from her eyes. The flowing blood shield collapsed, raining blood over the two bodies.

Porth

"Porth, use the hammer!" Zeraph yelled, using both hands to smash his giant shield into a demon's head. Bright blue light poured from his eyes, the skin started to crack near his eyes as more light escaped through. His light wings beat furiously, allowing him to sprint across the battlefield, smashing his shield into demons as broken teeth and blood flew with each heavy impact of his massive shield.

Porth held his bloodied mace in his right hand and looked up to see Zeraph continuing his rampage across the field; however, it seemed an endless amount of demons kept flooding from the rifts. He smashed his mace into the head of a demon, cracking its skull, causing it to fall backwards. Using his left hand, he reached behind his cape for the Hammer of Creation, but he hesitated for a moment. The power of this hammer is immense. Can it be used without being corrupted? He stood still for a moment, scanning the battlefield. It seemed that the endless waves of demons were swallowing everything in their path. They were losing the war badly and if there was any chance to turn the tides, he needed to use the hammer, Porth thought to himself as he saw a spear flying towards him from the corner of his eye. "Whatever the cost…" he whispered under his breath as he quickly grabbed the handle of the hammer.

Bright blue light exploded from his eyes as giant light wings folded behind his back. He swung the hammer, reflecting the spear into a demon's torso. Demons surrounded him as one leaped forward with a raised sword. Porth stepped forward, rearing his mace and when the demon drew closer he swung, smashing his mace into the skull of the demon, sending him backwards with such force along with a few more demons. His light wings spread open as he raised both his hammer and mace, hitting them together, creating a giant wave of light which erupted from the impact, causing the surrounding demons to fall backwards from the force. He then sprinted forward, swinging both of his weapons wildly, killing every demon in his path.

Demons tried to move out of the way but his speed was so fast they only saw a blur of light. They didn't even have the time to cry out before they died, they just fell dead to the ground where they stood. His wings beat heavily behind his back as he sprinted towards a giant demon which roared, lifting up its massive crude ax. But that did not slow him down, he quickened his pace and leaped up at the demon. He spread out his arms as time seemed to stand still for a moment. He grunted, using all of his strength to swing both the hammer and the mace, smashing them both into each side of the demon's head, making it explode into flesh and blood.

Demons watched the massacre in awe shortly before fleeing back to the rifts and into the depths of darkness. As more and more demons fled, Tern'natha leaped from the cliff, landing on the ground with a giant thud. He walked towards the paladin and stopped at an eye's distance away. Ker'es stood at the side of Tern'natha, looking forward at the paladin. Tern'natha held out his hand as a sleek obsidian spear appeared in his hand. He curled his slender, ash gray fingers around the spear, lifting it up then rearing quickly before hurling the spear at Porth.

The spear danced in the air for a few seconds before Porth held up his hammer and swung diagonally downwards deflecting the spear into the ground. Another spear ripped across the battlefield towards him; just before the impact he swung his hammer again, ricocheting it. The spear hit the ground at an uneven angle, making it spin rapidly before it struck a demon trying to flee. Tern'natha spawned another spear, rearing it up. Just when he was about to throw it, he felt the end get caught on something. He turned his head slightly to see Zary'Zadendra holding the backend of the spear.

"It's useless, while he is holding that hammer!" she said.

"Release your grip, or this one is going into your skull."

"Swallow it," Zary'Zadendra said while letting go of the spear and folding her arms together.

Tern'natha shook his hand violently and yelled out in anger. "Grrrrahhhh!" He threw the spear into the ground in front of him. The ground split into two then slowly started to pull apart. A stray sword fell into the chasm and eventually disappeared into the depths of blackness.

Gor'eck Kal was the first to enter the chasm, followed by Ker'es. Zary'Zadendra unfolded her arms and walked calmly to the pit and leaped into it. Tern'natha kept his eyes on the paladin who was standing perfectly still, his arms spread, holding a mace in one hand and the hammer in the other. Deep down he knew Zary'Zadendra was right, as long as he was holding the hammer, he couldn't kill that paladin. He took a step forward and plunged into the chasm, the light above him getting dimmer and dimmer until he was surrounded by blackness.

Porth watched the last Tormentor slip into the abyss before turning his head to see a familiar face. Zeraph's light blue eyes started to slowly fade, his whole chest which once shone brightly now started to become blood red. Porth extended his hand, holding the hammer to Zeraph but he shook his head and refused.

"You know you can still live?" Porth told him, opening his hand.

"…and what? Forever be forced to hold the hammer and if I ever let go I would perish instantly? That's not a life for me. I think I did more good in the world than bad… I'm okay with that," Zeraph replied as his voice started to become distorted. He sat down on the ground, gazing across the bloodied battlefield filled with thousands of corpses. Porth dropped the hammer, the light in his eyes faded to its normal color. He felt the burden of mortality slam into his body like a horse kick, knocking him down. He pulled himself up to a sitting position next to Zeraph.

Ryell walked towards Porth, kneeling down and slamming his twin fiery blades into the ground before sitting beside the paladin.

"Did we win?" Ryell asked.

"No. The burden is passed to our children and their children," Porth replied.

Chapter 2

(100 years later)

Soonifer

Anger. *Who needs paladins anyway?!* Soonifer sneered, thinking to himself while walking out of the capital. The giant wooden gates closed behind him as he walked furiously, kicking up dust. Why was he unable to understand the light? Why was his brother so talented at captivating his peers in awe, and all he received were laughs and jeers? The sun, high above the cloudless sky, beat down upon his black leather tunic, silver polished buttons lined down his chest, meeting his thick black belt. His princely dark pants were polluted with dust, even his black boots were scuffed with dry dirt. *It could not be that hard to become a paladin. Why didn't the divines bless me like they did my brother, Claudius?*

His thoughts were still in turmoil as he reached a small town that sat on the outskirts of the capital. He walked towards the small wooden fence that kept sheep corralled. He leaned on the fence, watching the sheep meander around, shifting his view towards the town and seeing people go about their business. He looked to his right just past the pen and saw a sheep laying on the ground. He pushed himself off the fence and walked towards the stray sheep, thinking to himself how careless the farmer was, allowing his sheep to wander outside the fence.

He was just steps away from the sheep when he discovered its underbelly ripped apart, blood staining both the carcass and the surrounding grass. Looking around, he saw a small trail of blood leading away from the dead sheep. He took a step back and could see that the trail would have led into the woods.

"I guess I can save the farmer some grief." He took a step forward, knelt down and put his hand on the open wound of the sheep. Closing his eyes, he concentrated his thoughts until darkness started to surround him. He could feel life essence draining from the surrounding area and pouring into the dead sheep. The darkness surrounding his thoughts began to dissipate and suddenly he felt a heartbeat against his palm. Opening his eyes, he saw gray light fill the sheep's eyes for a moment then slowly fade away. The sheep moved its legs, kicking around before getting up. "They underestimate dark magic; it can be used for good." He picked up the sheep, it struggled in his grasp, tilting its head as it attempted to bite him. "Gah! Maybe I should have left you dead…" Walking over to the wooden pen, he put the sheep down and it ran off to the other sheep. He turned around to see a jet black furred lycan pup with bright yellow eyes staring up at him. It let out a sharp growl, letting its mouth open as it panted with its tongue hanging out. He looked over at the group of sheep and then back to the lycan pup.

"I guess I owe you dinner. Come on, I know someone who can make us dinner." He walked past the pup and turned his head to see if it would follow. The pup turned its head but didn't move. He patted his leather pants and the pup started to follow.

By the time Soonifer and the lycan pup were inside the capital the sun had already started to set, dusk quickly approaching. "We are almost there. Alorah is going to love you," he said, turning his head and watching the pup eagerly follow behind. They stopped at an iron gate as a guard holding a torch approached. He wore the traditional city guard attire which was comprised of light plate mail with a sturdy leather strap that ran down from the shoulder, across the chest, hooking to the belt. His legs were also covered with light plate mail, tucked into heavy brown leather boots. The metal pauldrons carried the city guard symbol, a shield with a sword slung across it. The guard held out the torch trying to get a better view of the person.

"Identify yourself," the guard spoke, holding a torch in one hand and the hilt of his sword with the other.

"Prince Soonifer... and my friend here is ..." He turned his head to the sitting pup who was eagerly looking up at them with perked up ears. "Nox!" The lycan pup let out a sharp bark in excitement as the guard straightened his stance upon hearing the word 'prince'.

"Majesty!" the guard replied, bowing his head. "Where are you headed?"

"The Parrish estate," Soonifer replied, pointing to the gate. The guard nodded and released his grip on his sword and opened the iron gate, signaling for them to enter.

"Let's go, Nox!" Nox let out another sharp bark and followed Soonifer through the gate. The walkway was made of stone, the sides of the open yard filled with grass and a few trees which stood still as the moonlight quietly shone down upon them.

They came upon a decorated wooden door, the intricate curves and details lit by a wall mounted torch. He grabbed the iron ring, lifting it up to knock but the door opened first to his surprise and standing there was Alorah.

"Soonifer?"

"My lady." He bowed as the lycan pup dashed inside towards the smell of roasted chicken.

"Nox! Get back here!" he yelled, chasing after the pup as Alorah closed the door and followed them. A scream filled the kitchen as Alorah entered and saw one of the female servants hurriedly run out while Soonifer was holding Nox, but not before the pup had a chicken leg in its mouth. He put the pup down as it furiously gnawed on the chicken leg. Alorah couldn't help but laugh and walked closer to the pup. A few of the servants peered into the kitchen, watching the little beast finish up the chicken and start to gnaw on the bone. Soonifer grabbed another leg of roasted chicken and gave it to Nox. The pup instantly dropped the bone and began eating the leg.

"Well, Nox approves of your cooking," he said with a smile, looking at the servants who showed uneasy smiles while walking back into the kitchen.

"Where did you find him?" Alorah spoke softly, kneeling down to the pup and gently stroking its head.

"I found him on the outskirts of Irrend."

"That farm village just on the outskirts of the capital?"

"Yes, that one… and I owe him dinner." He walked over to the table, grabbed another piece of chicken and held it out for Nox who began eating it immediately. Soonifer sat down at the table, taking a fork and knife in hand and started to eat the roasted breast of chicken. Alorah stood up and walked to the table, sitting across from him, she began eating a thigh of the roasted chicken. She was in mid bite when she looked up and noticed Soonifer's dark brown eyes staring at her.

"Yes?" The kitchen was silent for the most part, except for Nox who was chewing on the bones.

"You're so beautiful," he said while looking into her sapphire blue eyes. Her cheeks turned red as she closed her eyes; she couldn't help but smile back. The first few strands of her blonde hair were braided, looking almost as if she wore a woven crown with the rest of her hair falling straight down to her shoulders. He pushed his empty plate forward and got up, stretching. He looked down at the lycan pup who was fast asleep with a chicken bone between its teeth.

Alora got up from the table as well and walked towards him. He welcomed her with open arms and she rested her head on his shoulder. "I must go, it's an early day tomorrow."

"Your trials, they are near?"

"Yes, the crucible that all paladins must endure."

"How long will you be away?"

"Three days," she replied, pulling her head away from his shoulder after which they stared at each other for a moment.

"That is a long time without seeing you," he lamented as she broke away.

"It is, but now you will have some company while I'm away." She smiled, motioning to the pup. He forced a smile back as Alorah started to walk out of the kitchen.

"I'm sure you'll do well," he said, keeping his eyes upon her. She paused for a moment and turned her head, showing another smile.

"I'm sure the divines have something spectacular in store for you, Soonifer," she promised before walking out of the kitchen and heading to bed.

"I'm sure they do," he said under his breath with a slight sense of sorrow.

Soonifer walked out of the kitchen into a large dark room that was lit by a roaring fire. He pulled a leather chair near the fire and sat down; sinking into the chair and staring at the fire. His raven black hair sat upon his shoulders, his elbows resting on the hard leather arms of the chair. His legs were crossed and the heels of his boots rested against the stone fireplace. The reflection of the fire danced in his dark brown eyes.

Chapter 3

<u>Soonifer</u>

Desolate. He woke up, opening his eyes slowly. His eyes looked around the room while his head remained still, the blurs of the room slowly starting to become clear. The once roaring fire in front of him had become ash. He noticed a red blanket covering him and slowly pulled it off, tossing it to the side. Moving his hands to his face, he rubbed his eyes, taking in a deep breath and letting out a long drawn out sigh. He stood and stretched, looking down at Nox who looked up at him with his tail wagging. He walked into the kitchen with Nox following, and approaching the table, he picked up a letter and read it:

Soonifer,

I hope this letter finds you well. I saw you struggling while you slept, and the fire had been long gone. I thought you were shivering so I put a blanket on you. Make sure to take care of yourself and Nox while I attend the final trials of light. The divines are always looking out for the ones who are in need.

Eternally yours,

    Alorah

"Alorah always talked about the divines…a bunch of garbage." His voice trailed off as he picked up a biscuit, putting it up to his mouth for a bite and turned around to see Nox sitting and staring up at him. He pulled the biscuit away and gave it to Nox. The pup took a bite, chewing slowly as bits of the biscuit fell from his mouth. The expression on Nox's face was as if he just ate a wild mushroom that didn't taste all too good. Soonifer couldn't help but laugh, while picking up another biscuit and taking a bite out of it. "Let's go," he said, looking back at Nox as the pup replied with a sharp growl.

The sun was at its highest when they reached the outskirts of Irrend. He noticed a small gathering of people at the entrance of the town and quickened his pace. When he got closer he noticed a majority of the people were guards of another town who had crests of a yellow sun on their chests. He remembered seeing that crest a long time ago in the capital but hadn't seen it since. Peering over the shoulders of a few guards, he could see a pile of dead bodies and just beside it, a few bodies that were separated from the pile. A guard was kneeling down and examining the separate bodies.

"That's him!" a man shouted, pointing at Soonifer as two guards followed him. He took a step back from the approaching man and could see another man emerge from the group of guards. This man wasn't poorly dressed like the man who yelled but instead was dressed rather well, as if he was a noble or lord.

"If you are looking for the prince-" Soonifer was cut off as the yelling man stopped in front of him, still pointing at him.

"This is the man that brought plague into our town!" Soonifer stared in disbelief as the guards placed their hands on their swords.

"I did no-" He tried to speak but was cut off again, this time by the well-dressed man.

"Is this him?"

"…well it looks like the man I saw."

"Is this him?" The well-dressed man asked again, this time with a little irritation in his voice.

"Yes! I am certain!" the man replied.

The well-dressed man stood an arms distance away from Soonifer, wearing a velvet red tunic with gold trim that ran along every edge of his outfit. He opened his arms and introduced himself.

"I am Hallowmis Vicar, baron of the city Solbris." He crossed his arms, concealing a star shaped ornament that hung off of his golden necklace. "…and who might you be?" he asked with his solid hazel eyes fixed upon Soonifer.

"I am-"

"Actually, I don't give a hell who you are," the baron exploded unexpectedly. "Seize him," he said in a calmer voice. The guards started to walk towards Soonifer but Nox leaped in front of the guards and let out a high-pitched growl. They stopped for a moment but realized the lycan pup was no threat and continued forward. Nox dashed forward and bit one of the guard's foot who jumped up and grabbed his foot, yelling in pain. Nox let out another high-pitched growl as more guards approached. Nox leaped forward, trying to bite another leg but one of the guards reared back and kicked the lycan pup in the throat. Soonifer saw Nox tumble backwards past him and stop, his body sprawled on the ground.

"Nox!" Soonifer yelled as he tried to run to the lycan pup but was quickly grabbed by the guards. He struggled in their grasp while looking at the motionless pup then turned his head to the baron. "Release me!" he yelled.

"You resurrected a sheep that is quite impressive." The baron took a step forward towards Soonifer and looked him directly in his eyes. "You don't look like a paladin, so perhaps you are a demon? Don't worry, I kill demons all the time." Soonifer struggled in the grasp of the guards once more as the baron pulled out a steel dagger and stabbed him in the chest. He yelled out in pain as the dagger was pulled out from his chest. Hallowmis struck him three more times in the chest, and before pulling out the dagger he spoke. "Three for my family." A guard handed the baron a cloth which he used to clean the dagger of blood before placing it in his sheath. Soonifer's head hung down, his eyes closed as he hissed in pain. When he opened his eyes, he saw his tunic saturated with blood and more blood spilled on the ground.

The guards threw him backwards and he let out a muffled groan when he impacted the ground. He clutched his chest and looked at his bloodied hand. The baron turned to walk into the town as the guards followed closely behind him. It became harder to breathe as Soonifer turned his attention from his hand to the baron who was walking away. His chest started to become cold as his vison of the group of guards slowly became distorted. He rolled to his other side and pulled himself towards Nox, reaching out an arm and placing it on the back of the pup. He closed his eyes and tried to concentrate but the pain was unbearable. He held his breath and for a moment there was silence, enough to force all of his energy into his hand and into Nox.

Soonifer felt his arm go cold. He could feel the weight of his body against the ground but that was about it. He felt his body slowly sinking into the ground until he no longer felt anything. He hesitated for a second before opening his eyes and felt as if he was falling. Soonifer forced his eyes open to see nothing but blackness. The slow fall suddenly changed into a rapid descent. He felt his body being twisted and jerked around with such force he couldn't do anything except fall. The drop seemed endless until everything stopped and then he felt nothing.

He laid there for a moment before sluggishly moving his arms and placing his palms against the ground. Pushing himself up, he stood on both legs and looked around. Still surrounded by blackness, he stretched out his arms and swung them slowly, trying to find any object hidden in the dark. He took a cautious step then another. His steps quickened as his eyes frantically looked around trying to find any sort of light. It seemed he had walked for miles but his eyes caught sight of two lights in the distance. His fast walk turned into a sprint and as he drew closer to the two lights it became clear that the lights were fire.

They were two slender skeletal dogs with their paws on fire, the sound of searing echoed as they walked. The pair of dogs stopped right in front of him and looked up. He could see the dogs had no eyes and slowly walked backwards away from them. They both opened their mouths, fire raged in their maw with some sparks spewing out to the ground. Loud screams of humans emitted from their mouths as they dashed for Soonifer.

One of the hounds leaped at him, but he reared back and punched it in the nose, sending it backwards. The other bit down on his forearm, its teeth digging into his body. He didn't feel any pain in his arm but instead he felt the beast's teeth tearing at his heart.

He pulled his arm close and clenched his other hand into a fist to furiously pound at the head of the dog. After the fifth punch he was able to free his arm from the dog's mouth. The beast fell to the ground as the screams stopped and the fire in its mouth faded. He looked at his forearm and could see the indents where the teeth had pressed. A loud scream broke the silence, startling him. He turned his head to see the other dog in mid-leap at him with its fiery mouth wide open. He quickly grabbed the dog's mouth with both hands, each on the top and bottom jaw. He could feel the intense fire against his heart as the dog tried to clamp down on his hands. He forced all of his strength to pull its jaws apart, letting out a yell as he ripped the lower jaw off from the head. The yells subsided as the fire disappeared from the mouth of the dog.

The silence was broken again by a deep, demonic sounding laughter. He turned around and could see two figures, one that had the head of a ram that stood almost a head taller than the other who had the head of a barn owl. "He killed my pets!" bellowed the ram-headed demon as his laughter quickly turned into anger. It stepped forward, stretching one of its four arms out as purple fire covered his hand, a giant obsidian hammer appearing in his grasp.

"Perhaps he can be of some use?" the owl-headed demon whispered.

"I don't care, I want to smash his skull in!"

"...But you do care about the tools? He just needs a little guidance." There were a few seconds of silence before the ram-headed demon tossed its hammer in the air as it disappeared. "Is there anything your eyes cannot see, Ker'es?"

Soonifer stood still as the owl-headed demon walked towards him and stopped at an arm's distance away. He looked into the owl's hollow black eyes and it felt as if the demon could see into his soul.

"You are fortunate enough to become a demon," Ker'es whispered as he turned to walk away. Soonifer followed behind for a moment and stopped.

"I want to see someone!"

"You don't give orders!" the ram-headed demon bellowed.

"A little encouragement will help," Ker'es whispered as he continued to walk and eventually disappeared into the blackness. The ram-headed demon huffed and moved towards Soonifer, reaching out to grab him by the neck.

"You have until nightfall." The ram-headed demon launched Soonifer upwards into the blackness.

Soonifer felt licks on his face and moved his head away. Opening his eyes, he let out a rough cough as he tried to breathe. *Was it all a dream?* he whispered to himself, moving his hand over to his chest and feeling the holes of where he had been stabbed. He frantically ripped his tunic and could see the scars of where the dagger had pierced him. He looked at the wounds with disbelief before turning his attention to the lycan pup. Nox was wagging his tail and seemed like he was barking but no sound came out.

"Nox?" The lycan pup jumped up at him with perked ears. He looked around and noticed the sun had already begun setting. "Shit!" He scrambled up and ran towards the capital as Nox followed behind.

The sun had nearly set as he burst through the doors of Alorah's estate. "Alorah!" he yelled, running into the den of the estate with Nox still following closely behind. A servant hearing the yelling, walked into the room.

"What is all this yelling about?" she demanded.

Soonifer disregarded the servant and ran into the kitchen. "Alor..." He stopped in mid-word, looking at the table and knew instantly that she wasn't here. He walked through the door and saw the last few orange steaks of the sun in the sky. A giant black rift appeared in front of him, the darkness of the void inviting him in. Soonifer turned around and looked at Nox.

"Stay here." The lycan pup watched him disappear into the darkness as the rift dissipated.   Soonifer reappeared back in the Nether. "Are you ready?" Ker'es whispered, his hollow black eyes fixed upon Soonifer. "Let's disappoint the divines."

Chapter 4

<u>Claudius</u>

Exhilaration. "Today! Few have stood in your place, held the same sword, worn the initiates' armor and said the sacred vows to become the bane of any demon's existence. You will endure the trials to become a weapon against darkness! A light that can never be extinguished! The highest honor that anyone can achieve, if completed, you will become a paladin!" Mentor Elle spoke with vigor in his voice in front of the initiates who listened eagerly and were about to embark on the crucible to become a paladin. "Cressia and the other mentors will be observing your journey to give guidance if needed. May the divines bless you."

Lance opened his small brown satchel and pulled an apple from it. "An apple, some slices of bread and a canteen of water. This doesn't look like a day's worth of rations to me." He put the apple back into the satchel.

"It's better than nothing," Claudius said, tying his ration to his waist.

"I guess… Good thing I already ate my fill of roasted pork this morning." Lance smiled, patting his stomach.

"I was thinking about having a race to see who could finish first. I hope all that pork doesn't slow you down." Claudius spoke nonchalantly as he finished tying his satchel. Lance's smile was quickly wiped away but turned into a grin.

"You know, I can't back away from a challenge. I accept!"

"Let's get started, shall we?" Mentor Cressia suggested, turning around as her white cape followed her movements. The initiates followed behind her, going through a set of wooden doors and into a nearby meadow where they walked towards a towering mountain. Claudius turned his head and looked at Nara, the first lycan ever to come this far to become a paladin.

"Nara, are you ready?"

"Of course! I cannot wait to see what the first challenge is!" she exclaimed, turning her head to Claudius, locking her yellow eyes on him. An initiate sneered at Nara's words. She started to show a frown when Claudius interjected.

"Don't mind her, Nara, I'm sure news would spread quickly to the Lycanian Kingdom that you bested Lance, a human, at becoming a paladin." Her frown quickly turned into a smile showing her sharp teeth.

"Lance, how are you doing back there?" Claudius yelled, looking back to see Lance sprinting forward, barreling into other initiates to walk alongside Claudius.

"What are you talking about? I'm going to best you, Claudius, I'm going to best all of you!" he yelled, moving his arm in a circle, pointing at everyone. "All demons will fear me!"

"And taverns too!" Claudius added.

"Hey, you can make fun but you know it's true, they will erect statues of me! Sing songs about me!" Lance bragged, waving his arm again in the air. "…and women would-"

"Shut the hell up, Lance!" an initiate yelled as others laughed at the jest.

They arrived at the base of the mountain that had a cave. Mentor Cressia stood in front of the cave, facing the group of initiates. "Our great divine, Hysolin, did not always walk the path of divinity. No, his early years were plagued by darkness and at times, he felt lost in the journey of life. Yet that did not stop nor slow him, he continued and ultimately found his place in life, to be a great paladin. You have all heard the stories, but now you must endure his experience. Before you is a cave that no sunlight or candle has touched. Each and every one of you is to traverse it with your own paladin's light."

Mentor Cressia held her right hand as a light radiated from it, and with her other hand she pointed to a pile of rusted swords near the entrance of the cave. "If anyone is unwilling to enter or wishes to quit now, please remove your sword and put it in the pile." She spoke, returning her hand to her side as the light dissipated.

"What if we get lost?" an initiate asked.

"You have plenty of time to complete this challenge. Mentor Elle awaits at the other side of the mountain, and if anyone does not complete this challenge by dusk, I shall come looking for you. May your inner light prevail"

44

"Last chance to turn back, Claudius," Lance whispered. Claudius placed his right hand around the hilt of his blade and pulled his sword from its sheath. The sound of metal rubbing against the leather caused everyone to shift their eyes onto him. Nara's eyes widened at the sight and even Lance looked a bit shocked. Claudius walked straight towards the pile of swords, walking past Mentor Cressia who was the only one who kept the shock hidden on her face. He stood in front of the pile of metal, complete silence descended as everyone watched on. Turning around, he looked at the group and could see Lance with his mouth wide open, shocked and speechless at what was about to happen.

"Looks like I'm going to have a head start!" Claudius yelled as his left hand instantly emitted a bright light. He quickly faced the cave and sprinted forward into the darkness. The group of initiates roared with laughter and even Mentor Cressia let out a faint giggle.

"That son of a whore!" Lance yelled, pushing initiates out of his way. He held his right hand into a fist but no light appeared. Fearing the look upon his peers' faces that he could not summon his light, he sprinted into the cave trying to catch up with Claudius. The rest of the initiates finished their laughter as each raised a hand

and entered the cave one by one until there were only two left behind. Nara was just about to enter but caught the sight of Seren who seemed reluctant to enter.

"Come on, you can do it," Nara urged as she walked towards her.

"I don't need your encouragement…" Seren said under her breath.

"Here, we can walk together and take turns with the light," Nara suggested as Seren hesitated for a moment before weakly replying with "okay." They both entered the cave together as Mentor Cressia watched them until their bodies had faded into the darkness of the cave. *I hope those two get along together,* she thought, remembering all the times that Seren would poke fun at Nara for being different and sometimes even harass her in the classroom. She looked at the pile of swords, some rusted, others bent and shook her head.

Lance

Blackness surrounded him, however that did not impede his progress. He sprinted through the long narrow paths of the cave with only the faintest glow from his hand giving him a brief sight of his surroundings. He stopped at a fork in the path and chose the left; he started to run but was met with a dead end, almost crashing into the wall. *You got to be kidding me.* He thought before quickly turning around and running back to the forked path, this time taking the right path. "Claudius!" he yelled as he continued to run into the blackness.

He saw a small glimmer of light ahead of him and instantly thought it was Claudius' light. Lance quickened his pace, sprinting at full speed but as he drew closer the light became bigger and he soon realized that the light was not from Claudius but from the exit of the cave. Exiting the cave, he quickly looked around and to his dismay he saw Claudius talking to Mentor Elle. He walked towards them and put one hand on Claudius' shoulder and shook it. "You won this time, but don't worry, I work well when I am at a disadvantage."

"Lance, I am glad to see you here." Mentor Elle spoke, turning her attention to him.

"Tell me, I surprised you, right?"

"Oh no, I have much faith in you, Lance."

"Thank you, Mentor Elle, you have been the most supportive of all the mentors," Lance said as Mentor Elle smiled and slowly nodded her head. Claudius noticed another paladin emerging from the cave and started to clap.

"Well done, Alorah!"

"Yes, well done indeed." Mentor Elle turned her attention to Alorah and smiled.

"Thank you, Claudius. Thank you, Mentor Elle," Alorah beamed while rubbing her right hand.

"Hey you didn't thank me!" Lance groused, crossing his arms.

"Oh, that's right, thank you, ass," Alorah replied with a grin on her face. Claudius couldn't help but laugh as Lance walked off a few paces and sat down, stretching his arms before he laid backwards on his back. "What are you doing, Lance?" Alorah said, putting her hands on her hips.

"Oh? I'm Lance now? I'm relaxing. I'm not going to stand all day waiting for the rest to catch up."

"He's got a point," Claudius agreed as he walked towards Lance and Alorah followed in suit.

He sat down across from Lance, the sun hidden behind a multitude of clouds as some rays of light slipped past. A cool gentle breeze whisked by as Claudius breathed in deeply and let out a long exhale. Alorah sat down across from them, reaching in her satchel and pulling out a fresh red apple, taking a bite into it.

"How is your brother?" Lance asked, breaking the silence.

"I am not sure, the last time I've seen him was when he stormed out of the lecture hall," Claudius replied.

"Wasn't it the time when Mentor Zurrel instructed him to recite the lesser light incantation?"

"Yes, the very one."

"And he started to babble like an idiot?"

"You know you are a real ass, Lance," Alorah interrupted, throwing her half-eaten apple at him. The apple bounced off of Lance's chest armor with a low metallic thud as he sat up.

"What?! It's true! He would be sitting among us if he didn't act a fool all the time."

"Sometimes I think Soonifer is not acting," Claudius stated as he crossed his arms. "When he stormed out of the hall, he seemed sincerely upset."

"He cannot comprehend the light like we do," Alorah added. Lance and Claudius looked at Alorah in disbelief.

"What do you mean?" Claudius asked.

"He told me before that he cannot understand the scriptures or incantations. He has tried countless times but with no success, it usually ends up with him cursing the divines."

"I have not seen him practice once outside the training grounds."

"He practices at my father's estate, in secret away from laughter, ridicule and asses." Alorah spoke with a little anger in her voice, directing it towards Lance.

"No need to be angry, I meant no offense, Alorah," Lance replied, raising his arms and then placing them on the ground at his sides.

"He has a good heart, this I know."

He looked towards the cave and saw four initiates exit and talk with Mentor Elle.

"Seems that more have passed the first challenge," said Claudius as Lance looked over and nodded.

"I wonder when the next challenge will be," Lance questioned as he laid back down on his back, resting his head upon his hands.

"I'm sure we shall soon find out," Claudius replied, seeing more initiates exit the cave. A long hour had passed when Mentor Elle gathered the initiates and spoke to them.

"There is a small spring up ahead. Even if you are not thirsty I would recommend that everyone take a drink. The next challenge is arduous and you will need your strength for tomorrow."

The group of thirteen initiates walked towards a giant cliff that rivaled the height of the capital castle itself. They stopped at the top of a small hill that held a tiny fresh water spring, a round shield laid near the edge of the water. Lance ran towards the spring and picked up the shield with both hands, quickly inspecting it. The shield was made out of steel, the front had a tarnished silver coat with golden writing that was so worn away the writing was illegible.

Lance dipped the shield into the spring using both hands and pulled the water filled shield up to his chest before lifting it further to his chin. He looked into the shield and caught a slight reflection from the water and remembered one of the stories about the divines. How Zeraph's last action in his mortal life was quelling the thirst of a dying knight. His legs were weak, though he had treaded past the many dead bodies and found the spring of water. Using a fallen knight's buckler shield he scooped water that was not tainted by spilled blood and carried it back to the dying knight. He knelt down and carefully held the shield as the knight quelled his thirst.

"Lance! What's the hold up?" a fellow initiate yelled out as Lance snapped out of his trance. He didn't yell back but instead called upon Claudius to come and take a drink. Claudius walked forward as Lance extended the shield, allowing Claudius to drink from it.

"Thank you, Lance," he said as he backed off from the spring. Lance then called forth Alorah and the other initiates to come forward and drink. Mentor Elle watched on silently and couldn't help but to show a gentle smile. She had observed Lance throughout the years and even though he could be proud and boastful at times, she knew he had a part of Zeraph's heart inside him. The last initiate finished as Lance dipped the shield back into the spring and pulled up another fill of water. Just at that moment, he looked out and saw two initiates exit the cave.

"Hey, look!" Lance shouted as the group turned around watching Seren and Nara run across the field towards them. The group started to clap as they arrived at the spring. Seren raced up to Lance and just as he offered the shield she grabbed it and quickly drank from the shield before returning it to Lance and walking off into the group.

Lance shrugged it off and filled the shield up with water again, offering it to Nara. She hesitated for a moment before leaning in and licked the water a few times before closing her mouth to drink deeply. "Oh, the water is so crisp, thank you, Lance. Have you drunk yet?"

"No, I haven't."

"Here, allow me." She took the shield from his hands and dipped it in the spring. She pulled up the shield to Lance's chin as he leaned in and drank from it, closing his eyes. She carefully watched him drink from the shield. He opened his eyes and caught a glimpse of Nara watching as she turned away from embarrassment, slightly blushing.

"You're right, the water is so crisp and refreshing, thanks, Nara." Lance said, taking the shield from her and placing it on the edge of the spring.

The group of initiates sat in small clusters of three for the night. Each group made their own small makeshift fire as the sun completely hid behind the horizon.

The next morning, Mentor Elle gathered them up and walked towards the cliff. With each step it looked as if the cliff was getting bigger and bigger until they stopped at the base of it.

Elle turned around, facing the group and spoke, "As many of you know, Kionta's life was full of strife, every step a journey and every day a hardship. From a farmer she became one of the greatest paladins to have ever walked Terrazel. From every false path she did not slow nor yield but remained stalwart and wore the visage of courage to meet every challenge she faced with tenacity." The group listened on as she continued. "Just as you have walked Hysolin's path, now you must climb to unimaginable heights as Kionta once did." She paused before finishing. "If you are unwilling to climb, place your sword in the pile." Mentor Elle pointed at the pile of swords, similar to the one before the cave. "If you cannot climb to the top you will fail this challenge. Mentor Thalen awaits at the top. I wish you all the strength to overcome this challenge."

The group of initiates looked up at the steep cliff towering above. It was a sheer vertical cliff that intimidated some while others looked in awe. An initiate stepped forward from the group and walked towards the cliff. The rest silently watched on to see if he would be the first to climb but instead he stopped, withdrawing his sword and tossing it in the pile before walking off, not even turning his face to the group, hiding his shame. Claudius walked towards the cliff, reaching up and grabbing hold of a small lip, he raised a leg searching for a platform to push himself off of and eventually found one. Slowly he climbed the cliff as the rest of the group watched on. Lance also watched on before realizing that Claudius was ahead in their contest. He darted towards the pile of swords, using a rope, he attached four swords together and placed the roped belt around his shoulder.

"What are you doing, Lance?" Mentor Elle asked.

"I need an excuse for why I didn't beat him to the top," Lance replied as a few laughs and whispers arose from the group. He raised an arm, finding a lip to climb on, pulling himself up as he reached up with his other arm to continue his pace. The rest of the group looked on as another initiate walked forward to the wall of the cliff and started to climb.

Nara looked up, seeing Claudius way up high on the cliff almost reaching the top, she turned her attention to Seren who seemed nervous. "Go ahead Seren, you can do it!" Nara called, trying to give her words of confidence. Seren didn't have the words to reply, she just stood there watching the others climb the cliff.

"Nara, I suggest you should go ahead and I'll stay here with Seren," Mentor Elle said as Nara nodded, walking towards the base of the cliff and jumping five feet into the air before grabbing lips of stone with her claws. Her tail hung under her as she climbed the cliff with much ease, even passing by fellow initiates.

"Well done, Claudius," Mentor Thalen spoke, nodding his head in approval.

"Thank you," Claudius replied as he stepped towards the ledge that overlooked a giant valley. He could see parts of the Silpine Forest and even parts of the capital from the sheer height of the cliff where he stood. The sun had started to descend, almost falling directly in front of him.

"This is the final test," Mentor Thalen instructed.

"What do I do?" Claudius replied, looking around but seeing nothing except the small cliff they were standing on. The mentor lifted his arm, pointing to the edge of the cliff.

"Porth was a great paladin, a person who stood for truth, knowledge and faith. At times when he felt lost he would let the light guide him, give him direction, but he needed faith to follow. Jump and embrace the light."

"You... can't be serious?" Claudius replied, peering over the edge before looking back at the mentor. Mentor Thalen nodded. "Well, here goes," Claudius whispered to himself as he breathed heavily for a moment before leaping off the cliff. His brown hair whipped behind as the air rushed against his face and body. He opened his arms, extending them wide as he clenched his teeth, his heart racing, beating madly within his chest. His vision started to blur, the colors of the ground, the trees and the sky all started to meld together. A light blue light outlined the blurred objects before light exploded violently, blinding him.

He no longer felt the air against his body nor the sensation of falling. He opened his eyes to see a familiar face, a face he had seen on paintings and statues that were over a hundred years old.

"Hello, Claudius." Porth spoke almost in a calm whisper but loud enough to be heard perfectly, a tone not completely angelic but holding great power.

"Am I dead?" Claudius replied in a faint voice.

"No, but there are greater things at hand that we must speak of," Porth continued, signaling Claudius to follow. He walked on what seemed like clouds but felt as if they were stone. Porth had a marble white cloak with golden lettering that followed the edge of his cape, the top covered one of his shoulder plates and was held together by a golden sun like sigil. They stopped at what seemed like the edge of a cloud, peering down below. Claudius saw parts of Terrazel that looked familiar; however, there was a large dirt road that stretched for endless miles, cutting through hills, valleys, mountains and even water. *How is that possible?* he thought to himself. Porth explained, "The time when demons will rise is near and there needs to be someone who can unite all humans, elves and lycans together to fight this evil. You are strong, but not strong enough to fight the hordes of unrelenting darkness; however, if you accept this burden, and it is a great burden, I shall share my gift with you."

"I don't have a choice, do I?" Claudius replied, standing next to Porth as he looked below.

"Let me show you," Porth whispered as he lifted his hand, placing it on Claudius' shoulder. Not a moment later, they appeared standing on the same dirt road. Claudius looked around, seeing a giant field that reached for miles before yielding to a massive mountain range on the left side of the road. To the right held the same open field, stretching for miles, eventually intertwining with an enormous lush green forest. The dirt road they stood on appeared to stretch for lengths unknown; he couldn't see the end.

Hundreds of what seemed like constellations of people ran past them, following the dirt road into the horizon. "What are they?" Claudius asked, keeping his eyes on them.

"Souls," Porth replied, starting to walk along the road as Claudius followed beside him. They walked into the horizon and to his surprise, the dirt road continued on to the next horizon. They steadily continued their walk, passing by souls who walked slower, souls who stood still or ones who sat at the edge of the road.

"Why have these souls slowed down while the others keep pace?" inquired Claudius.

"Much like children who cannot wait to grow, they were eager to take all of what life had to offer, only to find out the journey was longer than anticipated."

They came across two souls who had stood still, looking backwards upon the road. "What are they doing?" Claudius asked, stopping to examine them.

"They are looking back to the past, too consumed by it to walk. You may glance at the past but do not stare, young paladin," Porth replied as Claudius quickened his pace to catch up with the divine. Claudius caught sight of a soul who had sat at the side of the road, clutching what seemed to be a bright star.

"What is that soul holding?"

"A treasure. Tell me Claudius, what do you treasure?" They continued to walk upon the road as Claudius thought deeply for his reply.

"My friends."

Porth nodded at his answer and asked, "Your talents, abilities and skills?"

"I guess those could be treasures too."

"Accomplishments, achievements and deeds?"

"I agree."

"And memories?"

"I did not know so many things could be considered treasures."

"Many things can be treasures to us, each differ from soul to soul. If one loses everything, their treasures are the only things they have left to hold." Claudius nodded as they proceeded to walk along the road. He noticed how the once lush green grass that touched the road had turned gray, and even the outer edges of the road seemed to have started to wither away.

"What is happening to the road?"

"Evil, once at bay, has now taken root and threatens all who walk upon this journey."

"Why are you showing me this?"

"So that you may see what is at stake." The road had become narrower as more of the ground had become grayed with decay. Porth stopped walking, turned to Claudius and asked, "Will you bear the burden so light may forever exist?"

"I am honored and yet conflicted. I do not know if I am able to bear that task," he replied, looking into Porth's glowing blue eyes.

"Do not worry, young Claudius. Your heart will answer soon." Porth revealed a faint smile, reaching to his own side and pulling out a bright star. He extended his hand to Claudius and signaled him to take it. "Take one of my treasures and use it well."

Claudius slowly extended his hand and took the star. At that moment, light exploded violently blinding him momentarily, then quickly retreated as he opened his eyes to find himself standing on the ground. Confused, he looked around before looking up to the cliff from where he had jumped. *What happened?* he thought to himself before he felt a faint warm glow in his right hand. He closed his hand, clenching it into a fist as his hand became warmer, and then suddenly, a mace appeared in his hand. The ball was spiked as if it was the hairs of a lion's mane. A lion's open mouth was at the base of the ball where the handle was attached. He looked at it intensely before it disappeared from his hand and instantly he knew.

Lance

Lance reached the top of the cliff before he started to sprint towards the end of the flat. "Well done, Lance," praised Mentor Thalen. "Why do you have so many swords?"

Lance ran past the mentor and yelled in reply, "So I may have an excuse for why Claudius had bested me to the finish, mentor!" He neared the edge and leaped off as the roped swords flung behind him. His eyes widened at the height from where he had jumped as the air rushed through his hair. "Crap!" Lance yelled in realization of what he had just done. His heart raced within his chest as he clenched both hands into fists. Bright blue light erupted from within his eyes as giant light wings appeared behind his back, beating heavily, keeping him in stationary flight.

He looked below and could see Claudius standing with his hands up high, yelling, "Lance! Lance!"

He flew downwards toward Claudius and landed on his legs before the light escaped both his eyes and his back. He opened his arms and gave a heartfelt hug to Claudius.

"We did it, Claudius!"

"Yes, we did, brother!" Claudius replied, embracing Lance.

Nara grabbed the ledge and pulled herself up, brushing some of the dirt that had covered her armor. "Well done, Nara," congratulated Mentor Thalen as Nara's ears perked up, she turned to him.

"Thank you, Mentor Thalen."

"You are almost there, all you must do now is to jump." He coaxed, pointing his open hand towards the open valley.

"Jump...?" She asked with a little stammer in her voice, walking over to the edge and looking far below.

"Yes, this is the final test, Nara. Porth's leap of faith."

"Lycans are great climbers but not... so well fallers."

"I believe in you, Nara, you just have to believe in yourself."

She nodded, biting down on her own teeth. "I can do this, I've come this far," Nara whispered to herself. Taking a deep breath, she swung her arms forward to jump but her legs did not move, causing her to fall backwards on her butt. She turned her head to the Mentor. "I don't think my legs are cooperating with me."

"Perhaps a running start is in order?"

"Oh! Great idea, mentor!" Nara replied, scooting back a bit before getting up into a running stance. She clenched her claws and started to run but then quickly halted. "Has there ever been a paladin, other than a human, mentor?"

"I will speak honestly, in my mentorship, no. But that does not limit one's abilities whether they are human or lycan. I have watched you grow, Nara, and you possess great potential, I assure."

"Thank you, Mentor Thalen, for everything," she declared, taking a few steps backwards as the mentor showed a faint smile and watched on. Nara breathed in deeply before she sprinted across the flat and leaped off the edge. She descended quickly, her heart racing as her eyes widened, looking frantically. The mountains, the forest, the grass all started to blur and she quickly moved her claws in front of her face, covering her eyes and forcing them shut. She did not feel the air brushing against her fur but instead felt stillness and warmth. She opened one eye and peeking through her claws she saw the vast Silpine forest.

"Nara! Down here!" Lance yelled from below. Nara removed her claws from her face and looked down to see the two paladins waving their arms at her.

"Lance!" she yelled back, waving an arm.

"Come down!" Lance yelled again. She nodded to herself, slowing her light wings until her paws touched the ground. Lance opened his arms for a hug but instead was met by a tackle from Nara.

Hundreds of people, including the King, watched on silently as the initiates spoke their vows and accepted their lightblades. Claudius stood in front of Mentor Zureal who held a lightblade with both hands, one holding the blade and the other the hilt.

"Will you bear the burden so light may forever exist?" Mentor Zureal questioned as Claudius looked at the lightblade before shifting his eyes to the mentor's.

"Absolutely," answered Claudius, opening both hands and extending his arms, receiving the sword.

"A moment?" Mentor Elle asked Lance as he nodded and followed her out of the room, down the hallway and into her office. "What's this all about, Mentor Elle?" Lance asked as she unlocked a large wooden chest in the corner of the room.

"Did you know your grandfather was a paladin, Lance?" she asked, looking over at him.

"Wait, really?" Lance replied with surprise plastered all over his face.

"Indeed. He was an outstanding paladin!"

"My father has never mentioned that before."

"That is strange…" Mentor Elle's voice trailed off as she rummaged around in the chest. "Ah! Here it is!" she blurted as she picked up a giant Warhammer from the chest and handed it to Lance.

"What?" Lance inquired as he took the weapon from Mentor Elle.

"It was your grandfather's; I knew he would want you to have it." She spoke while Lance examined the Warhammer with a huge smile. The two hammerheads of the hammer had a lion's fierce face on it with two sapphires as eyes on each face. The silver finish of the weapon had started to fade away with time and usage, but the weapon was beautiful nonetheless.

"Thank you so much, Mentor!" beamed Lance, still smiling as Mentor Elle nodded. "I have a dire question though…" Lance continued as his smile faded into a serious face.

"Yes, what is it?"

"Do you know any…greater healing techniques or anything of that sort?"

"Why are you asking this? Those abilities are quite dangerous for veteran paladins let alone newly initiated ones."

"The only reason I am standing in front of you, as a paladin is because of Claudius. If he were to ever become injured...and I was unable to help, I could never forgive myself," Lance explained as Mentor Elle searched her thoughts, weighing the decisions and finally looked at Lance with stern eyes.

"Yes, but I warn you, only use this in dire circumstances, got it?" she warned as Lance firmly nodded.

Chapter 5

Lance

Excitement. "I cannot wait to see our griffons!" Lance exclaimed while walking alongside Claudius up the pathway towards Griffon's Peak, which was a hatchery and training ground for griffons just on the edges of the capital. "Perhaps I shall get a giant griffon so that I may sleep while on travel or be a fighter, able to kill demons at my side or maybe a majestic one where everyone who watched me fly would be filled with envy!" he continued before turning his attention to Claudius. "Aren't you excited?"

"Of course, I've always dreamt of flying."

"Well, you certainly don't show your excitement."

"My mind is consumed with trying to decide on a name."

"Shit! A name... that thought had escaped from my mind." They finished walking on the stone stepped path that wrapped around the giant hill, reaching the entrance. There was a wooden fence that encircled the land on top. A giant wooden barn sat on the edge of the grassy plateau with a small wooden house attached to it. Lance pushed open the fence and started to sprint towards the small wooden house as Claudius closed the gate and casually walked in the same direction. Claudius walked past a giant oak tree that sat in the middle of the lot, the only thing that gave any sort of shade against the sun. It was relatively quiet except for a few wind chimes that would occasionally play with the wind.

Lance knocked on the wooden door of the house. A few moments later a lady opened the door and stepped outside. "Oh, greetings!" She spoke to the two paladins with a smile.

"Hello!" Lance replied.

"Good morning, and your name is?" Claudius questioned.

"Cathevne, I am the stable master here at the griffonary and your names?"

"Claudius and this is my brother, Lance." He raised his hand towards Lance who was almost shaking in excitement.

"I haven't had any visitors for quite some time, would you care for some tea?" she asked, taking one of her hands and combing it through her long curly brown hair.

"Oh, no, we are here for our griffons!" Lance replied.

"Ah, judging by your armor, you are the newly appointed paladins?"

"Yes, we are," Claudius replied.

"You two are quite early, I thought the paladins were coming around afternoon."

"We are; however, my brother here could not wait any longer to receive his griffon." Claudius replied, pointing to Lance who was still trembling with anticipation.

"I see, griffons are marvelous creatures and if I for one would be receiving a griffon, I wouldn't be able to wait either." Cathevne smiled again. "Come now, I'll show them to you." Cathevne walked towards the barn door as Claudius and Lance followed closely behind. She grabbed the iron handle of the giant wooden barn door and pulled. As she did, various sounds of sharp whistles and squawks erupted from the griffons inside. "Remain here, please," she instructed the paladins as she walked into the barn and greeted the griffons, "Hello, darlings!"

Claudius crossed his arms as he turned his attention to Lance who had an enormous smile on his face while his eyes were glued to the dark interior of the barn. A few moments had passed when Cathevne emerged from the barn holding a griffon in her arms as another followed closely behind her steps, both griffons about the size of a small round shield.

Lance's smile faded drastically, changing into surprised disappointment. "…what are those?" Lance questioned.

"Your griffon chicks," Cathevne replied. "There you go," as she gently pushed the griffon chick into Lance's chest, he moving his arms to hold onto it. It leaned forward and sniffed Lance before letting out a high-pitched whistle. Lance lifted the griffon chick up to his eye to inspect it.

"I thought we were getting… you know, full grown griffons."

"Oh, you will. They grow pretty fast," Cathevne replied, kneeling down and gently scooting the griffon chick towards Claudius. He knelt down, uncrossing his arms and extending his right arm towards the griffon chick. It lifted its head towards his hand and sniffed before walking closer. He placed his palm on the griffon chick's head and gently rubbed as it let out a soft coo.

"They're beautiful," Claudius sighed with his eyes fixated on the griffon chick's light brown feathered body.

"She's beautiful," Cathevne replied with a smile.

"…They don't look deadly," Lance spoke as he continued to eye the griffon chick.

"Well, not yet anyways, they are still babies," Cathevne replied, standing up and looking at Lance. "Have you picked a name for her?" Cathevne continued.

"Fuzzlebutt!" Lance blurted out followed by a short laugh. The griffon chick reared back its head and slammed it into Lance's head causing him to fall backwards. He landed on his back with a thud as the griffon chick flapped her wings in mid-air, landing on his chest. "…okay perhaps a better name is in order. Surina it is then!" Lance announced with a half-smile as he lifted his head up to see the griffon chick sit upon his chest, letting out a sharp squawk in approval. Claudius and Cathevne both erupted in laughter at the event. Claudius poked the griffon chick's yellow beak before reaching under and gently scratching her chin. She tilted her head up, letting out a soft coo.

"Sundra," Claudius decided with a smile.

"That is a fine name, Claudius," Cathevne replied.

Their reception was interrupted as they heard the wooden gate close from a distance. They turned their head in that direction to see a paladin walking towards them. The group stood up as the paladin drew closer and stopped, resting his left arm on the hilt of his lightblade and his right on his hip.

"Claudius?" The paladin asked.

"Yes?"

"You are being summoned to Light's Reach."

"May I ask why?"

"To further your Paladin's training. I am to be your guide to guarantee your trip to be a smooth one."

Claudius took a moment to think but that name was foreign to him, the only exception was his father had said that name a few times. He nodded his head to the paladin before kneeling down to Sundra and giving her a gentle pat on the head. "Be well," he whispered to her as he got up to face Lance. "Try not to drink yourself into oblivion."

"Safe travels, brother." Lance grinned while hitting his hand on Claudius' shoulder.

"Shall we proceed?" Claudius spoke facing the paladin.

The paladin nodded and replied, "It's three days travel by horse."

"I cannot wait for my griffon to grow," Claudius replied back as they both walked towards the gate.

Chapter 6

<u>Soonifer</u>

Agitated. "Where are we going?" Soonifer asked as he followed Ker'es for quite some time, with nothing but darkness surrounding them. Ker'es replied with silence. Eventually he could see a double row of pillars that seemed to lead towards a throne. Black iron torches hung from the pillars but even the fire dared not let out a sound. Lesser demons stood in front of each pillar, standing straight, their eyes looking forward in a statuesque pose. Ker'es stopped at the base of the stairs that led to an obsidian throne, extended his right arm signaling Soonifer to stand beside him. Soonifer cautiously stepped to Ker'es' side and looked up. He saw a massive lion's head made of stone that hung over the throne, its mouth open, showing its teeth as liquid fire poured from its mouth. He lowered his gaze, seeing a slender figure sitting upon the throne in an unusual way. The demon leaned against one arm of the throne while its legs were hanging over the other arm, with its face looking up into the blackness.

"Tern'natha, I require a favor," Ker'es whispered.

"...and that is?" The demon spoke in a rough sounding voice.

"Teach this one your spear."

The demon broke his gaze from the ceiling and looked below, his fiery red glowing eyes fixated on Soonifer. Soonifer could clearly see the demon had a lion's head on a human body. The demon pushed himself off the throne and stood up, taking a moment before walking down the short flight of stairs.

"This?" He pointed to Soonifer. Ker'es remained silent but the answer was clear. The demon stopped in front of Soonifer, he could see the deep red glowing eyes glaring at him. His face was ashen gray and his mane even darker.

After a moment that seemed forever, Tern'natha spoke in a rough, deep voice. "We are even."

Ker'es tilted his head before taking a step back and disappeared completely into the blackness. "Come, little demon." Tern'natha spoke as he walked off into the distance. Soonifer hesitated for a moment, looking around to find Ker'es nowhere and with little reluctance he followed the demon. The demon stopped walking near a massive hole that spanned miles. The whole area was better lit than the throne room. Peering up he could see strange black figures flying around and every so often they would release a purplish fire followed by a faint ghostly roar. He wondered if those beings were dragons; however, in all the books and stories that were told, all dragons had perished long ago. Then again, he just encountered two beings he had never imagined, one with an owl's head upon a man's body and now a lion's head upon a man's body, so anything seemed possible.

"Let's hope you don't fall into the pit," Tern'natha threatened, lifting his right hand, palm facing up. Soonifer noticed a scar on the palm of the demon's hand but before he could say anything, his hand was engulfed in a purple fire. A second later an obsidian spear appeared in the hand of the demon as the purple fire disappeared. Tern'natha tossed the spear to Soonifer who quickly caught it with both hands. The spear was extremely cold to touch but weighed next to nothing. He examined the spear for a moment before catching a glimpse of the lion-faced demon disappearing into thin air and reappearing far away. He was slightly confused at what was happening before he noticed the familiar purple flame appear in the demon's hand. The second the spear appeared in the demon's grasp, he reared back and threw the spear at Soonifer.

Quickly evading the attack, Soonifer tossed himself to the right, landing on the cold rocky surface. He looked up to see the demon in mid-throw. Soonifer pulled his spear close and rolled out of the way. The spear crashed into the solid ground where he just was, letting out a sharp metallic ring. He quickly pulled himself up, fixing his eyes upon the demon. Tern'natha hurled another spear which Soonifer narrowly dodged as he threw his own spear at the demon. The spear flew in the right direction but missed the demon completely. Tern'natha let out a foul laugh before proceeding to throw a multitude of spears at Soonifer.

Soonifer closed his fist, trying to spawn a spear like Tern'natha but he couldn't focus with a horde of spears flying at him. Sharp metallic rings echoed as each spear crashed into the ground. Soonifer ran, pulling a spear out from the ground as he steadied his aim for a brief moment and let out a grunt, hurling the spear at the demon. This time his aim was true, however Tern'natha simply took a step to the left, avoiding the spear completely. Soonifer stopped running as he reached a massive rock wall that stood towering behind him. He narrowed his eyes, watching the demons each throw. Soonifer mimicked the demon's moves, stepping only a few steps to either right or left instead of running around. Spears flew past him and collided with the rock wall behind him. As soon as the next spear flew past him, he turned around and ran towards the wall, leaping up the wall, grabbing a spear with both arms and pulling it out from the wall. He thrust himself off the wall with his legs, tilting his head back, he could see the demon upside down. He threw the spear with both arms using all of his might, twisting his body so he landed on his feet. He quickly bolted towards the wall and pulled a spear out to hurl it just left of the demon.

Tern'natha stepped to the left, dodging the first spear before noticing the second spear flying at him. He threw out his hand and grabbed the spear, stopping it mere inches from his face. He threw the spear down at the ground in anger as it let out a metallic clang. Tern'natha closed both of his hands as purple fire engulfed both of his fists. A spear appeared in each hand as Tern'natha's eyes glowed a bright red. He threw with increased fury, hurling a spear from each hand. Soonifer dodged as many spears as he could before the sheer number of spears was too much.

A spear slammed into the side of his torso, the intense force pushing him backwards, making him unable to move as he caught glimpse of another spear flying straight towards him. He closed his eyes and grit his teeth, hastily accepting his fate before hearing a metal clang. He opened his eyes in confusion, seeing Ker'es in front of him as the spear flipped uncontrollably in the air before hitting the ground.

He noticed Ker'es held a dagger in each hand before they disappeared. Shifting his eyes down to his body he could see the spear protruding from his torso. Wrapping both hands around the shaft, he pulled the spear out. A sharp pain pulsed throughout his body as he threw the spear to the ground. He pressed his right hand over the wound as warm blood seeped through. He walked forward, standing diagonally from Ker'es. Tern'natha had stopped an arm's distance away from Ker'es, not even acknowledging Soonifer's wound.

"I was just having a little fun," Tern'natha spoke as his eyes returned to a normal soft red glow. Ker'es remained silent as Tern'natha sneered, shaking his head. He walked forward, holding out his right arm as purple fire engulfed his hand. Ker'es turned, facing Soonifer. He stood his ground, not moving as the lion-headed demon walked towards him and stood in front of him. Soonifer hoped that Ker'es would intervene if Tern'natha tried to pull another trick.

"…and my spear you shall have." Ker'es smiled, slamming his hand on Soonifer's shoulder. His hand felt like an icicle, so cold that his shoulder felt as if it were burning. He tried to hold in the pain but it was too much to bare as he let out a horrific yell.

"Rrrraaahhhh!" Soonifer tore his hand from his wound and grabbed Tern'natha's wrist, trying to remove his hand but his wrist too was icy cold. The pain was too great, everything started to turn black.

Soonifer opened his eyes, feeling as if he had woken up from a dream. There stood Tern'natha in front of him and Ker'es beside him. Tern'natha let out a deep demonic laugh as he turned around, disappearing into the blackness.

"Summon a spear," Ker'es whispered. Soonifer lifted his arm and curled his hand into a fist, mimicking Tern'natha's actions. A purple fire erupted, engulfing his hand. He widened his eyes in amazement before slowly opening his palm. An obsidian spear appeared in his hand as the fire vanished. Bewildered, he wrapped his fingers around the spear, instantly feeling all the warmth escape from his hand. The longer he held the spear the colder his hand seemed to become. His hand started to become numb before he tossed the spear aside, letting out a clang as it hit the ground before disappearing. He could not believe what had just happened, he shifted his attention to Ker'es, whose hollow black eyes were still fixated upon him.

"Heal yourself," Ker'es whispered.

"How..?" Soonifer replied, looking down at his torso, blood still seeping through the wound. The only thing he could think of was to cauterize it. He clutched his hand into a fist and once again the purple fire erupted. He pressed his palm against the wound, feeling an uncomfortable coldness before the sensation stopped. He removed his hand as the fire disappeared and to his amazement the wound had completely healed. "I don't understand," Soonifer spoke, looking up to Ker'es.

"In time, you will," Ker'es whispered. "You are to steal the Hammer of Creation from the Citadel of Light."

"Me...?" Soonifer replied, a little confused by the fact. "Am I ready to do such a task?"

"No, you will fail," Ker'es whispered. Pride suddenly flooded into Soonifer as his eyes flashed bright red.

"Then why are you sending me to my doom?" he bellowed, clutching both of his hands into a fist. Ker'es remained silent and still, his gaze locked on Soonifer. Soonifer's red eyes dimmed back to normal as he looked down at his hands which he opened to see his palms before looking back up at Ker'es.

"I'm sorry... I don't know what just happened," Soonifer spoke in his regular voice.

"This is not under my instruction but Gor'eck's."

Soonifer let out a long drawn sigh before reluctantly nodding his head. Ker'es slammed his foot into the ground and a few seconds later a demon appeared next to Soonifer. He turned his head and examined the demon. She had short black hair, with the similar red glowing eyes that he had. She wore a strange black robe that covered most of her body although the parts of her that were revealed showed her ashen skin. A single black candle stood on each of her shoulders with a purple flame crowned on top. She had a chain sashed around her shoulder that crossed her chest and rested at her waist. There was an odd black book tied to the chain which rested against her waist.

"Tormentor Ker'es, what can I do for you?" Her voice was soft and calming. Not loud nor deafening but something truly gentle. Soonifer quickly became entranced by this demon.

"Take him to the rift, see that he gets to Light's Reach."

"Understood," the demon replied, nodding her head.

Ker'es disappeared instantly as the demon turned to Soonifer and signaled for him to follow. Soonifer followed her down a corridor of stairs that seemed to descend endlessly in a spiral. The only source of light were torches mounted on the stone walls.

"What is your name?" Soonifer broke the monotonous sound of stone steps.

"Edge'knol," she replied.

"My name is S-" he began to speak but was cut off.

"Soonifer," she finished. "There has been quite a lot of talk about you."

"Talk?" Soonifer asked curiously.

"Yes, I keep track of all demons that reside in the first level of the nether."

"How does one do such a task?"

"Perhaps I can show you sometime, but you are currently tasked with an objective and shouldn't stray from it."

"Fair enough," Soonifer said to himself.

They arrived at the end of the stairs which led into a giant room that held hundreds of doors. Some doors were wooden, others made of stone. Some doors had chains wrapped around them while others had iron bars sealing the door shut. In the middle of the room was a lectern comprised of two demons facing away from each other as each raised an arm holding a map.

Edge'knol held her arm as purple fire engulfed her slender hand, then placed it on the lectern, moving it slowly. The floating doors began to move in a circular direction following her hand movements. She stopped moving her hand as a black door appeared in front of them. She walked towards the door and opened it as Soonifer followed. They entered into a room with two giant demons standing in front of them with their arms crossed.

"Light's Reach, please," she asked as the two demons turned, facing each other. The demon on the left withdrew an obsidian dagger which glowed a dark purple. Turning its back against them, the demon reared back and stabbed the air, quickly pulling its hand downward. Soonifer looked onward and saw that the dagger seemed to have cut the air and created some sort of rift from which light appeared to seep through. The demon sheathed its dagger, then pushed both of its hands into the rift and grabbed a hold of it. The other demon did the same, grabbing a hold of the rift and simultaneously they pulled the rift apart. Soonifer widened his eyes, seeing trees and a blue sky, something he thought he would never see again.

"Try not to die," Edge'knol spoke as the rift closed behind him.

Chapter 7

Claudius

Eagerness. The bright sun beat against his back as his cape dangled in the air. Claudius wasn't sitting on his horse but was leaned up near the horse's neck in excitement, anticipating his arrival to Light's Reach. He could see three small stone keeps that sat up on a small cliff which guarded the road to the main fortress. He squinted his eyes, barely seeing the top of the Citadel in the horizon.

"He-yah!" Claudius yelled, snapping the reins to his horse as he raced behind the paladin who was escorting him to the Citadel.

"We are only a few short moments- "The other paladin yelled before he was cut off. Claudius saw a spear slam into the right side of the paladin, knocking him off his horse.

"By the divine!" Claudius yelled as he pulled the reins upwards with all of his might, signaling his horse to halt. The horse stopped while he looked at the paladin to see he was not moving, with a spear going through his upper torso. He turned his head in the direction from where the spear was thrown to see another spear dancing in the air towards him. He threw himself off his horse, evading the spear as the horse let out a startled neigh before running off towards the Citadel.

Claudius felt his muscles tense, his heart racing as light flooded his eyes and he pushed himself off the ground and flew towards the attacker. He saw the being spawn another spear and hurl it at him. Claudius unsheathed his lightblade quickly and deflected the spear. Only yards away, he lifted his sword into the air, readying for a downward strike but as he drew nearer he hesitated and froze.

"Soonifer!?" Claudius yelled as he released his ascended form, landing on his feet. Soonifer stood still, remaining silent but in a combative pose. "Where have you been, brother? You have been missing for a month now!" Claudius expressed.

"You have no idea.... what I have endured," Soonifer replied. Claudius lowered his blade but kept it ready, seeing his brother with new found red glowing eyes.

"A lot of people are asking questions about your involvement with the plague in Irrend, let alone you just killed a paladin!"

Soonifer stared forward at his brother but remained silent. Claudius grit his teeth in anger, seeing his brother show no remorse for the actions he had committed.

"If you only took your paladin's training seriously then none of this would have happened!" Claudius yelled, raising his left hand and pointing at his brother. Soonifer's heart raced as pride flooded his mind, he recalled always standing in his brother's shadow of achievements and accomplishments.

"No more!" Soonifer roared, his eyes exploding in bright red as he clenched his right hand, spawning a spear and lunging at Claudius who parried the attack and swung downwards with his blade. Soonifer quickly pulled the spear towards himself and raised it above him with both hands, blocking the attack. He pulled the spear down and quickly swiped the spear at Claudius. The tip of the spear ripped into the chest plate but did not scathe his body. Claudius fumbled backwards before regaining his balance, his left hand ran against his chest plate which he examined closely. He saw no blood and stepped forward, pushing off against the ground and charging at Soonifer, sword raised.

Claudius swung his sword diagonally only to have it blocked again by Soonifer's spear. He quickly drew his sword in and lunged his blade forward, stabbing Soonifer's torso. The tip of the blade pierced Soonifer's tunic with ease and his body much easier. Claudius pulled his sword back as thick black blood followed, more blood pouring profusely from the wound. He thought that the damage inflicted would have subdued his brother but he was wrong. Soonifer retaliated back, swinging his spear wildly with increased ferocity. Claudius blocked each of the attacks as metal clanged with every strike. His hand started to hurt from the sheer force of the incoming attacks. Soonifer jumped up towards him, rearing back his arm before jabbing his spear at Claudius. He tried to deflect the blow with his sword but it was too powerful, knocking his sword from his grasp. Soonifer jabbed at Claudius with his spear, thinking quickly, Claudius grabbed the spear and yanked with all his might, pulling Soonifer close.

Claudius reared back his arm and closed his hand into a fist as light

surrounded his hand, spawning Porth's mace. He full-fledged

swung the mace, cracking it against the side of Soonifer's head.

Soonifer released the spear, stumbling backwards but Claudius

pursed after him. Pulling his mace towards him, he unleashed a

powerful backhand swing with his mace at Soonifer who barely

dodged the attack. Claudius reared back his arm for another attack

but Soonifer leaped forward and grabbed a hold of his chest plate.

Soonifer reared back his head and slammed in into Claudius who

fell backwards, closing his eyes in pain as his back slammed

against the ground. He opened his eyes to see Soonifer standing

over him with a spear in hand. He couldn't move before Soonifer

slammed the spear into his upper torso. The sharp pain pulsed

throughout his body as he let out a yell.

"Arrrgggh!" Claudius let out as he reached for the spear

but Soonifer pulled it out with his left hand. He reared back his left

arm, holding the spear high up into the air with the spearhead

pointing down at Claudius. Soonifer grit his teeth as he started to

pull his arm downwards but stopped when he felt three sharp pains

pulse through his body. He looked at himself to see an arrow had struck him in his right shoulder, his upper chest and lower torso.

He looked outward in the direction from where the arrows had been shot and saw an elf who had just released another arrow. The arrow cut through the air rapidly and found its mark, hitting Soonifer's chest. He let out a demonic yell, turning his body towards the elf and lifted the spear, readying to throw. Claudius turned his head and caught sight of his sword, quickly turning his body to grab it. Using all of his might, he pushed himself off the ground and swung his sword upwards, slicing Soonifer's left hand, cutting it clean off. Soonifer let out another demonic roar before falling backwards. The ground shook violently for a moment as the earth split into two, revealing an endless black crack. Soonifer fell into the hole, staring up at the crack as he continued to descend into darkness. With his right hand he grabbed an arrow that was stuck in his chest and ripped it out. The light got smaller and smaller until once again he was surrounded by blackness.

Claudius looked onward and caught eyes with the elf. She turned around and slipped back into the Silpine forest. He pulled himself up and clutched his chest with his left arm, groaning in pain. *Who was she?* He thought to himself and decided to run after her. When he entered the forest, he knew the elves were not friendly towards humans but he wanted to know the name of his savior. Quickening his pace, he passed trees and bushes and eventually saw the familiar elf. He further quickened his pace and caught up to her, reaching out with his right hand he grabbed her arm.

She quickly turned around, looking at Claudius and yelled, "Stop!" Claudius froze in his place but noticed her eyes were not on him but looking behind him. He released her arm and turned around to see a giant stone golem with its arms raised to attack but frozen in place. Claudius fell backwards in surprise, crawling backwards with his arms and legs away from the golem. "It's okay, Rockstead," she assured as the golem obeyed and rested its arms against its body.

"...I can see why humans don't enter the Silpine forest," Claudius said, catching his breath while looking at the elf.

"Yes, most humans are smart enough to stay out," she replied sternly.

"I'm not most humans, I'm a paladin and I just wanted to say..." Claudius paused as he let out another groan clutching his chest. "...Thank you for saving me," he finished, letting out a long heavy breath. She whistled and pointed at the ground behind the paladin as the giant golem moved as instructed and with a thump, the golem sat down on the ground.

"At first glance you could have mistaken it for a large pile of rocks…" Claudius spoke. The elf let out a sigh and pulled Claudius to the golem. He sat on the ground and rested his back against the golem and looked at the elf. The elf kneeled down next to him.

"Help me take off your chest plate," she demanded as he did what she asked. He undid the chest plate and tore it off, revealing his blood stained shirt. She pulled the shirt apart to gain access to the wound and pulled off her necklace. She opened the small stone vial and poured the liquid into the wound. Claudius held his breath in anticipation of pain but instead he felt a soft warm touch on his wound. He looked at his torso to see his wound had completely healed.

"Lunnah," she whispered, wiping the blood away from the area while taking small peeks at his face.

"What?" Claudius replied bewildered at what just happened.

"That's my name."

"Oh, yes… that's right. Thank you, Lunnah, and I was referring to what just happened…? What did you pour in my wound?"

"Water from our sacred tree," she answered, her hazel eyes no longer hard but soft.

"That's amazing! Can you get more?"

"Yes, but it's rare, not often do trees cry." Claudius shifted his gaze from Lunnah to his wound, examining it.

"Yeah… buildings in the city don't cry that often either," he said, his voice trailing off. Lunnah smacked his torso in response to his words. "Ow! What did you do that for? I was only joking."

Lunnah playfully sneered, "Oh, you'll be alright."

"Yeah, thanks to you. You saved my life." Claudius spoke again, turning his attention to her before looking at his right hand. He curled it into a fist and light started to escape from his hand until a mace appeared. He held it for a moment before it disappeared. "Still got it!" He exclaimed with a smile.

"Wait! I've seen that mace before!" Lunnah cried with a little surprise in her voice.

"This?" Claudius asked as he summoned the mace again and held it in front of her.

"Yes! It has been ages ago but I recall seeing another human with it," she replied, reaching out and touching the mace. She ran her hands against the spikes that imitated the mane of a lion. At the end of the ball was a lion whose mouth was open where the handle was attached. "This is exactly it but... he died." Her voice cut off as she delved deep into thought.

"What do you remember?" Claudius asked curiously. There was silence between them both, only the soft brushing of leaves against the wind echoed in the forest with an occasional animal that let out a call.

"...I was only a child then, I had wandered, exploring the forest and I caught sight of two beings fighting, the one had red eyes similar to the one we saw earlier while the one wielding the mace had blue," she recalled. "I went to go check what had happened, but both of them were on the ground dead."

"Could it be him...?" Claudius whispered to himself.

"Whom?"

"A divine, well... the previous life of a human before becoming a divine."

"I don't understand." Lunnah shook her head as her long dark brown hair waved.

"Me neither," Claudius conceded. "I must go to the Citadel of Light. They were expecting us before we got attacked," Claudius remembered as he tried to get up.

"No, stay." Lunnah reached and placed her palm on his chest. "I shall go and see what has become of that man and return, while you should rest," Lunnah commanded. Claudius thought it over and reluctantly shook his head and agreed. He watched Lunnah walk away and vanish among the forest.

Chapter 8

<u>Soonifer</u>

Darkness. Soonifer continued to fall deeper into the nether, his initial descent was one filled with fear, loneliness and sorrow but this time he felt as if he were returning home. He grabbed the shaft of the last arrow that was sticking in him and ripped it out. He held it in front of him as purple fire engulfed his hand and the arrow too. The arrow caught on fire and quickly burnt away into nothing as he placed his palm on his chest, healing the last of the arrow wounds.

Anger fills his mind. *How could I be weaker than my brother? When I have been through nothing but torment, pain and darkness...* He whispered to himself as he landed on his feet, catching himself with his right hand on the ground and stood up to find himself in a similar room where Tern'natha was, except some of the pillars were broken. He looked onward and saw the ram-headed demon sitting upon an obsidian throne. He had four arms, two of which rested upon the arms of the chair while the other two were crossed against his chest.

"I see you have brought me no hammer," the ram-headed demon growled, a demonic tone echoing after each word. "I have no use for you." At that moment, one of the greater demons standing in front of a pillar stepped forward and faced the throne.

"Let me slay the Demiah!" The ram-headed demon raised one of his hands in acknowledgement before putting his hand back down on the arm rest. The greater demon turned to Soonifer and started to walk towards him with a wicked smile. Soonifer clutched his hand into a fist as it exploded into a purple fire. He pressed his palm against the stump of his other arm, cauterizing it. He glared at the approaching demon who stood a little over seven feet tall and with each step it took, the ground trembled. He closed his hand once again as a spear appeared. He quickly threw it at the greater demon who managed to evade it completely. The greater demon quickened his pace to a full-on sprint. Soonifer spawned another spear and hurled it at the approaching demon. This time the demon swung its massive arms, deflecting the attack. The greater demon raised its arms for a downward strike but just as he reached his target, Soonifer cartwheeled towards the greater demon's side, catching himself with his right arm and pushing himself off the ground, landing behind the demon. Purple fire erupted in his hand as another spear spawned, which he threw with all of his might. The spear slammed into the back of the demon as it let out a terrifying roar. The demon reached behind him and grabbed the spear, ripping it out from its back and throwing it on the ground where it let out a clang against the stone ground.

The greater demon turned around, facing Soonifer and once again charged at him with its arms flailing wildly in the air. Soonifer spawned another spear but this time he charged the demon head on. As the two met, Soonifer leaped in the air, raising his arm and slamming the spear into the chest of the demon. The demon roared again in pain as it swung its arms, knocking Soonifer backwards. He landed on his back and grunted in pain, raising his head to see the demon grab the spear and pull it out from its chest and throw it on the ground again. The greater demon snarled as it ran towards Soonifer. He scrambled to get up and once again ran to meet the demon. He spawned another spear but this time he aimed lower and hurled the spear at the left knee of the charging demon. The spear crushed into the knee of the demon causing it to stumble forward and eventually fall forward. Soonifer clutched his hand as yet another spear appeared in his hand and with all of his might he slammed the head of the spear into the head of the demon. He felt the skull collapse as the entire front end of the spear pierced the head of the demon. He released the spear and turned around, facing the ram-headed demon as the greater demon collapsed to the ground with a heavy thud.

Soonifer breathed heavily as his eyes glowed a furious red, closing his right hand into a fist, another spear appeared. He clenched the spear tightly, ignoring the cold bite of the spear. Suddenly, Ker'es appeared beside the ram-headed demon. Ker'es stared at Soonifer for a moment before turning his attention towards the ram-headed demon.

"He shows potential," Ker'es whispered. The ram-headed demon sneered in response and remained silent for a moment before finally speaking.

"So, what do you suggest?" he inquired as a demonic echo shadowed his words.

"Give him the rank he has killed for," Ker'es responded. There was an uncomfortable silence before the ram-headed demon stood up and spoke.

"Welcome, Greater demon Soonifer." Ker'es disappeared and reappeared in front of the new greater demon, however Soonifer's eyes were still locked on the ram-headed demon.

"Come," Ker'es whispered as he turned around and walked between a pair of pillars, slipping into the darkness. Soonifer took a few steps in the path that Ker'es walked before abruptly turning around and hurling the spear at one of the demons who stood against a pillar. The spear pierced the head of the demon as the spearhead crunched into the stone pillar. Soonifer then turned around and disappeared into the darkness.

Soonifer followed Ker'es down the familiar stone stairs where he had walked previously with Edge'knol. He did not know what to say but instead embraced the silence. He stopped at the demon statue lectern and placed his hand on the map. The doors quickly shifted as an obsidian door appeared in front of them. The door opened revealing a dark room. Ker'es entered and Soonifer followed. Ker'es stopped at the edge of what seemed to be a circular pool of water that seemed to almost mimic a mirror. Ker'es looked down at the pool and spoke.

"What is the most thing you desire?" Soonifer thought for a moment, delving deep into his thoughts. He could think of a few things he desired the most, to have been successful at the paladins' academy, to be his brother's equal and to be at Alorah's side. He returned back to reality and walked towards the pool, stopping just at the edge, he looked up at Ker'es before looking down at the pool. He was in complete shock that he saw himself standing by Alorah's side, hand in hand. The one thing he noticed most about the image was that they looked happy, an emotion that seemed to have become distant as of late.

"Put your left arm into the pool," Ker'es whispered, breaking the silence. Soonifer obeyed, as he started to kneel down, he could see the image of Alorah fade away while his reflection stayed. He slowly put his left arm into the pool and stopped when his elbow touched the water. He suddenly felt something grab his stump of a hand and tried pulling his arm out but it was too powerful. Before long he felt a painful sensation shoot up his whole left arm as he yelled out in pain. He grabbed the edge of the pool with his right hand and pressed against it and eventually whatever had his arm let go. The commotion sent three ripples throughout the pool before becoming perfectly still. He looked at his left arm and to his amazement, he had a new left hand. Pulling his left hand close he examined it. It was as if his hand had never been cut off. Opening his palm he could see a slit going across his palm and before he could touch it with his right hand it opened. A black eye was looking directly at him but before he could do anything, his palm closed. Soonifer closed his hand into a fist before opening it and yet the slit remained.

"What is this eye that is embedded in my hand?" Soonifer asked, standing up.

Ker'es remained silent for a moment before replying, "Ko'vik's eye." Soonifer looked at his hand once again in confusion.

"…and my hand miraculously healed? What does this pool really do?"

"Come," Ker'es commanded while walking out of the room and once again Soonifer followed.

They stood in the room filled with doors before Ker'es pressed his hand on the lectern and closed the door.

"Do you remember the place where Tern'natha toyed with you?" Ker'es whispered. Soonifer took a moment to collect his thoughts, remembering a rocky flat surface next to a giant bottomless black pit.

"Yes" he replied.

"Imagine yourself there, your feet standing upon the rocky ground. Do not use your eyes to picture yourself, that is folly. Instead simply imagine and it shall be so," Ker'es whispered as he disappeared completely.

Soonifer stared at where Ker'es had previously stood in bewilderment. *What?* He thought to himself before remembering what Ker'es had just said. He closed his eyes and pictured himself standing on the rocky surface near the pit and instantly he could feel the shadows of the nether cling to him. He felt his whole body become consumed by darkness and yet he didn't struggle. For a split second he felt weightless before opening his eyes and suddenly he felt the burden of his body. He looked around and there he was, standing on the familiar rocky surface and in front of him, the bottomless black pit. He turned his head to the right and there stood Ker'es, looking back at him.

"Give me your right hand," Ker'es whispered. Soonifer raised his right hand before him with his palm facing up. Ker'es placed his hand on Soonifer's and instantly he felt his hand burning. He could feel his flesh searing from Ker'es' hand and as he yelled out, his human tone turned into a deep demonic one. The pain was beyond unbearable but he dared not pull his hand away. Ker'es removed his hand and instantly Soonifer clutched his right hand into a fist as purple fire erupted. A black obsidian dagger appeared in his hand as the fire vanished. He gripped the dagger tightly and started to feel the similar intense burning feeling again. He released the dagger and it fell, turning to dust as soon as it touched the ground. He looked at his hand before turning his attention to Ker'es, who stared at him for a moment with his familiar hallow black eyes before whispering, "There is two." Ker'es stomped on the ground with his leg as three demons with bows in hand appeared from the shadows in a triangle formation with Soonifer in the middle.

They wore no clothing, thus exposing their ashen skin except for a loin cloth and a leather quiver. They reached back, grabbing an arrow and aimed in unison as Ker'es disappeared. They each aimed at Soonifer who quickly clutched both hands into fists. Purple fire erupted, engulfing both hands as a dagger appeared in each hand with the blade pointed inward towards him. At that moment, the three demons released their arrows with the snap of their bows. Soonifer felt the familiar burning sensation in his hands and started to sear. He noticed time had seemed to slow down; the three arrows were merely drifting in the air towards him. He ran forward, lifting his right dagger up and slammed the tip of the dagger against the arrowhead, sending the arrow spinning away. He quickly turned around and deflected the other two arrows in the same manner.

He released the daggers from his grasp, time seeming to continue as normal as the demons reached for another arrow. Soonifer spawned a spear and hurled it at one of the demons, slamming it into the chest of the demon, knocking him down with the sheer force. The two remaining demons released their arrows, this time they zipped through the air towards Soonifer. He turned around and caught a glimpse of the arrows and spawned his daggers just in time to deflect them. The demons readied their bows and fired another volley of arrows. Soonifer closed his eyes for a moment, imaging himself standing behind one of the archers.

As soon as he felt the shadows take hold of his body, he opened his eyes to find himself standing behind one of the archers. He raised both of his arms and slammed both daggers into the neck of the archer who collapsed instantly, falling to the ground. The last demon frantically fired a barrage of arrows at Soonifer who deflected each one while walking towards the demon. As Soonifer got close, the demon dropped its bow and ran away. Soonifer released the daggers and spawned a spear, raising it to throw at the retreating demon. The spear slammed into the demon's skull, killing it instantly.

Ker'es appeared next to the greater demon. Soonifer looked at his hands for a moment to see if he had incurred any damage from the daggers but he had none.

"I have another task for you," Ker'es whispered.

"Will I fail this time?" Soonifer replied hastily. There was a short silence between them before Ker'es continued.

"I recommend another greater demon accompany you for this." Ker'es lifted his leg up to stomp.

"May I make a suggestion?" Soonifer offered, stopping Ker'es who placed his leg back down. "I have someone in mind."

The night was dark as a cool breeze ruffled the leaves of trees. Soonifer pushed the wooden doors of the Parrish estate open. He looked around and could see everything was as he last remembered.

"Nox!" Soonifer yelled. Suddenly, he could hear the rampart legs of the wolf running down the wooden stairs. The wolf pup had grown quite big since the last time he saw him. Nox sat at the bottom of the stairs looking at Soonifer. "Do you remember me?" Soonifer asked while walking towards the wolf. Nox tilted his head for a moment before full-on sprinting towards Soonifer, leaping at him. Soonifer caught Nox in mid-air wrapping both arms around him. Nox tried to lick his face before trying to gnaw on his worn leather tunic. Soonifer turned around and started to walk out of the building.

A servant quietly peered from the wall seeing a person walking outside. She slowly crept across the room to see the person walking into a black rift while holding the wolf. The second they entered the rift, it closed and the rift vanished into thin air. She quickly closed the wooden doors, locking it before turning around to see Alorah there with a sleepy expression.

"Who was that?" she asked in a sleepy tone.

"Oh, it was nothing my lady, please return to your chambers," the servant replied as Alorah sleepily nodded her head and walked off.

Soonifer stood at the edge of the pool while holding Nox with both arms. "Are you sure, Ker'es?" he asked while looking at Nox. He shifted his attention to Ker'es who stared back silently. He let out a sigh and lowered Nox into the pool. Taking a step back, he watched as the last few ripples reached the edge of the pool before becoming completely still. Just as he was about to take a step forward to see if anything had happened, a giant, jet black lycan burst from the pool as water splashed everywhere and landed on the opposite end of the pool. It turned around to reveal a pair of red glowing eyes. Soonifer stared in marvel at what had happened and finally managed to utter a word.

"Nox?" Soonifer queried. The giant lycan leaped across the pool and on top of Soonifer, knocking him to the ground, standing over him on all fours and licking his face. Soonifer reached up with his right hand and patted Nox's head.

Chapter 9

Blackness. Light Warden stood tall, unyielding to the Nether. Light itself poured from his bright blue eyes as he stared into the boundless abyss. Nothing escaped his stalwart gaze, letting no shadow or demon past him. His left hand clenched into a fist at his side while his right held firmly to a fiery sword, waiting to strike at will. A pair of light wings folded behind him which gave his silver lined armor a faint white glow. The massive portal behind him led to the realm of the living, in front was the Nether and in between was a long bridge made of light. The bridge was brightest where the Light Warden stood and as it reached farther into the void, the color of the bridge slowly faded, matching the color of the blackness. The Light Warden continued to stare into the abyss knowing that thousands of demons stared back, watching his every move.

A large shadowy hand flew from the darkness straight towards the Light Warden, its flight speed incredible but unparalleled against the Light Warden's reflexes. He swung his sword diagonally upward, horizontally, then finally diagonally downward in a single motion. Giant waves of light escaped from his fiery blade forming an upside-down triangle, ripping the shadowy hand apart. The waves continued exposing the blackness, killing any demon caught in the light/path. Hundreds of demons ran from the waves before the light dissipated and the shadows returned, concealing the horrors of the Nether.

"Kavas, I miss you." The Light Warden lowered his sword into a resting stance while standing perfectly still, the only thing moving were the flames on his sword. His gaze was forward but his mind (elsewhere) was not, the voice familiar but where had he heard it from? He searched his thoughts, trying to recollect the voice until he felt something press against his right shoulder and at that moment he remembered. Maurea. It seemed ages ago since he heard her voice, let alone the memory of her which was so distant.

"Have you forgotten me, love?" He heard the voice again, even feeling a harder tug on his shoulder armor. *It can't be, she can't be here,* he thought. He felt a kiss on his cheek. The Light Warden widened his eyes in surprise as he turned his head to the right to see if she was really there and instantly died. The shadows of the Nether slowly crept across the bridge, swallowing the light it had emitted as if night approached day.

Chapter 10

Claudius

"I hope to see you soon," Claudius spoke, looking into Lunnah's soft hazel eyes.

"So, I can save you again?" Lunnah replied with a slight giggle.

"If it means I can see you again then I shall stand in danger's way once more," he declared with a smile.

"I'll see you around, paladin," she teased, turning around quickly to hide her smile as she strode off into the Silpine forest.

***

"Who are you?" one of the paladin guards asked as Claudius arrived at the giant wooden gate of Light's Reach.

"I am Claudius… I was supposed to arrive earlier but was attacked by a demon. He killed my escort," Claudius replied, shaking his head.

"Yes, we were expecting you two, and we've retrieved his body. It was a damn shame, paladin Karthus was a great man! May the divines give him peace." The guard spoke while lifting his arm and signaling the guard in the tower above to open the gates. The massive wooden gates opened slowly, revealing a giant of a man standing inside.

"Claudius!" the man shouted and walked hastily towards Claudius.

"Hello?" Claudius questioned with a little confusion in his voice. The large man stood before him and reached out with his hand. Claudius reached out in return and grabbed his wrist.

"I cannot believe my eyes, how you have grown into a man, a paladin no less!" the man bellowed.

"Do I know you, friend?" Claudius asked again, releasing his hand and placing it at his side.

"I doubt you would remember me, you were just learning how to walk when I last saw you! My name is Kaypel, I am one of your father's close friends!"

"Ah, that would explain it."

"Please, come in! We have much to discuss and plan!" Kaypel said, turning his body and pointing his hand inside the courtyard. Claudius nodded and walked inside as Kaypel walked beside him, the massive wooden doors closing behind them.

They entered a giant stone room that was well lit by the many torches that hung on the walls with a large candle chandelier hanging from the center of the ceiling. A colossal rectangular mahogany table sat in the middle of the room accompanied by various mahogany chairs at the side. An assortment of scrolls and parchment were strewn about on the table. Claudius looked around the room and could see statues of various paladins in heroic poses.

"Claudius! Welcome!" Another paladin spoke who was standing at the end of the table. Claudius walked towards him and noticed he wore the same ceremonial armor that Kaypel wore. The armor was trimmed with brilliant silver with a dark blue cape attached to the pauldrons. He had only seen a few around the capital in his life. Claudius extend his hand towards the man who excitedly grabbed his wrist and gave a hardy squeeze.

"Who are you?" Claudius questioned.

"Oh, please forgive me, I am paragon Arywin. I have heard news of your completion of the academy and could not wait to see you in person!"

"Thank you, paragon, for the warm welcome," Claudius spoke as they released their hands.

"I can see paragon Kaypel has already met with you," he said, glancing at Kaypel before returning his gaze to Claudius.

"Yes, he was very kind" Claudius replied, but noticed something disturbing Arywin. "I sense something troubling you, what is the matter?"

Arywin let out a deep sigh and walked over to the corner of the table and signaled Claudius to follow.

"Look here," he said. Claudius followed and looked at the map of the known world. He looked around the map, seeing the massive mountains in the north followed by the Silpine forest and eventually looked at where Arywin was pointing. He was pointing to the keep that sat at the southern side of the capital.

"Yes? What about that place?" Claudius questioned.

"Do you know the significance of that place, Claudius?"

"Sorry, No, I do not."

"It's where the Eternal Gate is located." Claudius thought for a moment, remembering a brief lecture about the Eternal Gate.

"…isn't that supposed to be the bridge between this world and the Nether?" Claudius suggested.

"Yes, and we have just received word that the Light Warden there has just died."

"What does that mean?"

"It means we have a very limited amount of time to select another to become a Light Warden."

"And if we don't?" The conversation fell silent as Paragon Arywin shifted his eyes downward to think before looking back up to Claudius.

"Hordes of demons would be allowed to enter our world without resistance." Claudius looked at Kaypel and turned to Arywin.

"How long does it take to find a new one?"

"The selection process is difficult. In theory, any paladin can become a Light Warden; however, once you enter the Eternal Gate you cannot come back," Kaypel explained.

"A death sentence?" Claudius replied.

"It's a price we must pay to keep our world from demons," Arywin replied while walking away from the map and standing at the other side of the table. "The life of a Light Warden is demanding, there is no communication, no rest, and you are constantly being attacked by the demons of the Nether… this is no task for the weak," Arywin continued as he grabbed a letter off the table and shook his head. Claudius pushed himself off the table and delved deep into his thoughts. *Was this his life's purpose? To become a Light Warden? Divine Porth mentioned nothing of this…* He snapped back to reality and looked directly at Paragon Arywin and firmly spoke.

"I'll be the next Light Warden."

"Wait! Let's not be so hasty!" Kaypel interrupted as he briskly walked towards Claudius. He placed his hand on Claudius' shoulder. "I am heartfelt that you would volunteer but that is a big decision to make, Claudius."

"How long will it take to reach the Eternal Gate from here?" Claudius asked as Kaypel pulled his hand off his shoulder.

"Three days or so." Kaypel crossed his arms. "What did you have in mind?"

"Let's depart for the Eternal Gate and perhaps on the way you can fill me in all the details about being a Light Warden," Claudius replied with a smirk.

"Your mind is set on this?"

"Someone has to do it."

"Very well, I'll send instruction for horses and supplies," Kaypel agreed, placing his left hand on the hilt of his lightblade, turning around and walking out of the room.

"You are brave, Claudius, your father would be proud," Arywin beamed, reaching for a quill and fresh parchment before proceeding to write a letter. Claudius walked towards the map, giving it one last look before walking out of the room.

Claudius and Kaypel rode out of Light's Reach with the heavy sun on their backs. A gentle breeze accompanied them on their trip south to the Eternal Gate. The miles seemed short as they paced along the countryside. He looked upward and could see the giant, blue, cloudless sky, with no doubt in his mind that he would see the sky again. Claudius could see a giant city with stone walls in the distance. The city was well lit with torches in watch towers and in the market, a haven from the approaching darkness of the night.

"Let's rest there!" Kaypel yelled pointing at the city as he turned his head to Claudius. Claudius nodded in agreement as they rode on towards the city. The well-worn dirt road was lit with stone torches that lined alongside the road. They were stopped at the gate of the city by a multitude of guards wielding steel halberds.

"Halt!" one of the guards cried out, holding his left palm in the air. The two paladins obeyed, pulling on the reins of their horses as the guard walked towards them. "What is your business?" the guard questioned, looking up towards them.

"We seek shelter for the night," Kaypel replied, placing his hand on the hilt of his light blade and pulling the sword halfway out, exposing the glowing white blade.

"Paladins! Welcome to the City of Kionta. May her blessing embrace you!" the guard yelled as he stepped back and signaled the other guards to move.

"Thank you, friend." Kaypel sheathed his sword and snapped the reins as he rode into the city. Claudius followed closely behind looking around and he could see the thick stone walls that shielded the city from any outside attacks. The hooves of the horses clacked as they transitioned from dirt to the polished stone floor of the city. The night had stolen the sky but the city was still much alive as the denizens walked about their business.

"Claudius, would you like to see Kionta's statue?" Kaypel inquired.

"Of course," Claudius replied while his eyes darted around, seeing all the marvelous stone buildings that covered the city. "How come the capital isn't this nice?" Claudius wondered as they rode along the polished stone streets of the city.

"Because the capital isn't sacred or a pilgrimage site," Kaypel replied.

Claudius laughed and said to himself, "That is true." They stopped in front of an inn and dismounted from their horses. Claudius patted the side of his horse as he tied the reins to the post.

"Here," Kaypel signaled Claudius to follow. "It's just a small walk ahead," Kaypel continued. They approached the center of the city where Claudius caught sight of the statue's head. As they walked closer he could see that the statue was well over 15 feet in height. Kionta stood tall with her head looking straight. The butt of her halberd was planted into the ground as she held the pole with an outstretched arm. She wore the traditional paladin's armor that was worn in the godless era, her left hand resting on her hip.

There was a statue of a man at her side which stood about half the size of her. His facial expression showed fearlessness as he held a sword with both hands. "Kionta and her champion, Thandel," Kaypel described as the two paladins stood at the base of the statue. Claudius could see the hordes of roses that were left by the people of the city at the statue's base.

"It's beautiful," Claudius breathed.

"Indeed. Let's retire for the night, shall we?" Kaypel replied.

"If you don't mind, I'd like to stay for a moment longer."

"Of course, the inn is back where we left our horses," Kaypel spoke before turning around and walking off.

Claudius felt a strange sensation ever since he had walked close to the statue. He remembered how he encountered Porth and wanted to try the same with Kionta. Closing his eyes, he held his breath for a moment, upon opening them light flooded his eyes as light wings grew from his back. At that instant everything turned to white and he heard a silvery voice.

"Greetings, paladin." Claudius turned his head to reveal a lady who resembled the statue and mustered a single word in reply, "Kionta?"

"That is I and who are you?"

"I am Claudius, surely Porth has talked to you?"

"I have first watched you since you laid eyes upon my beloved city. We divines live very much separate lives now," Kionta explained. "Shall we walk?" she continued as Claudius nodded his head in agreement. As they walked down the street of the city, Claudius noticed that it was nearly empty.

"Tell me, where does your journey take you, paladin?"

"I am headed to the Eternal Gate. The Light Warden there was recently killed and I volunteered to take his place."

"Ah, the life of a Light Warden is a solemn one as such, a divine. You are valiant, paladin."

"Is that my rightful path?"

"You ask me as if I know all the answers and I assure you, I do not," Kionta insisted, turning her head to look at Claudius and seeing the confusion in his face. "We are divines, our power and knowledge are extensive, they are not, however, infinite," she added, looking forward. "In some stance you hold greater power than we do." There was a short pause in the conversation as they continued to walk along the stone street. "I am confident you will do great things on whatever path you choose to follow." The look of confusion faded away on Claudius' face as he revealed a gentle smile.

"Your kind words comfort me," Claudius said as Kionta stopped and turned to him.

"Extend your hand," she instructed as Claudius followed. She softly held her left hand under his and in her right hand she held a star that radiated brightly with light. She placed the star in his hand and with both hands she closed his hand into a fist. "Take this, perhaps it shall aid you on your journey." Her touch was warm and soft as if embraced by a distant lover. "His ebb is beautiful as the Vivian Ocean and his flow is destructive as the northern frost, treat him well."

Claudius looked at his hand and before he could look up at Kionta and thank her, her image disappeared. Claudius found himself standing in front of the statue at night alone. He looked around and could see a few people still outside wandering the streets. He closed his right hand into a fist as light started to slip out between his fingers. Suddenly, a magnificent silvery white halberd appeared in his hand. He pulled it close to examine the head and could see very intricate lines engraved in the blade as a faint light emitted from the weapon. He opened his palm, allowing the halberd to vanish. It being nightfall he hurriedly walked towards the inn.

Entering the noisy inn, Claudius scanned the well-lit room and could easily find Kaypel sitting at a table with another man. Kaypel caught sight of Claudius and raised his left arm in the air, signaling him to come over.

"The world is becoming a more dangerous place; this city is the only safe haven from demons." The man spoke as Claudius sat down across from Kaypel.

"Light's Reach, the Capital, this City, Blackrock Mountains, Urogorth Wastes and the Silpine forest," Kaypel intoned, counting the cities with his fingers before taking a drink from his mug.

"Blackrock... You can't be serious?" the man replied.

"Demons aren't going to be climbing those forsaken mountains to fight vampires, now are they?" Kaypel spoke as Kaypel and the man both laughed. "Claudius! You finally decided to join us. Arven here has kept me in good company," Kaypel continued.

"You are too kind, sir," Arven replied, drinking the last bit of his ale.

"Yes, I got a bit distracted," Claudius explained.

"You don't have to become a Light Warden if you have any doubt in your mind," assured Kaypel.

"No, no, it's not that. I just walked down the street with Kionta, is all." Claudius replied lightheartedly.

Kaypel and Arven both let out a hardy laugh as Arven got up to say, "You paladins must come through this city more often. Another on me?"

"I cannot say no to mezzleberry wine!" Kaypel replied, revealing a smile and nodding his head.

"And for you, Claudius?" Arven asked, looking at the paladin.

"Honeyed milk, thank you."

"The best honeyed milk, it shall be!" Arven exclaimed as he left the table and headed towards the barkeeper. Kaypel directed his attention to Claudius.

"The rooms have already been arranged, your room is upstairs – second from the right. We set out at dawn," Kaypel said, reaching in his pocket for a bronze key and leaning over the circular table sliding it towards Claudius.

"Thanks, Kaypel," Claudius reached out to grab the key, placing it in his pocket.

Arven returned back to the table juggling three mugs and placed them on the table. He pushed the mezzleberry wine towards Kaypel and placed the honeyed milk in front of Claudius and grabbed his own mug before plopping back down in his seat.

"Thanks, Arven." Claudius and Kaypel spoke almost in unison as they reached for their drinks. Claudius raised his mug to his lips and took a sip, the cold milk mixed with a light honeyed taste quenched his thirst. Placing the mug on the table he questioned Arven.

"As a citizen of this city, how well do you know the lore of Kionta?" Avren gulped the last of his ale and slammed it on the table while wiping his mouth with his hand.

"Well? I've lived in this beautiful city my entire life. I know the legend more than the story of my own life! Over a hundred years ago Kionta was born in this very town. Back then it was a small farming community – rather than the large fortress of a city it is now. She had encountered a paladin who rode a griffon, Dondadas. His face chiseled, his hair was brown as the farm rich dirt and his eyes blue as the sky." Arven continued, moving his hands as he told the story. "Every time he arrived, she was there to greet him and every time he left on another campaign against demons, she would wish him well. Until... he didn't return with the other paladins." Arven paused as both Claudius and Kaypel waited eagerly for him to continue. "Some say she was heartbroken, others say she wanted revenge but the truth is, it was both. She couldn't watch people like Dondadas die and do nothing about it." Arven's excited voice turned back to normal as he continued. "So, she stole a horse and set out to the capital to become a paladin."

"Wait... she stole a horse?" Claudius interrupted as Kaypel let out a hardy chuckle.

"You didn't know that? And you yourself are a paladin?" Arven replied.

"Uh, I guess that part was left out of what we were told," Claudius returned as he picked up his mug for another sip.

"She battled many demons and even fought in the godless war. She was the one who killed Lord Volten, the supposed father of the vampires. Chopped his head clean off!" Avern exclaimed, slamming his hands on the table. "Sadly, she fell upon the battlefield but rose as the first divine." Arven finished, leaning back in his chair as Kaypel clapped his hands excitedly.

"Well done, a true storyteller!" Claudius smiled as he clapped his hands as well.

"Thank you, shall you paladins have another?" Arven asked standing up.

"No, it's very late and we set out at sunrise," replied Kaypel, standing up.

"Thanks for your company, Arven," Claudius added, pushing his mug towards the center of the table before standing up.

"I wish you well on your journey, paladins," Avern said with a smile and walked to fetch another ale for himself.

"I'll see you in the morning," Kaypel spoke to Claudius as he nodded in agreement. He walked up the small flight of wooden stairs and entered his room. The room was small, containing a lantern on top of the wooden table in the corner with a simple wooden chair. The other side of the room contained a wooden bed with two linen blankets. Claudius closed the door and stood next to the wooden table, taking his armor off and placing it on top of the table. Taking his cape off last, he hung it over the chair and plopped into the bed. The small window above the bed let some of the moonlight into the room. He raised his right hand in the air and closed it into fist. Light poured from his hand as the halberd appeared in his grasp.

The halberd emitted a soft glow, mixing with the moonlight as it shone a ghostly silver in the dark room. He stared at the weapon for a few minutes, thinking of the conversation he had with Kionta. He opened his hand, causing the halberd to disappear. Claudius closed his eyes and fell fast asleep.

Chapter 11

<u>Soonifer</u>

Delirious. "Who would like to recite the paladin's prayer?" Mentor Cressia asked, standing in front of the class of initiates. Her eyes scanned the stone room until she caught sight of an initiate who wasn't paying attention. "Soonifer, please stand and recite the prayer." Soonifer let out a mellowed sigh and stood up. His eyes were locked onto the mentor as he tried remembering the prayer but could only recollect a few words.

"...the light... protect..." He paused for a moment as all the initiates looked onward, trying so hard to remember but his mind was blank. "Unyielding...shall..." Soonifer tried to continue but was stopped as the room erupted in laughter. Mentor Cressia showed disapproval in her face as she shook her head while

Soonifer looked at his brother Claudius, the only initiate who wasn't laughing.

"Why do you not take your studies seriously, brother?" Claudius spoke with a stern tone in his voice. Soonifer held his tongue, knowing his brother would never understand and ran towards the door. He grabbed the iron handle then pulled the door open as light erupted, nearly blinding him. The light quickly subsided as Soonifer hastily stood up with his eyes glowing bright red, he spawned a spear holding his arm readily to throw it. He scanned the room and realized he was in Ker'es' throne room. *What was that...?* Soonifer whispered to himself as he tossed the spear to the ground. The spear let out a XXXetallic clanging noise as it fell down the obsidian steps before disappearing. His eyes returned to a soft red glow as he looked down at his side to see Nox awake from the noise. Soonifer knelt down and placed his hand on Nox's head and rubbed it gently.

"Sorry, rest easy." Nox closed his eyes as Soonifer stood up and looked around the room, seeing stacks upon stacks of books. Soonifer pushed the giant wooden doors of the library open and walked in. The room was dead silent except for the soft sounds of quills writing upon parchment. He looked around seeing numerous books crammed into the many dark wooden shelves. The room was well lit with an abundance of torches hanging from the stone walls, along with a giant chandelier in the middle of the room. Walking a little further, he stopped to see a multitude of floating books with quills writing in them. The sight captivated him as he stepped forward to see what the quills were writing.

"Oh, hello, Soonifer," a soft voice spoke behind him. Soonifer turned around to see Edge'knol looking at him with a little interest.

"Hello, I was just looking at these books," Soonifer replied.

"They are interesting, aren't they?" she said, walking towards the books, reaching out and grabbing a book and pulling it down.

"What are the quills writing?" Soonifer asked.

"These books are the lives of greater demons, and the quills are writing down their every action. Here, come see." Soonifer stood next to her and looked down at the book, his eyes following every stroke the quill made.

I stood next to greater demon Edge'knol, she showed me my infernal book.

"Wait… is this my book?" Soonifer questioned, looking at Edge'knol.

"Indeed, it is," she answered as she nodded her head and raised the book back to its floating position.

"Why is it recording my actions?"

"There are books for almost every demon, their actions are written and once they die their book is pooled into the Book of Infernal Knowledge."

"I see and what does this Book of Infernal Knowledge contain?"

"It contains the recollections of all demons."

"Can I see this book?"

"I don't see why not," Edge'knol spoke with a slight smile as she walked off with Soonifer following close behind.

It felt like he walked past hundreds of shelves until they finally arrived at the center of the library. She stopped only steps away from the lectern which held a stone statue of a demon who held up the giant book. The parchment was an ashen gray color with a giant black feather writing on the page. The ink was a ghostly maroon color before drying into a blood red lettering.

Soonifer stepped towards the book but was stopped by Edge'knol's words.

"I have to warn you, the knowledge of this book will be all encompassing to your eyes. It will try to satisfy your innate hunger for knowledge but if you are weak, it will consume you. I am here if you wish to stop reading at any moment."

Soonifer's eyes glowed bright red as he felt his eyes being ripped out, gritting his teeth he felt unable to move. Everything went black for a moment as he felt a soft hand cover his eyes. He heard Edge'knol's voice whisper, "Are you okay?"

"I think I am now...?" Soonifer replied as he felt being turned around by her. He opened his eyes slowly to see Edge'knol's soft red eyes glowing at him. He sat down and rubbed his head as she sat down beside him.

"The first time is always the hardest," she spoke, reaching out and holding Soonifer's left hand and examining his palm. "It seems that you too have been blessed by Kovick'kal, you hold his eye in your hand."

"Is that what that is? I received it when I entered the pool to heal my arm," Soonifer explained, looking at his palm. "Who is Kovick'kal?" he asked.

"He was a powerful wizard who lived hundreds of years ago."

"A wizard of the Nether? No mages have ever treaded Terrazel."

"Not in your lifetime, even time has forgotten his name."

"There once was a time mages existed?"

"That is perhaps a question you should ask the book another time," Edge'knol spoke.

Soonifer showed a little disbelief in his face but remained silent. "You don't believe me? Would you like to see one of his creations?" she continued, looking at him. Soonifer narrowed his eyes in interest and nodded his head. They both stood up as Edge'knol walked out of the library with Soonifer close behind.

They stood before the giant black pit where Soonifer first learned of his infernal spear. "Here," Edge'knol spoke as she started to walk near the edge of the pit. He followed behind her as the ledge they walked on became narrower. As they walked towards the other side of the pit, the entire area was dead silent. He looked down into the black pit and felt as if hundreds of thousands of eyes were watching his every move. They arrived at the other side of the massive pit and walked into a giant opening in the rock wall. As they journeyed further, Soonifer noticed how the rocky, desolate landscape had slowly started to shift into a forest type setting, however instead of lush green leaves, brown bark or even green grass, everything was gray.

"Where are we?" Soonifer questioned, looking around.

"The Sapphian forest," Edge'knol replied.

"How come everything is gray?" Soonifer asked.

"It's what happens when love fades away."

Claudius

Claudius finished putting on his armor as a loud knock sounded from the door.

"Sweet prince, are you up?" Kaypel inquired. Claudius reached for his lightblade on the wooden table and pulled the sword from the sheath as light radiated from the blade. He put the lightblade back into the sheath and attached it to his leather belt. Turning around, he opened the wooden door to see Kaypel standing there holding two apples, of which he tossed one to him. Claudius caught it with one hand and looked at the green apple.

"The sourness will wake you up, let's depart," Kaypel urged as he walked off with a smug grin.

"Thanks," Claudius replied, closing the door behind him as he took a bite into the sour apple. As they raced across the dirt road on horseback, Claudius looked back at the city and felt Divine Kionta's watchful eye upon him. Turning his head forward to set his eyes on the next destination, the Eternal Gate.

Claudius could see Castle Vernahs in the distance, miles away, a giant staggering stone fortress that overlooked the miles and miles of flat ground. "We're almost there!" Kaypel yelled as Claudius nodded his head and ushered his horse on. Claudius and Kaypel were met with almost a dozen paladins at the gate.

"Halt! Who goes there?" one of the paladin bellowed as he raised his hand signaling them to stop.

"The next Light Warden!" Kaypel replied, pointing his hand at Claudius. The entire place fell silent as the paladins looked over at Claudius.

"Is this true?" the paladin in charge questioned, taking a step closer towards the two.

"Indeed," replied Kaypel as he shook his head.

"What is your name… Light Warden?" The paladin asked looking up at Claudius.

"My name is Claudius." The other paladins looked at each other and a few whispers were exchanged as they continued to look onward at the two paladins.

"The very same Claudius that is the son of the king?"

"Yes, that is I," Claudius answered, nodding his head.

"The next Light Warden is the son of a king? I wouldn't have ever imagined." The paladin spoke before pausing, almost deep in thought. The paladin then snapped back into reality as he yelled towards the castle. "Open the gates!"

"Please, come in." The paladin spoke, taking a step back and signaling them to enter.

Kaypel turned his head to Claudius and revealed a grin as he snapped the reins of his horse to move forward.

The two paladins entered a giant courtyard and dismounted off their horses.

"I'll take your horses to the stable," one of the paladins spoke as he grabbed the reins and led the horses away. Claudius and Kaypel walked side by side on the stone steps that led to the center of the courtyard which held a medium-sized pond.

"There it is," Kaypel spoke as he pointed towards the pond. Claudius narrowed his eyes, seeing the pond in the distance.

Suddenly, he heard a group of footsteps and turned his head to see a large group of paladins walking towards them and noticed the person in front wore the same armor as Kaypel.

"Ronnick!" Kaypel yelled, walking towards the group to meet them as Claudius followed.

"Kaypel?! What brings you to these parts? It must be important considering you never leave Light's Reach."

"Escorting the next Light Warden," Kaypel replied, once again pointing to Claudius. Ronnick's eyes widened as the group of paladins formed a half circle around them. Ronnick seemed speechless but didn't show it in his face.

"Yes, I just received word that the next Light Warden has arrived." Ronnick turned his attention to Claudius. "As much as I am delighted that we have found the next Light Warden so quickly, I'm not too sure if it should be the son of the king," Ronnick shared.

"My choice to become a Light Warden benefits everyone in Terrazel far more than if I were to be the next king," Claudius replied.

"Wise words," Ronnick replied, taking a pause in thought while looking at Claudius. "Very well, tomorrow morning you shall be the 5th Light Warden." Ronnick finished as he held out his hand to Claudius. Claudius grabbed Ronnick's wrist firmly as the group of paladins cheered, chanting, "Claudius! Our next Light Warden!"

The next morning, Claudius exited the great hall where a quiet breakfast had been held. Walking down the hallway, he was stopped by an older man who was using a polished wooden cane to hold himself up.

"Excuse me, young man, care to exchange a few words?" The gray haired man asked as his eyes looked upon him.

"Sure, I have a moment," Claudius replied as he followed the man into his quarters. The man hobbled across the room and sat down on a square wooden chest that was at the head of the bed and signaled with his free hand for Claudius to sit in the wooden chair nearby. Claudius sat in the chair, placing one hand on his thigh while resting the other on the table.

"Your name is Claudius, right?" The man queried, placing his cane in his lap and holding it with both hands.

"Yes, after my father," Claudius replied.

"A great man and a courageous son."

"Kind words, I don't think you have told me your name."

"My name is Ferrell; I am the head mentor here. I've been a paladin all of my life. I have been on many campaigns, fighting countless demons in my day until my leg was crushed." Ferrell pointed to his lame leg as he continued. "Have you killed any?"

"No, I have not been given the chance."

"Not a single one yet you wish to become the Light Warden?" Ferrell spoke with his eyes widening in surprise.

"I feel when the opportunity presents itself, I will be able to handle it," Claudius replied firmly.

"I mean no offense to your skills or capabilities but there are more demons in the Nether than there are blades of grass in the world." There was silence between the two as Ferrell stood up, using his cane to hobble over to the armor rack which held a full paladin's armor. He reached out with his free hand and touched the armor, following a large scratch on the worn chest plate with his wrinkled finger.

"I offered to be the next Light Warden…" Ferrell's voice trailed off for a moment before he continued. "But Ronnick believes I have lost the skills I once had. He keeps telling me that my knowledge in demonology is best given to the new paladins than if I were to be a Light Warden." Ferrell spoke with a long drawn out sigh. Ferrell turned around and looked at Claudius. "Could you help me get into this armor? I want to look at least representable when you enter."

"Of course," Claudius replied.

"Thank you…Light Warden," Ferrell whispered.

Claudius stood in the courtyard seeing Kaypel and Ronnick with the entire garrison of paladins looking upon him in silence. He took in a deep breath and walked towards them. The sound of his boots hitting the stone echoed through the courtyard. He could see a few clouds hang across the early blue sky as if time stood still. He finally arrived at the pool, standing in front of Ronnick who tried his best to hide his emotions underneath his stern face, but his eyes gave him away. Ronnick held out his hand as Claudius received it strongly.

"Ascend before you enter the pool, the demons will try to strike you as soon as you enter." Ronnick spoke before releasing his arm, taking a step back. Claudius nodded his head and stood only steps before the pool, looking around. Everyone remained silent as all the goodbyes had already been said. Claudius looked at Kaypel who stared back and gave a single nod in gesture.

He stood at the edge of the pool and looked down, seeing the dark murky body of water. Claudius clutched both of his hands into a fist, closing his eyes, he took in a deep breath. Light radiated from his body as giant light wings appeared on his back. Claudius opened his eyes as light poured out. Extending his right arm, a halberd appeared in his grasp. He jumped into the pool head first as he grabbed the staff of the halberd with both arms, rearing it back for a strike.

He felt the cold water consume him for a split second before finding himself standing on a long bridge that seemed to lead nowhere but into darkness. He swung his halberd as a giant wave of light erupted from the swing, a second ghostly halberd followed closely behind the first swing, letting out a second wave of light. The wave of light tore through the darkness, killing hundreds of demons while the light from the wave revealed thousands of demons lurking in the shadows. As the light faded away, darkness quickly reclaimed the space. Claudius stood still, looking forward into the darkness. There was no silence but constant dark whispers of incoherent words.

Soonifer

Soonifer stopped to look around, noticing how the rocks, grass and trees were all gray. The only thing that held any color were small dark blue flowers. "This is a strange place…" his voice trailed off as Edge'knol stopped and walked back over to where he was.

"Indeed it is, let's continue," she replied.

"What is this…feeling?" Soonifer asked looking at his hand. He felt a warm glow from his body that seemed to slowly expand.

"I'm sure with time you'll remember," she assured Sonnifer as she started to walk off. Soonifer didn't think much of it as he walked off. As they walked away from the center of the Sapphian forest, he noticed the vegetation had started to decay until eventually there was nothing. Edge'knol quickly extended her hand, pressing it against Soonifer's chest.

"Stop!" she ordered, taking her arm from his chest and pointing it towards a small speck of light in the distance. Soonifer narrowed his eyes, trying to fixate on the small speck of light. "That's the Eternal Gate," she spoke, returning her hand and placing it on her hip.

"Can we go closer?" Soonifer questioned.

"No."

"Why not?"

"If the Light Warden attacks, we don't want to be caught in the way."

"What can they possibly do to us?" Soonifer replied with a sneer as he spawned a spear in his right hand. Rearing back, he hurled the spear at the speck of light and turned his head to Edge'knol, revealing a sly grin. "See? Noth-" Two giant waves of light raced across the cavern, obliterating any demon caught in its path. The waves of light illuminated the area temporally, revealing thousands of demons retreating from the light. The light was so bright that Soonifer held his right arm up against his face. A giant gust of wind howled past the two as the waves of light eventually faded away, darkness returning. Soonifer lowered his arm and dared to look at Edge'knol who tried to hide her smile behind a stern face.

"See you there," Edge'knol spoke as she disappeared into the darkness. Soonifer turned his head to look at the speck of light in the distance before darkness surrounded him.

Claudius

He stood still with his halberd at the ready, awaiting anymore incoming attacks when suddenly a paladin stood next to him. He looked at him and could see the familiar armor designs that the man wore.

"Claudius!" the man bellowed as he swung his light blade, a giant wave of light erupting from the sword. Claudius stared at the man in disbelief.

"Leave this place! You have your entire life, I have already lived mine." The paladin said as he pushed Claudius backward into the Eternal Gate. The light escaped his eyes as he let out a deep breath, gasping for air. His whole body was soaked with water as the crowd of paladins surrounded him. He wiped away the water from his face and tried to open his eyes as the bright sun shone heavily down upon him. Claudius finally opened his eyes to see Kaypel and Ronnick trying to get him up.

"What happened?" Claudius spoke weakly.

"That old fool, Ferrell, leaped into the pond," Ronnick replied as they pulled Claudius up onto his legs.

"That was him? He looked much younger when I saw him."

"The ascended form paladins take does much more," Ronnick replied.

"I need to lay down, I do not feel well," Claudius whispered. Kaypel nodded his head as he grabbed one of Claudius' arms and put it around his shoulder, helping him walk.

"To the barracks," Ronnick ordered as he and a few paladins rushed ahead to get things in order.

**

Claudius opened his eyes to find himself in bed, looking around he saw Kaypel sitting on the bed next to him. "You're awake! How are you feeling?" Kaypel asked.

"Better, I guess," Claudius replied as he rubbed his eyes with his hand.

"You have done something no person has ever done before, enter the Eternal Gate and leave...alive." Kaypel reached over to the wooden nightstand and grabbed a plate of fruit and placed it beside Claudius. "You need to eat something." Claudius reached over, grabbed a handful of pomegranate seeds and shoved them in his mouth. He bit down as the juice exploded in his mouth, quelling his slight thirst. Claudius cleared his mouth and spoke.

"Am I a disgrace?"

"Because you lived? No. Whatever burden you had as Light Warden is now to that paladin."

Claudius let out a long sigh before looking straight up at the ceiling. "Clear your mind and rest easy, Claudius," Kaypel said before getting up and walking out of the room. Claudius moved his right hand in front of his face and clenched it into a fist. He felt as if he had aged over 50 years, his hands were slow and sluggish. Daring not to move, he placed his hand at his side and let out a rough sigh before closing his eyes and falling into an empty sleep.

Chapter 12

<u>Claud</u>

Excitement. "Claud! Are you ready yet?" his father yelled from downstairs as the young boy rushed down the wooden stairs.

"Yes, I am, father!" Claud replied as he stood by the door. His father walked up to Claud and ruffled his hair and smiled. They stepped outside into the bright sunlight as Claud looked up to his father with wide eyes and asked, "What's the surprise?"

"You'll get it when we meet your uncle."

"Uncle Renner?"

"That's right"

"Yay! He's my favorite!"

The two arrived at the steps of the stone castle as the guard's signaled for them to enter. "Morning, Zedson," the guard spoke to the father while standing at attention.

"It's a fine morning indeed," the father answered while nodding his head as they past the guard and entered the castle. To his surprise, the king and a few of his advisors were in the atrium before the grand hall. The young boy sprinted towards the king with open arms while yelling.

"Uncle Renner!"

"That'll be all," the king instructed the advisors as they left the atrium. The king turned his attention to the young boy, knelt down and embraced him with a hug. "How's my favorite nephew doing?"

"Great! Father tells me that you have a surprise for me!?" The king released the boy and stood up, looking at the boy's father.

"Did he?"

"Yup!" The boy exclaimed.

"Well, it is true. Come, let's go to the throne room." The boy could hardly keep himself from sprinting as his father followed behind.

The three entered the throne room where they were greeted by one of the king's advisors. He wore a dark purple opulent robe and had his right hand clutched into a fist.

"Here you go," the man spoke in an age-worn voice as he opened his palm to the boy, revealing a gold ring that held the king's royal colors of blue and silver. The young boy widened his eyes in surprise as he looked up to the advisor and asked.

"For me?" The advisor nodded as the boy took the ring and examined it. He noticed within the colors was an engraved figure of a lion. "It's marvelous," Claud whispered.

"Go ahead, put it on," the boy's father urged. Claud slipped the ring on his right ring finger and held it up.

"From this moment on, you are officially the royal messenger, the carrier of the king's words," the advisor proclaimed as he gently clapped his hands, the king and the boy's father joined in clapping.

"It's a big responsibility but I believe you can do it, Claud," the king spoke firmly. Claud shifted his attention from the ring to the king and replied.

"I won't let you down, uncle!" The advisor reached into his pocket and pulled out a sealed piece of parchment and handed it to Claud. The young boy took the parchment and examined it, noticing that it had a red wax seal that carried the similar lion figure as his ring.

154

"Your first duty is to deliver that to the Baron of Solbris, Hallowmis Vicar." The boy nodded in acknowledgement but had a confused look. "Worry not, the king has arranged an escort for you." The advisor added.

"He has?" Claud questioned.

"Just outside, go look for yourself," the advisor replied. Claud bolted towards the exit as his father walked towards the king.

"I cannot thank you enough, your majesty."

"Please, Zedson. It's the least I could do for my nephew."

Claud pushed the giant wooden doors apart, as the sun's rays poured in. He quickly walked forward to see his cousin Malzek standing in front of a small group of knights on horses.

"Malzek!" Claud yelled as he ran down the steps to meet his cousin. They both widened their arms and hugged in embrace.

"I'm glad to see you, cousin!" Malzek exclaimed as they let go of one another.

"And I as well!" Claud replied.

"Are you ready to depart?" Malzek asked, looking down at his cousin. Claud looked back at the castle, seeing his father nod. He nodded back and turned to Malzek.

"Yes, I am." Malzek lowered himself and interlocked his fingers forming a step. Claud placed his foot on Malzek's hand as he was boosted up onto the horse. Claud held the horse's reins firmly in his hand. Malzek mounted his horse and ushered the horse to walk forward next to Claud's.

"Don't worry, I'm here to protect you," Malzek sternly spoke before revealing a smile. "Alright, let's go!" he ordered the small group of knights as he snapped the reins of his horse. The giant wooden gates of the capital closed behind them as they departed towards Solbris.

They arrived at Solbris as the sun was already in mid-fall. A loud horn was blown from the guard below to allow the knights to enter the walled city. The interior of the city was maintained very well as rows of buildings lined each side of the stone street. Malzek led the group towards a giant keep and stopped at the signal of a group of guards stationed outside.

"What is your business here?" one of the guards demanded.

"We seek an audience of Baron Hallowmis, we have a letter for him," Malzek firmly stated.

"I'm sorry but the Baron is not seeing anyone today," the guard replied, placing his hand on the hilt of his sheathed sword.

"Are you impeding the royal messenger's duties?" the knight rebutted. The guard showed confusion in his face, turning his head to see the other group of knights before facing Malzek.

"I see no royal messenger."

"Claud, please come forward." Malzek motioned as Claud ushered his horse forward so the guard could see him.

"This boy?!" The guard laughed as the other guards also let out a soft chuckle.

"Yes, selected by the king himself. Go on, Claud, show him," Malzek ordered. Claud lifted his hand, showing the royal signet to the guard as they quickly fell into silence. Malzek dismounted his horse and walked to Claud. The young messenger reached into the leather satchel and grabbed the rolled parchment. Malzek helped Claud dismount his horse. The guard reached out with an open hand expecting to be given the parchment but Malzek pushed the arm away. "This message is to be given to the Baron directly," Malzek sternly spoke. The guard paused for a moment, narrowing his eyes at the knight but eventually stepped aside and ordered his own guards to let them pass. Malzek signaled to Claud to walk up the stone steps towards the keep's door. Claud obeyed, walking the stone steps as if each step was a mountain. Malzek followed closely behind.

The two entered the keep and found themselves in a great hall that was makeshifted into a throne room. A steward of the keep gathered them and brought them to the end of the great hall where the Baron sat in a beautifully crafted wooden chair.

"Your highness, these two seek your audience," the steward spoke before taking a step back.

"...and who are you?" the Baron questioned in an almost snobby tone.

"Claud, the royal messenger," the boy answered.

"Malzek, his personal bodyguard," the knight added. "He bears a message from the king, addressed to you." Malzek nodded to Claud, as the boy walked towards the Baron and handed him the rolled parchment. A few armed guards stood in front of the pillars of the great hall but the room was filled with silence. The Baron broke the wax seal and read the letter. He promptly rolled the letter back up and held it in his hand.

"You may leave now," the Baron commanded with a little anger in his tone. Malzek nodded his head and walked towards the exit as Claud walked beside him. The Baron crumbled the parchment as he closed his hand into a fist. "Jathaya!" he yelled as the captain of the guard quickly ran to his side.

"Yes, your highness?" the captain spoke in a stern but concerned tone.

"Follow and kill them just beyond the outskirts of Solbris. Make it look like bandits," the Baron instructed, keeping his eyes upon the giant wooden door.

"Kill the royal messenger?" the captain asked a little hesitantly.

"Yes, that child is a clear agent of evil. We wouldn't want demons running around in guise."

"But he is just a child –"

"Yes, but evil comes in many forms. I can differentiate between what is good and evil, you disagree Captain?" The Baron spoke sternly as the captain stood in silence.

"No, of course not, your highness. It shall be done," the captain replied as he walked off. The Baron opened his hand, letting the crumbled parchment fall onto the table.

The two stood outside as Malzek signaled to the group of knights that they had accomplished their task. "You did well, Claud," Malzek commended, giving Claud a pat on the back.

"Thanks, Malzek!" Claud exclaimed with a smile as they walked down the stone steps. "Are we going to head back to the capital?" Claud questioned as he mounted his horse with Malzek's help.

"No, we are going to stay at an inn for the night and will depart in the morning. Once you get used to travelling, then we shall travel at night," Malzek replied.

(Malzek orders

knights to leave)

They entered the wooden inn, the main room crammed with many wooden tables and chairs filled with citizens talking to each other. Malzek walked directly towards the innkeeper and placed five silver coins onto the wooden counter and requested, "Two of your best rooms please." The innkeeper looked down at

160

the coins and nodded his head before reaching under the counter for something. He placed two bronze keys on the counter and scooped up the silver coins with his hand. Malzek grabbed both keys, turning around he signaled Claud to follow as he walked up the stairs to their rooms. Malzek stopped in front of one of the doors and turned around to face Claud.

"Here is your key and that is your room," Malzek pointed to the room opposite of his. "I want you to have this," Malzek added, unhooking his sheath and handing it to Claud. Claud slowly reached out with his hand and grabbed the sheath, examining the well-worn hilt of the sword before looking at his older cousin.

"....Really?" Claud uttered in surprise.

"Yes, a real knight's sword. It shall be yours when you complete the knight's academy," Malzek replied. Claud leaped forward and wrapped his arms around his cousin.

"Malzek, you're the best!" Malzek smiled and patted Claud on the back.

"Head to bed now." Claud let go and nodded, entering his room. Malzek entered his dark room, tearing off his armor and placing it on the small table. He fell backwards into the bed, closing his eyes and wishing for better days.

The next morning, Malzek stood at the end of his bed, finishing tightening his left pauldron. He stepped out of his room and knocked on Claud's door. Almost immediately the door opened with Claud standing there holding the sword. "Sheath that – and did you get any sleep?" Malzek asked. Claud grabbed the sheath from the table and sheathed the sword.

"Nope, not a wink! I was too busy imaging fighting demons!" Claud exclaimed. Malzek sneered playfully.

"Come on, let's go."

Malzek helped Claud upon his horse then hopped onto his own horse. They left the city of Solbris to begin their journey back to the capital. Just as they reached the outskirts of Solbris, Malzek heard the sounds of yelling mixed with horse hooves beating into the ground.

"Halt your horse, Claud!" Malzek shouted as they turned around and waited for the group of soldiers to catch up. The soldiers halted once they were almost a sword's distance away. Three of the soldiers dismounted and looked upon Malzek.

"Off your horse, I must speak with you immediately." Malzek looked a little confused.

"What is so urgent that you followed us so hastily?" he asked as he dismounted off his horse.

"Your death!" one of the soldiers shouted as he swung his sword downward, maiming Malzek's left shoulder.

"Claud, Run!" Malzek shouted as he ripped his sword from its sheath and slashed one of the soldiers across the chest. Claud snapped the reins of his horse and quickly galloped away.

"After him, you fools!" one of the soldiers on the ground yelled as the small group of soldiers on horseback chased after the royal messenger. Malzek deflected multiple attacks using his sword and when one of the soldiers raised his arm to attack, he forcibly swung his sword cutting the soldier's arm clear off. Blood gushed from the wound as the soldier let out a roar in pain. One of the soldiers slashed his sword at Malzek but it was quickly parried into the air as Malzek leaped forward, slamming his sword into the chest of the attacker. Malzek pulled his bloodied blade from the chest of the soldier and looked towards the remaining lone soldier. He charged towards him with his sword in the air and swung downward. The soldier tried to block the attack with his sword but the attack was so powerful it knocked the sword out of his hand. Taking advantage of the situation, Malzek reared his sword back and slammed the hilt of his blade into the face of the soldier. The soldier's body hit the ground with a loud thud as Malzek turned around and quickly hopped on his horse to chase after the pursuers.

Claud turned his head and looked back to see three soldiers chasing after him but in the distance he could see Malzek trying to catch up. "He-yah!" Claud yelled, pushing his horse to gallop faster as his cape danced in the wind behind his back.

Malzek snapped the leather reins, trying to force his horse to run even faster. He could see he was slowly gaining distance on them but it seemed a lifetime away.

The soldier who was closest to Claud was almost an arm's distance away. He leaned forward and reached out with his hand to grab the messenger's cape but the cape was flickering wildly in the air. The soldier grunted loudly and finally grabbed the tip of the cape and pulled the cape backwards with all of his might as Claud was torn from his saddle, tumbling backwards and landing on the ground on his head. The three soldiers halted their horses as one of them dismounted to inspect the boy. He knelt down and rested his hand on the twisted neck of the boy and nodded his head to the others. At that moment, Malzek swung his sword, cutting one of the soldiers on horseback's head clean off as he rode by. The head hit the ground with a soft thud as the body quickly followed.

Malzek halted his horse and turned around before charging towards them. The soldier on the horse moved into position to challenge the knight. Malzek rushed his horse next to his while shifting his entire weight onto his right side and slammed his shoulder into the soldier, knocking him clean off. The last soldier scrambled onto his horse and started to ride back towards Solbris. Malzek hopped off his horse and knelt beside Claud, inspecting his cousin. He placed his hand over the boy's head and closed his eyes.

"I'm sorry, Claud..." Malzek whispered as he opened his eyes in anger and clenched his teeth. He hopped back on his horse and chased after the lone soldier. He could see the soldier periodically looking back towards him as he continued to chase after him. They reached Solbris and the soldier yelled for help to the tower guards, pointing at the knight. Malzek ushered his horse forward while holding his sword in the air for a strike. Malzek heard a metallic ring before his left arm shot up in pain. He looked down to see a crossbow bolt lodged in his arm. As he looked up he could see a volley of bolts flying towards him. Two bolts pierced his chest as he groaned in pain but continued to ride forward. Another bolt snapped by, barely missing him. He almost reached the soldier before a bolt slammed into his neck causing him to cough up blood while it also seeped from his wounds. Malzek fell off his horse with a loud thud, still holding firmly onto his sword as the world started to become black.

***

"Have you had any word of their return?" the king asked in a concerned voice.

"I'm sure they are fine, your majesty," the advisor calmly reassured.

"It has been several days…" The king's voice broke off.

"Perhaps they decided to visit some of the out-lying villages on the way back? The season is quite beautiful now."

"Send a scout," the king ordered.

"At once," the advisor replied, giving a slight nod with his head before turning around and signaling to one of the knights to venture out and investigate. The knight nodded and departed immediately.

Chapter 13

<u>Zedson</u>

Quandary. The scout busted through the wooden castle doors of the capital as everyone inside looked onward towards the knight. The king hoped to see his nephew follow behind the scout but as the scout quickly walked towards him, deep inside he already knew the answer. The scout knelt before the king and raised his right fist up, opening it to reveal the royal messenger's signet sitting on his palm. The room was in total silence, awaiting some sort of answer. The king slowly picked up the ring and clenched his hand into a fist. Zedson ran into the room and stood next to the king, looking around frantically.

"Did they find them?" he yelled.

"Yes, Malzek and the royal messenger have been slaughtered by bandits," the scout answered as he stood up.

"Are you absolutely sure?" the king asked. The scout shook his head.

"Yes, I pulled the ring off his finger myself. I can lead you to their bodies." The king nodded.

"Send a legion! I want to find whoever committed this vile act!" the king yelled as knights scrambled out of the castle doors. The scout gave a single firm nod and ran out with the others.

The king turned to Zedson and spoke. "We will investigate this, I promise you." Zedson's eyes began to tear as he tried his best to hold back the sobs, shaking his head violently, he ran out the castle doors without a word. "Give me a parchment and quill, I need to reach out to my son," the king ordered as his advisor ran to fulfill his request.

Zedson reentered the throne room as it quickly fell silent. The king motioned Zedson to come before him and he complied. Then he turned to his captain to question him. "Captain, tell us what you have found."

"Very well, your highness. We have recovered two bodies, one identified as Malzek the other to be Claud. We have questioned many citizens of Solbris, yet none heard of any incident outside its walls. A few of the guards however, did mention there have been bandits about on the outskirts of the city. We have sent numerous knights to possible locations, yet we have found nothing."

"Thank you, captain, you may be dismissed." The king spoke as the captain nodded and walked out of the throne room.

"What more can we do?" Zedson urged.

"Right now, we wait for any new information that may be discovered by the scouting parties," the king replied.

"You are asking of me the impossible, Claudius…." Zedson replied.

"If the knights cannot find anything, I will send a team of paladins to investigate the matter. I have already sent a letter to my son requesting him to return to the capital. He will personally lead the investigation." Claudius added, "The service for your son will be in a few hours, if you wish to go see him now, his body is at the cathedral."

Zedson left the throne room abruptly. He stood on the steps of the castle and noticed the sky was light gray, so many clouds that not even a single ray of sunlight could get through. He let out a deep sigh and headed towards the cathedral. He pushed the heavy wooden doors of the cathedral and entered. His eyes first caught sight of two wooden coffins that stood on the floor in front of the altar. He slowly walked toward the coffins and with each step he took he remembered all the time he had spent with his son. He stood in front of the two coffins and saw that one of them had the royal messenger's ring on top. He walked towards it and pressed his right hand on the coffin's top for a moment before taking the ring. Leaving the cathedral, he quickly rushed home.

Entering the modest stone house and closing the door behind him, the room was all too quiet without his son. Placing the ring in his pocket, he walked over to the small wood pile, picking up a few logs and placing them in the fireplace. He grabbed a small tin of tinder that sat on the lip of the fireplace and lit the logs on fire. The unsettling silence soon was driven out of the room by a roaring flame. He walked over to pull out a wooden kitchen chair and placed it facing the fire. Sitting down, he leaned back into the chair while reaching for the ring with his right hand. He pulled it out and held the ring in front of his face, examining how the light of the fire would gently make the gold ring glow. The thought of someone killing his child rolled over and over in his head. "How could one be so evil?" he muttered to himself while staring at the ring. Hours passed by as the once roaring lion of a flame slowly faded into soft crackles.

Immediately he was surrounded by blackness but heard a soft whisper.

"What aches your soul?" He dared not answer but instead looked around, seeing nothing and stretched out his arms searching for anything in the dark.

"Stop," the voice whispered and this time he obeyed.

"Where am I? Who are you?" Zedson frantically asked.

"Ask from the heart," the voice whispered as Zedson's mind shifted thoughts quickly before taking a moment to breathe.

"Who killed my son?" he demanded, yelling into the blackness. Zedson spoke again but this time his voice trembled with sadness. "I have no swordsmanship... I am no knight or warrior...please...I will do anything..." There was a brief silence before an image of a brown-haired man with hazel eyes appeared in his mind. That man wore a star shaped ornament on his necklace. The voice whispered again.

"Young lamb, extend your hand and feel just a sliver of my power." Zedson felt compelled by the voice to do as instructed

171

so he extended his arm out with his palm facing up and held it very still. He felt skeletal fingers touch his palm, their touch icy cold. He wanted to pull his hand away but his desire for revenge weighed more. His entire hand started to shake as if he was touching electricity. He tried his hardest not to yell and instead bit down on his tongue. The pain was so intense that his hand had become numb and now his whole arm had started to shake vigorously. The pain shot into his arm and he could no longer hold all the pain inside. He opened his mouth and yelled as if all of his light had faded away.

Zedson slammed his feet on the ground and abruptly opened his eyes. He found himself standing up in his house and noticed the fire had become mere cinders. "Was it just a horrid dream?" he whispered to himself as he quickly lit several candles and held out his hand to the flame. He could see three black burn marks on his hand and began to shake in fear. Inspecting his hand further his mouth dropped open. Using his left hand, he touched his tongue and looked back at his hand to find some blood. He clutched his right hand into a fist and could feel darkness travel from his arm to his hand. The color of his hand started to become darker until he opened it. The darkness vanished just as fast as it came. He quickly grabbed his leather brown robe and wrapped it

172

around himself. He grabbed the royal messenger signet and carefully placed it on his left hand. He exited his house and mounted a horse towards Solbris.

Zedson arrived at the gates of Solbris just as the sun had started its ascent towards the sky.

"Halt, state your business, traveler!" one of the guards shouted as Zedson held out his left hand to show the royal signet.

"I bear a message from the king directly to the Baron, Hallowmis Vicar." The gate guard took a step back and raised his arm to signal the gate operators to let him enter. Zedson snapped the horse's reins, guiding the horse towards the keep. Once again, he was stopped by guards but he held out his left hand showing the ring which allowed him access. Pushing the two wooden doors inward, he walked steadily into the throne room. The room was filled with silence as the guards and Hallowmis himself stared forward to the robed man.

"What news does the king have for me, messenger?" the Baron inquired fingering a star shaped ornament that dangled from his neck, all the while his captain of the guard stood at his side.

"Death," Zedson whispered as he lifted his face up to match the Baron's. He then extended his arm out as if he was trying to reach something.

"What did you say?" the Baron demanded.

"DEATH!" Zedson yelled as the guards clenched their weapons in attention and pointed their blades towards the man in robes, awaiting a command by the Baron. Zedson's hand slowly turned completely black as all in the throne room watched on. Zedson threw his hand towards the Baron as black lightening shot out of his hand. The Baron quickly grabbed his captain and pushed him forward taking the full attack. The captain's body tumbled down the steps as the smell of searing flesh filled the room.

"KILL HIM!" the Baron screamed as the entire room of guards charged at the robed man and struck him down instantly. The Baron walked down the steps and examined the body of the captain which seemed as if he'd been struck by lightning. The Baron walked towards Zedson's corpse as the guards took a step back. He knelt down and pulled off the ring and examined it. "From now on, no one from the capital may enter my city. Clean this mess up," the Baron snapped.

Chapter 14

Claudius

Homecoming. Five months after returning from the Eternal Gate, Claudius has exceeded in his paladin's training and increased his bond with Sundra. He and Lance has been summoned by his father. "Thank you for arriving so fast my son, Claudius," greeted the king, taking a brief pause before he continued. "Lance, I send you two on an important task, to find who is responsible for the murder of our royal messenger but above all, our dear nephew." The two paladins nodded and knew how important the task was at hand.

"Absolutely father, we shall find and bring them to justice," Claudius promised.

"Our investigators cannot find much, but I would start your search at Solbris," the king remarked. The two paladins nodded before leaving the palace.

"Pretty serious, huh?" Lance said.

"Must be," Claudius replied. They hustled down the stone steps as Lance let out a sharp whistle. Surina turned her heard towards Lance and let out a fierce squawk. "My father is counting on us, I won't let him down," Claudius spoke as he mounted onto his griffon. Lance hopped onto his griffon and roughly brushed Surina's head.

"Let's ride!" Lance yelled as the two griffons flapped their massive wings and flew into the air.

The two paladins arrived at Solbris, flew over the outer walls and stopped at the small mass of guards that surrounded them. The guards drew their swords and stood their ground as the paladins dismounted their griffons.

"Put your needles away, we aren't interested in you," Lance spoke while giving Surina a rough brush across the neck. Surina was ready to tear any guard who came close while Sundra took a defensive stance.

"We cannot let you enter, by the order of the Baron," a guard yelled while standing in Claudius' way.

"You will move aside. The death of the royal messenger has prompted a royal investigation and anyone who gets in my way defies the king himself," Claudius replied in a calm but unsettling tone. The guard grit his teeth, showing conflict in his face before he ultimately nodded and took a step back.

"Let them pass! Make way!" the guard shouted to the other guards as they obeyed.

"Thank you," Claudius spoke as he walked up the stairs. He turned his head towards Sundra and let out two sharp clicks, his griffon walking up the stone steps behind him.

"Let's go, girl!" Lance yelled as Surina flapped her wings excitedly and followed behind Lance. The two paladins entered the keep, their griffons following close behind.

Hallowmis and his royal court stopped in mid-walk to see the two paladins and their griffons.

"Hello?" the Baron questioned.

"We are looking for Hallowmis Vicar," Claudius explained as the Baron pointed to himself with both hands.

"And you two are…?" Hallowmis asked.

"Name is Claudius and this is my brother, Lance."
Claudius briefly pointed to Lance.

"Ahh... young Claudius – the last time I've seen you, you were just a small boy. It must be pretty important for the king to send you all the way here."

"Yes, we are here to investigate the murder of the royal messenger and a few knights."

"Very well. I am about to eat dinner; would you care to join me?" Claudius turned his head towards Lance.

"I could use a bite," Lance replied as Claudius nodded in agreement.

"Sure, we will accompany you," Claudius spoke as he turned towards the Baron. At that moment, the new captain of the guard appeared in the doorway and ushered for the Baron's attention. Hallowmis whispered a few things to his court before turning his attention to the paladins.

"Please follow my advisor, I have something to attend to," he spoke with a forced smile. The two paladins nodded as they followed the small group into the dining hall with their griffons following closely behind. Once the two paladins had left the area, Hallowmis stepped outside with the new captain of the guard. "I thought I told you not to let anyone from the capital inside, *Captain*." Hallowmis hissed, showing anger in his voice.

"Griffons! They were on griffons, they simply flew over the walls!" the captain replied, pointing at the sky. The Baron was about to speak but held his tongue, knowing the flaw in his logic before abruptly walking back inside the keep.

Hallowmis entered the dining hall as the rest of the court were already seated and eating. He walked steadily towards the head of the long wooden table and sat at the head of the table. A royal red opulent cloth covered the table with a wide assortment of meats on top of polished silver plates. Hallowmis reached over and grabbed a roasted chicken leg and bit into it then looked over at the paladins to see Lance picking up a hefty turkey leg, holding it up beside him as Surina snapped her beak at the meat with a crunch and furiously gobbled it down, bone and all.

"Is that necessary?" Hallowmis was a little irritated.

"Necessary for my griffon to eat or to baby my griffon? I can let her eat from the table if you so wish," Lance replied as he brushed Surina's neck feathers while she let out a soft coo.

"No, no... that's fine," Hallowmis replied with a sigh. "So... how may I assist you paladins?" Hallowmis continued.

179

"We need two rooms for the duration of the investigation," Claudius spoke while grabbing a turkey thigh.

"I can accommodate that, as well as two rooms in the stables for your er... griffons," Hallowmis replied, taking another bite into his meal.

"Oh, you don't need to do that, our griffons will stay with us." Lance spoke as he grabbed the last piece of turkey meat from the plate and tossed it to Surina which she caught in mid-air. Hallowmis finished his leg, gently set the bone down on his plate and sighed once again.

"Very well. My advisor can show you to your rooms." An older man in purple robes stood up from the table and motioned them to follow him.

"Thank you for the food, Hallowmis." Claudius stood up from the table and walked towards the advisor.

"I am stuffed!" Lance spoke out as he climbed on top of his griffon. "What about you?" he whispered to Surina as she let out a soft coo while Lance rubbed her head. Surina followed Claudius as they exited the dining hall. Hallowmis glanced at his captain who stood up from the table and walked over.

"Make sure you keep a close eye on them," Hallowmis instructed as the captain nodded and left the hall.

Chapter 15

Soonifer

Emptiness. Soonifer walked alongside Ker'es and for a short while there was nothing but silence. "Now is the time… for you to rise," Ker'es whispered as Soonifer listened carefully. "Your ascent starts with retrieving the Blade of Life, one of three powerful tools used to become a god," he continued. They arrived at the Book of Infernal Knowledge. Ker'es stepped forward and moved his hand just above the book as the pages obeyed, turning until he stopped moving his hands. Ker'es stepped aside and motioned Soonifer to come forth and examine the book. He obeyed and stepped forward.

The words on the pages emitted a soft red glow, inviting him to take a closer look. *Soonifer looked deeper and suddenly saw a* beautiful silver dagger which held intricate designs across the blade, as the entire piece pulsed light green like a heart. The dagger was placed into a leather brown sheath where even the blade was concealed, the glow emitting through the sheath. There was a man cloaked in a dark leather tunic, his face hidden under a hood as he held a bow. His back was pressed against the trunk of a tree he was peering around to see a stag. He leaped from behind the tree and pulled an arrow from his quiver, firing it from his bow. The arrow pierced the stag's heart. A thud echoed as the body of the beast hit the ground. The hunter ran to the corpse and pulled out the arrow, placing it back into his quiver. He grabbed the dagger and thrust the blade into the stag. Not even a moment later, the stag's head rose from the ground. The hunter pulled the dagger out of the body in shock as the stag quickly got up and kicked the hunter's head before sprinting off into the forest. The hunter grabbed his head in pain and cursed out words. He looked at the dagger with scornful eyes.

"Wretched mages enchanted this dagger with healing properties!" The hunter pushed himself off the ground and picked up the dagger. "What use is a dagger that cannot kill?" he mumbled to himself as he examined the dagger. He shrugged it off as he found a giant stump of a tree nearby. He slammed the dagger in the center of the stump and walked off into the forest. The dagger filled the tree with life as the old and decaying bark turned anew.

The tree stood a giant among the other trees and the leaves themselves emitted a soft green glow.

Everything suddenly became dark. Soonifer blinked his eyes repeatedly before he realized his eyes were covered by someone's hands. He turned around to come face to face with Edge'knol. "Hmm! Hi," she spoke, revealing a sly smile which quickly faded away when she caught sight of Ker'es and took a few steps back.

Soonifer turned to face Ker'es and questioned, "Where is the dagger now?"

"The Silpine forest," Ker'es replied with a whisper.

"The home of the elves?" Soonifer questioned again.

"The very same!" Edge'knol interrupted.

"Before you depart, I want you to have something," Ker'es whispered. Soonifer kept his glowing red eyes upon Ker'es hollow black eyes until Ker'es suddenly disappeared into the darkness.

"Huh? Where did he go?" Soonifer questioned.

"He's with Gor'eck Kal," Edge'knol replied. Soonifer sneered as the shadow surrounded him.

He too disappeared into the blackness and quickly found himself in front of Gor'eck the Tormentor of Anger sitting upon his obsidian throne with Ker'es standing at the throne's side. His two sons and greater demons, Urreck and Airoth, stood at each side, beneath him.

"Gor'eck, I am sending Soonifer to retrieve the Blade of Life," said Ker'es.

"Finally! Some usefulness out of him!" bellowed Gor'eck.

"Yes, but in order for him to get the dagger, he has to destroy the tree and your weapon. Your curse is the only one able to do that," Ker'es whispered. Gor'eck let out a crude smile as his ego filled.

"Very well, come forth, weakling," Gor'eck summoned Soonifer. Soonifer held back his tongue, his pride being slightly damaged by the Tormentor's words, he obeyed, walking up the obsidian steps towards the Tormentor of Anger.

Soonifer stood in front of Gor'eck the Tormentor who placed one of his hands on Soonifer's head. It felt as if his head began to sear with fire. Soonifer closed both of his hands into a fist, trying to endure the pain. The pain in his head became more intense as his fists started to shake, holding in so much anger. Just as he couldn't stand anymore, the searing pain quieted down into a dull ache. Gor'eck removed his hand from Soonifer's head and just as Soonifer was about to calm himself, the Tormentor reared back and punched Soonifer in the head, knocking him backwards down the stairs. Gor'eck let out demonic laughter as his sons did the same. Soonifer quickly got up and clutched his right hand into a fist as purple flame engulfed his hand. The fire vanished as a spear appeared in his hand. Gor'eck stopped laughing as his eyes narrowed, awaiting an attack. His sons quickly got into a defensive stance. Soonifer's eyes filled with anger as they glowed a very dark red, fixated upon Gor'eck. He glanced quickly to Ker'es who showed no emotion or sign but Soonifer knew very well that this wasn't what Ker'es would have wanted. Soonifer turned around and let out a demonic yell as Ker'es swung the spear in the air, cutting a rift. The bright light of the sun poured through the rift. Soonifer leaped into the rift as it quickly closed behind him.

"Did you teach him that?" Gor'eck asked Ker'es.

"No," Ker'es replied with a whisper before vanishing into the darkness.

Soonifer stood in front of the tree line that led to the Silpine forest. A moment later, a purple rift opened beside him and out jumped Nox before the rift closed. Nox immediately licked the cheek of Soonifer who responded by roughly rubbing Nox's head.

"Let's do this," Soonifer spoke, clenching both of his hands into a fist as purple fire engulfed his hands, leaving an obsidian dagger in each. Soonifer took a step towards the forest as a single arrow shot near his foot. Looking up, he could see a few elves hiding among the trees with their bows drawn upon him. He lowered himself before leaping towards the forest. A barrage of arrows rained upon him as he twisted his body in mid-air, deflecting the arrows with the blade of his daggers. Nox leaped into the trees and thrashed his claws into an elf before springing onto another branch and doing the same. The bodies of elves would fall from the trees, hitting the ground with a loud thud. Soonifer landed on his feet, blocking two more arrows with pin-point precision. Soonifer threw his dagger up into the branches of the tree as an elf fell downwards. Soonifer quickly spawned a spear and hurled it upward, instantly killing an elf. Nox leaped down next to Soonifer as the last elf fell from the tree branches. Soonifer noticed an arrow had struck Nox in the shoulder. Grabbing the arrow shaft, he pulled it out of Nox's shoulder. Nox shook his head in slight pain as Soonifer's hand engulfed in purple flame again. He placed his hand where the arrow had wounded the lycan. The sound of searing flesh ensued before Soonifer pulled his hand back.

"Better?" Soonifer asked as the wound became completely healed. Nox nodded his head with his mouth ajar, breathing heavily. "The outer and inner forest are the most heavily guarded, we shouldn't run into many more elves until we get closer," Soonifer spoke as he spawned a spear. "Let's find trouble." Soonifer continued as they walked deeper into the forest, leaving behind an entire band of dead elves.

The Silpine forest fell into an uneasy silence. A stag walked over and lowered its head as it took a mouthful of grass. A twig snapped in the distance. The stag lifted its head up in alert, only to catch a spear to the head. The spear was thrown so hard that the impact broke the stag's neck as it collapsed to the ground. As they approached a crystal blue river, Soonifer could see the forest become more alive on the other side. The trees were bigger and the vegetation was much greener. Nox leaped into the river and began swimming to the other side. At that moment, a volley of arrows were shot at them, the sounds of which crunched into the tree bark. Soonifer took an arrow in his shoulder before quickly turning behind a tree. He ripped out the arrow and snapped it in half with his hand as rage started to fill his heart. He spawned a spear and leaped out from the tree. He hurled the spear which slammed into the torso of an elf, pinning it to a tree.

"Nox! Paw!" Soonifer yelled as he leaped into the river, spawning his twin daggers. Nox turned his head to Soonifer and threw his arm in the air. Soonifer deflected multiple arrows with his daggers as he landed on Nox's paw. Nox launched Soonifer to the other side of the river as he blocked more incoming arrows with his daggers. He leaped at an elf and cut his bow in half before stabbing the elf three times in the chest. Nox reached the shallow end of the river and sprinted towards an elf, tearing him to shreds before leaping onto another elf and digging his claws into his flesh, nearly severing his limbs. Dozens of elves became only a few as they fled deeper into the forest. Soonifer spawned and hurled a spear that slammed into the back of a fleeing elf. The two ran deeper into the forest, finding themselves at the edge of the main elf encampment. Circular wooden tree houses wrapped around the trunks of massive trees. Small wooden rope bridges connected to each house, forming a web-like village suspended in the upper level of the trees. The once quiet forest had now become more alive as elves peered out of their houses and elf sentinels stood with bows drawn on the intruders.

A purple fire exploded from Soonifer's hand as a giant obsidian hammer appeared. He sprinted towards a tree, rearing the hammer back and with all of his might, slammed the hammer into the tree. A loud snap echoed in the forest as the giant tree roots lifted out of the ground and the tree went down. The rope bridges snapped as the tree hut smashed into the ground. Elves fell downwards, screams erupted from the chaos. The elf sentinels fired arrow after arrow at the intruders as Nox leaped onto the trunk of a tree, his sharp claws digging into the wood as he launched himself from tree trunk to tree trunk until he made it to the wooden huts and began killing elves. Soonifer ran towards another giant tree and slammed the hammer into the base of the trunk. The tree roots lifted up from the ground as dirt shot into the air. More rope bridges snapped as the tension of the falling tree grew too much. The screams of the dying elves were masked by the thunderous boom of the massive tree slamming into the ground. Soonifer wasn't finished yet, the redness of his eyes grew more intense as anger seared into his heart. He sprinted towards another giant tree as an arrow snapped into his back, the pain ripping into his flesh comparable to a finger tap. He leaped into the air, rearing back the massive hammer once again and hitting the base of the tree in full contact. The tree fell down as the big wooden tree hut smashed into the ground.

Soonifer laid his eyes on the massive tree that stood in the center of the floating tree village. He looked up and could see the leaves emitting a soft green glow. The tree trunk of this particular tree was about three times as big as the others. Amidst the chaos, Soonifer ran towards the tree and with full force slammed his infernal hammer into the base of the tree; however, the tree didn't budge, only a few chunks of wood splintered off. He reared back and slammed his hammer again as more chunks of wood and bark flew into the air. Soonifer tossed his hammer into the air, as it disappeared he spawned his twin daggers and began furiously slashing and digging the blades into the tree. Pieces of wood ripped from the trunk as the inner part of the tree glowed a strange dark green. He could feel the dagger's presence, almost calling to him, which only increased his ferocity. Enough damage to the base of the tree left it unbalanced. Soonifer slammed the daggers into the tree and left them there as he spawned the gigantic hammer once more. He swung the hammer into the tree as the top portion of the tree began to descend to the ground with a loud thunderous boom of wood snapping. The tree hit the ground with such force that the entire ground shook. Soonifer laid his eyes upon the hilt of the dagger still embedded in the tree. He tossed the hammer to the side as he approached the dagger and firmly wrapped his hands around the hilt. A strange sensation filled his arm as he pulled the dagger from the stump of the tree.

"The Blade of Life..." Soonifer whispered holding the dagger close to him as he examined it more thoroughly, noticing the silver blade was decorated with intricate designs. The guard of the dagger looked similar to a leaf. Soonifer squeezed the dagger as he slammed the blade into his own chest. He let out a muffled cough as if he were just punched in the chest. He couldn't breathe, his entire body felt as if it was slowly being squeezed. He opened his mouth and let the cool air in, and at that moment, all and any pain left his body and the feeling of his body being squeezed ceased. He looked around and could see that everything was a little brighter in color and he felt unburdened.

"Nox!" Soonifer yelled as he pulled out the dagger from his chest. The world returned to its dreary colors along with the pain. Soonifer fell to his knees, catching himself with his free hand.

He felt as if the pain of the entire world sucked into him. He felt the sharp pain of the arrow still stuck into his back. He reached behind him and grabbed the arrow, ripping it away from his flesh. He dropped the arrow as he stood up. Nox leaped from the high tree branches and landed with his feet on the ground with a thud. He ran towards Soonifer with his mouth ajar, panting heavily. Soonifer placed his free hand on Nox's head and stroked back his blood-soaked fur. He could tell Nox was happy to see him with his tail wagging excitedly. Soonifer peered to the side to see Nox's side and back riddled with a few arrows and dagger wounds. He then placed his hand on the lycan's muzzle and lowered it down.

"This is going to hurt only for a little bit," he whispered as he slammed the Blade of Life into the shoulder of the lycan. Nox's eyes dilated a bit as his muscles flexed. He stopped panting for a bit before he breathed in deeply, his eyes returning to normal. "Feel better?" Soonifer asked as Nox shook his head repeatedly. Soonifer turned to Nox's side and began pulling the arrows from his body, dropping them to the ground. As he pulled the last arrow out, he snapped the arrow and purple fire engulfed his hand. He pressed his hand against the wound, healing the flesh, as the sound of searing flesh emitted. Soonifer pulled the dagger out of Nox as the lycan stretched his muscles. "Good as new?" Soonifer asked as the lycan shook his head. "Let's return," Soonifer spoke as he spawned a spear in his free hand and slashed the ground, splitting the ground wide open. He leaped into the hole as Nox also jumped into the hole, the ground resealing behind them.

Chapter 16

Claudius

Determination. Claudius and Lance took flight on their griffons, leaving the city of Solbris. The brisk, cold air kissed the cheeks of the paladins as the sun started its climb towards the sky. "Where shall we travel first?" Lance yelled.

"Sentia, then perhaps Goven Hills!" Claudius replied. Lance looked around, seeing the vast fields and meadows they passed. He held the leather reins with his left hand, reached over with his right and brushed Surina's neck feathers as she let out a loud "Kaaa!" They reached the small town of Sentia and descended, landing in the center of the marketplace where people had already started to organize their wares for sale. The town had slowly started to come alive as merchants rolled their wagons and wheelbarrows to their shops.

"Excuse me, what rumors have you heard concerning the royal messenger?" Claudius questioned a patrolling guard.

"Royal messenger? I haven't heard any such news in quite some time, why do you ask?" the guard replied.

"The royal messenger and a few knights were murdered some days ago. I am investigating their disappearance."

"Oh, how tragic. I do hope you find the culprits." The guard frowned but showed some sympathy.

"Thank you, and have you heard anything concerning bandits or highwayman on nearby roads?"

"No, I haven't heard of any disturbances in quite a while. The only thing that comes to mind was some cattle thievery a few months ago." The guard spoke while eyeing the pair of paladins. "You don't look like regular guards, who are you exactly?"

"We are paladins!" Lance abruptly stated.

"Paladins? Aren't you supposed to be fighting demons? Not trying to catch bandits?"

"Generally, but this was a request by the king," Claudius replied.

"I see, have you checked with the guards in Goven Hills just north of here?"

"No, but it's our next stop. Thank you for your time."

"Aye, may the divines grant you favor."

Claudius and Lance mounted their griffons and took off into the air as the people in the market paused to watch the paladins leave the city.

They arrived to the town of Goven Hills which sat in the middle of a collection of smaller hills. The two paladins descended and landed in the town's marketplace. The crowd of people momentarily stopped their actions to watch the pair of paladins arrive. Three guards ran up to them with their hands on the hilts of their swords.

"Halt, we are paladins investigating the murder of the royal messenger and several knights!" Claudius announced as he hopped off his griffon.

"Besides, my griffon here could take all three of you alone!" Lance challenged while dismounting his griffon and giving a rough rub on Surina's head, causing her to let out a soft coo.

"Right, interesting to see paladins around these parts. How can we be of help?" one of the guards asked as all three of them took their hands off the hilts of their swords.

"Do you know any whereabouts of bandits or highwayman around these parts?" Claudius questioned.

"There was a man who was robbed of his purse several days ago, however the culprit was found and the man's purse was returned to him," the guard replied. The guards glanced at the griffons and back towards the paladins.

"They are beautiful creatures," the lead guard admired.

"Indeed they are, even though they take up more than half the bed!" Lance replied, giving a look at Surina to which Surina stepped forward and gave Lance a playful nudge with her head. "Hey! You watch that, you don't want to mess with this!" Lance yelled at Surina while pointing to himself. Surina spread her wings and let out a sharp "kaa!" Surina leaped at Lance as he wrapped his arms around her neck. She twisted her neck out of his grasp and leaped at him once more, this time knocking him to the ground, metal clinks emitting as she pecked at his armor. "Hey hey! No pecking!" Lance yelled as he grabbed her beak with both hands, struggling to stop her pecking at his armor. The three guards erupted in laughter, seeing the entire charade going on. Claudius revealed a smile as Sundra turned her head towards the event.

"Is… this normal?" a guard inquired, halting his laughter momentarily.

"All the time!" Claudius replied. Lance used all of his strength to flip Surina on her back as he jumped on her belly and began to furiously rub her stomach. She spread her wings out and let out rough coos as dust was brushed into the air from the griffon's wings.

"I am sorry we are of no help, but perhaps you should check Sentia?" the guard suggested.

"No, we actually came from there, checked there first. It was the closest place to Solbris," Claudius replied.

"Solbris? I would stay away from there, that place is not quite right…"

"Agreed. I get that feeling too."

"I know it's a longshot, but perhaps there is some information to the west, a small farming town."

"Kolloth!" one of the other guards shouted

"Yes, Kolloth – that's the one" the lead guard remembered.

"It's worth a try, thank you" Claudius replied

Lance walked towards the group brushing the dirt off his armor "Now where were we?" Lance asked.

"I think you were getting beat by Surina," Claudius replied.

"Careful now," remarked Lance, getting most of the dirt off his armor.

"Or what? You'll tickle me too?" Claudius replied as the guards erupted in laughter.

"Hey, I am the victorious one!"

"Indeed you are!" Claudius agreed, hiding his smile.

"Shall we eat something? I have become quite hungry after that victory."

"There is beef stew that my brother makes, his shop is nearby," offered one of the guards.

"That sounds great!" Lance said as Claudius nodded in agreement.

"Here, let me lead the way." The guard gestured as Lance clicked his teeth, to which Surina rose up from the ground and followed.

The sun had already begun its descent from the sky as Claudius and Lance flew through the air on their griffons toward the small town of Kolloth. They landed near the marketplace, however many of the merchants had already left.

"They seem to close up early," Lance surmised, still mounted on his griffon.

"Perhaps we should check elsewhere?" Claudius asked before they both heard a man yelling.

"Kayhe! Where are you?!" shouted the man. Both paladins turned their heads towards the man who was approaching. "Curse the divines! Please…where…" the man's voice trailed off as he stumbled upon the two paladins. Lance slid off his griffon and walked towards the man as Claudius remained on his griffon letting out a sigh.

"What is your problem?" Lance questioned the man, placing his hands on his hips. The man took a moment and studied Lance before replying.

"It doesn't concern you, silver spoon!" the man replied with noticeable disgust.

Lance took a few steps toward the man.

"Silver spoon?" Lance replied, crossing his arms.

"Yes, by your armor you seem to be well off!" the man sneered.

"I was a farmer before I became a paladin and it seems like I'm doing far better than you, pitchfork!" remarked Lance which seemed to surprise the man. Claudius hopped off his griffon and briskly walked over to the two.

"Please excuse my brother. What is the matter?" Claudius asked in a much more sympathetic tone. The man took a deep breath and let out a long sigh.

"My sister has gone missing for weeks now. The rest of the town has given up, but I still come out here every day in hope of her return. However, I am starting to have my own doubts."

"What is your name?" Claudius asked.

"Allister."

"And your sister's name?"

"Kayhe."

"We are actually in the middle of investigating the murder of a royal messenger and a few knights. Have you heard anything about that?" Claudius asked.

"Uh…no I haven't, sorry."

"If it makes you feel any better, we can try to help find your sister after," Claudius offered.

"That would be great, thank you! Are you… royal guards from the capital?"

"No, we are knives" Lance replied.

"What?"

"Knives, a type of food utensil - much like a spoon except used to cut things" Lance blurted out barely holding back his laughter.

Claudius shot Lance a look "We are paladins. Generally, we are fighting demons, however in special circumstances we help in other matters" he interrupted.

"I see." Allister crossed his arms.

"I understand how you feel, my own brother went missing a while ago" Claudius added as Allister nodded in deep thought.

"Would you like to become one?" Claudius asked as Allister quickly showed surprise in his face; a little showed in Lance's too.

"I'm… not sure."

"It could help find your sister faster." Claudius suggested as Allister's face quickly showed interest.

"How long does it take to become one?"

"Years."

"Years?" Allister questioned as his interest began to fade.

"Yes, but we will inform the king of your situation and we'll have active search parties for your sister in the meanwhile," Claudius remarked.

"Okay, I'll give it a shot," Allister replied, giving a confidant nod.

"Great!" Claudius agreed as he reached in his leather satchel and pulled out two gold coins which he handed to Allister. He looked confused but took the money.

"What is this for?"

"Buy yourself something good to eat tonight and a horse to ride to the capital tomorrow. Ask the capital gate guards directions to the paladin academy and once you are there, tell them your story and my regards," instructed Claudius.

"Absolutely, thank you, kind sirs!" Allister spoke as he stepped forward and gave Claudius a hug. He broke off and was about to give Lance a hug before Surina leaped at him with her wings spread, letting out a loud growl. Allister fell backwards as Lance let out a laugh.

"It seems that I don't give out hugs, she's a bit jealous," Lance chuckled while he patted Surina's head as the griffon folded her wings.

Claudius helped Allister up and held his wrist, whispering, "Be strong." Allister nodded and walked off.

"What the nether was that all about?" Lance questioned Claudius.

"You don't kick a man when he's down, Lance."

"Yeah, but you'd kick me?"

"True, because you are an ass!" Claudius replied with a laugh. "Besides, we could always use more paladins, right?"

"Right," Lance agreed with a nod. "I need a drink after that."

"There is an inn over there. I'll buy you a drink for not thrashing that guy."

"Thanks, but I don't need to do anything when I have her around," Lance spoke as he roughly rubbed Surina's neck.

They entered the inn as a few patrons turned, many looking up to see unfamiliar faces with griffons walking into the room. The air was warm and filled with talk and laughter. The two paladins walked towards the bar, their griffons following them with their massive bodies brushing against the wooden tables and chairs.

"Two rooms please," Claudius spoke to the innkeeper who had a strange look on his face.

"That will be five silver each and your..." the innkeeper's voice trailed off as he leaned to the side, looking at the griffons. "...griffons can stay in the barn out back with the horses," the innkeeper continued. Claudius frowned as Lance stood beside him and reached in his leather purse, pulling out a handful of silver coins and placing them on the table in a messy pile.

"Our griffons stay with us," Lance said sternly.

The innkeeper eyed the silver coins before looking up at Lance, as a patron of the inn shouted "Can my horse stay in a room too?"

"Does your horse have wings?" Lance replied turned his head with a sly smile, matching the banter of the man as the inn erupted in laughter. Lance turned his head back to the innkeeper, awaiting a reply.

"Of course, your griffons may stay in the rooms upstairs," the innkeeper conceded as he scooped the pile of silver coins with both hands. Lance placed one of his hands on top of the innkeeper's hands, stopping his action in place.

"As many drinks as I can muster and as much food as my griffon desires," Lance chuckled, revealing his giant grin.

"Absolutely!" he replied as Lance released the innkeeper's hand. Claudius smiled and placed his hand on Lance's shoulder.

"Thanks, Lance. I'm going to retire early, don't stay up too late," Claudius warned as the innkeeper placed two copper keys on the table. Claudius picked up one and walked towards the stairs as his griffon followed. Lance picked up his key and placed it in his leather satchel before turning to the innkeeper.

"Ale and some of your best food," Lance spoke as the innkeeper nodded and rushed into the kitchen. Lance turned around and walked to a table in the center of the room. He sat down and pushed two chairs away making space for Surina. The innkeeper rushed to the table and placed a tankard of ale and a bowl of something in front of Lance. "What's in the bowl?" Lance questioned, grabbing the tankard of ale and taking a sip.

"Beef stew with an assortment of vegetables, our signature and best dish, like you asked," the innkeeper replied with a smile.

"Thank you!" Lance pushed the bowl towards Surina and she quickly ate the contents of the bowl. The innkeeper was surprised that the food was for the griffon and not for the paladin and walked away. A few patrons took a seat at Lance's table as they held their own tankards of ale.

"So... who are you?" a man asked the paladin.

"I am a simple farmer and this is my flying horse!" Lance replied taking another drink of his ale. The people at his table roared into laughter as more people in the bar directed their attention towards Lance.

"No, but really, who are you?" the same man asked.

"My name is Lance. I am a paladin and this is my beautiful griffon, Surina." Surina lifted her head from the bowl and let out a loud squawk before pushing the bowl towards the center of the table with her beak. Lance drank the last of his ale and slammed the tankard on the table and shouted, "More ale and stew!"

"Of course!" The innkeeper shouted back as he rushed back into the kitchen and brought out a fresh tankard of ale and another bowl of beef stew, placing it on the table. Surina quickly ate the contents of the stew as Lance grabbed the tankard and began drinking it. The people in the room watched in awe, seeing the massive beast eat the stew as Lance continued drinking.

"Are paladins allowed to drink?" a person asked as Lance stopped drinking for a moment and pondered before responding.

"I don't think I have read the rules entirely but if you shall find one, please with haste, inform me," Lance finished as he gulped down another drink and the room erupted with laughter. More patrons turned their attention towards the center of the room, moving their chairs and such. "Careful! Don't get too close to Surina or she will attack!" Lance shouted as a man dared against his words to touch Surina's wings which Surina responded to with a firm headbutt to the man's forehead. The crowd of drunken people erupted once again with laughter and cheered. "Innkeeper, more please!" Lance shouted as the innkeeper rushed to the table with more ale and another bowl of stew.

"You are going to need more money to pay for these," the innkeeper informed Lance, holding the ale and bowl. The crowd of people quickly turned silent awaiting the answer. Lance reached into his leather purse and leaned forward towards the middle of the table. Everyone in the room watched carefully as Lance dumped the contents of his purse onto the table. A small mountain of silver coins sat on the wooden table, putting everyone into shock, their mouths open to see so many coins in one place. Lance sat back down and turned his head to the innkeeper with a giant grin on his face.

"Ale and food for everyone!" he shouted as the entire inn roared with a cheer. The innkeeper was in complete shock as he placed the tankard and bowl on the table while shoveling the silver coins into his brown apron.

"Lance! Lance! Lance!" The crowd of drunken people chanted as Lance grabbed his tankard and held it in the air, the crowd following suit.

"For truth, justice, and women!" Lance yelled as he took a deep drink of his ale and the crowd followed suit. Surina once again quickly ate the contents of the bowl, however this time she batted the bowl off the table with her claw and let out a loud squawk. The innkeeper returned with a tray of tankards, handing drinks to people left and right as the room erupted with loud chatter.

Later, the room was hushed with silence as everyone listened to Lance's stories, even the innkeeper was captivated. "And I stood at the edge of this massive cliff, which even clouds would brush my legs... and I leaped off!" Lance took a moment to drink from his tankard.

"How did you survive the fall?" a lady asked. Lance slammed down his tankard on the table.

"With my wings of course!" he replied, waving his arms in the air.

"What wings?" a man questioned.

"Yeah... I don't see how anyone could have survived a jump like that," another man added.

Lance placed his hands on the table, lowering his head and closed his eyes. Everyone watched, quietly waiting for the would-be paladin to do something. Lance shook his head and looked up as the crowd started to whisper among each other.

"Does anyone have a blade?" Lance shouted. Several people held daggers in the air as Lance pointed to a man. "You, stand up," Lance ordered as the man obeyed.

"Try and kill me," Lance dared as the man's face showed question and intrigue. More whispers and chatter fell among the crowd as they looked on. "Come on now, don't be afraid!" Lance shouted at the man. The man nodded as he ran towards Lance with the dagger in the air. The man was just a few steps away from the paladin before Lance's eyes exploded with a glowing bright blue color while giant ethereal blue wings flared up behind him. Lance quickly grabbed the man's wrist with his left-hand and grabbed the man's tunic, flipping him onto the table as empty tankards flew into the air. The light in Lance's eyes, body and wings faded instantly afterwards as he stood there. The entire crowd of people gasped and remained silent in awe, witnessing what had just happened. Suddenly, the crowd erupted in a cheer as Lance raised both arms into the air.

The morning sun's rays poured through the dusty windows of the inn as Lance climbed on top of Surina. "Let's go to our room upstairs" Lance urged as Surina started to walk through the crowd of people who were chanting, "Lance! Lance! Lance!" Lance met Claudius at the top of the stairs. "I can see you had a good time," Claudius stated.

"Something along the lines of that. I'm going to bed... I'm tired," Lance replied, mumbling a few words.

"Get some rest, we return to the capital when you wake," Claudius ordered as Lance drunkenly nodded and Surina walked into an empty room. Lance plopped onto the bed with Surina plopping into bed on top of him. Claudius walked downstairs to find some people half asleep on tables, some people leaving the inn, a mass of tankards lying everywhere. He turned to the innkeeper and handed him the key.

"Could you please remind the other paladin to return to the capital when he wakes?" Claudius asked.

"Yes, of course!" The innkeeper replied taking the key. "You paladins are always welcome to my inn!" the innkeeper continued with a big smile.

"Thank you," Claudius replied with a gentle smile and a low sigh. Claudius exited the inn and mounted on his griffon. "Let's return home," he told Sundra as she took flight into the skies.

Chapter 17

<u>Soonifer</u>

Noiseless. Soonifer handed the Blade of Life to Ker'es who examined the dagger. It emitted a dark green glow that pulsed every second.

"Well done, Soonifer," Ker'es whispered as he handed the dagger to Edge'knol. "Hide the dagger in his book," he instructed her as she nodded.

"Come with me," she spoke to Soonifer as she walked off into the darkness. Nox turned around and followed her. Soonifer stared into Ker'es' eyes and this time he didn't see the familiar emptiness but instead saw approval. Ker'es vanished into the darkness and so did Soonifer.

Soonifer appeared in front of the library's doors and pushed them open. He walked inside and saw Nox sitting nearby and Edge'knol walking towards him with a sly smile. "It's done, hidden from any prying eyes," she declared. "You know, you are the first demon in quite some time to retrieve one of the three tools."

"Am I?" Soonifer replied as she nodded. "I don't feel accomplished…I don't feel much of anything anymore," he continued. She showed a slight frown before showing an uneasy smile.

"Well, I think your actions are quite interesting, more so than other demons." Edge'knol spoke as the purple flame danced upon the candles that stood on her shoulders.

"Have you been reading my book?" Soonifer questioned.

"Occasionally," she replied, tilting her head trying to downplay it off.

"Could I see the Book of Infernal Knowledge?" he asked.

"Of course," she replied as she turned around to walk towards the center of the library. They stood before the giant book as it emitted a dark red glow. "Is there something in particular you would like to see?" she asked.

"Tern'natha," Soonifer replied as Edge'knol turned around and moved her delicate hands above the book, the pages turning rapidly, following her hand motion. She stopped moving her hand and the pages stopped turning. She took a few steps back and signaled Soonifer to look. Soonifer stepped forward, gazing deep into the book and was met with blackness.

***

The king wore a mixture of armor and royal attire. Metal plates lined up with golden trim and a long blood red cloak that rested upon his back. A fierce lion's head amulet hung from his golden necklace. A young man dressed in red and black silk stood next to the king. The king placed his arm around the young man as they both walked slowly forward. Elegant marble statues of the king in heroic stances lined the hall.

"My son, you are ready to become a warrior – just like your father." They stopped in front of a statue where the king held his sword out into the air and a multitude of dead soldiers lay at his feet. "I single-handedly slew a mountain of men who dared raise their sword against me. You must learn to be brave just like me." The king spoke as they continued walking to another statue of the king landing the final blow against another king who was on his knees. "Mercy is weakness, pride is strength." The two continued to walk as everything turned black except the echoes of their footsteps.

Suddenly, the young man was in a room filled with various weapon racks that lined the walls. Even more assortments of maces, daggers, clubs and swords rested upon tables that lined the outer room. The prince held his sword with both hands nervously.

"Again!" the teacher shouted as he swung his sword at the prince. The prince blocked the first attack but when the teacher quickly swung again, the prince tried to block the second attack and dropped his sword on the recoil. The sword hit the ground with a metal clang as the teacher sheathed his sword.

"I cannot use this sword with such finesse as you do, teacher. Such intensity at close quarters frightens me," the prince said while bending over to pick up his sword. The teacher let out a sigh and snatched the sword from the prince, walking over to the side of the room, he placed the sword on a table. He turned his head to a barrel of spears and grabbed one. Walking over to the prince, he handed him the spear.

"See that target? Throw the spear at it," the teacher instructed. The prince nodded as he gripped the spear firmly and raised his arm. He hurled the spear towards the target as the spear danced in the air for a second before slamming into the middle of the target. The teacher turned his head from the target to the prince in shock. The teacher ran to the side of the room

217

and grabbed the entire barrel and dragged it towards the prince. "Throw more!" the teacher exclaimed as the prince smiled.

"Father, I have mastered my weapon!" the prince exclaimed.

"The sword?" the king asked.

"No, the spear!" the prince replied as the king frowned before slamming his fists into the armrests of his throne.

"The spear is a coward's weapon!" the king shouted as the prince's smile quickly faded. The weapons teacher stepped forward.

"Sire, your son has displayed incredible mastery over the spear. Even veteran spearman cannot compare with his talent." The teacher spoke in the prince's defense. The king was unhappy but nodded, hearing the teacher's plea.

"Teach him everything, I want him to be the best," the king ordered as the room began to fall apart until nothing but blackness was left.

The prince stood on a high cliff holding a spear with two legions of archers behind him as a giant red flag of a fierce lion waved behind him. He saw two giant armies charge at each other and when they met an explosion of screams and metal echoed in the air. "Attack!" the prince commanded as he hurled his spear into the enemy lines while a volley of arrows followed his spear. The prince caught a glance of his father fighting in the front lines; however, he spotted a group of enemy knights on horseback, charging towards them from the side. "There! Focus all of our arrows on the knights!" the prince ordered.

"Sire! Five legions of knights are breaching the barricades. They will get us!" the captain next to the prince remarked.

"No! My father is more important! He will save us! Fire now!" the prince ordered as wave after wave of arrows and spears fell down upon the enemy forces, killing the entire squad of knights charging the king. The king had nearly decimated the entire opposing army, however the five legions of knights had broken through the barricades and captured the prince. One of the soldiers thrashed the prince before grabbing onto the belt that crossed his chest plate. Another enemy soldier blew a horn which made both armies below stop attacking.

"I have your son!" the enemy king yelled as he signaled the soldier to bring the prince to the edge of the cliff. "You will surrender your armor, weapons and horses to me, in exchange for your son's life," the enemy king continued.

"You have lost the battle! Your men are few in number, only five legions of knights remain!" the king yelled back from below.

"Yes, but I hold your son's life!" the enemy king replied as the prince struggled in the soldier's grasp at the edge of the cliff.

"I have never lost a battle! It does not change today!" the king from below yelled.

"Father!" the prince exclaimed, struggling against the soldier's grasp once more.

"Very well," the enemy king replied as he gave the signal to the soldier. The soldier tossed the prince over the ledge as the prince flailed his arms against the rushing wind of the descent.

"Father!" the prince shouted once more before the world around him turned to black.

***

Soonifer turned his head to Edge'knol who seemed a bit surprised. "Is everything okay?" she softly whispered with a worried look on her face.

"My hand…" Soonifer replied, taking his left hand and holding it up to his face. He could feel the eye of Ko'vik moving in his hand. "It feels like it's on fire…" Soonifer continued as he curled his hand into a fist. Edge'knol walked towards him and held his fist, which she gently opened and slid her fingers across the palm of his hand.

"You hold tremendous power, Soonifer," she told him, changing her gaze from his palm to his glowing red eyes.

"Do I?" Soonifer replied. She nodded her head.

"You have his eye, so you are able to draw power from him," she said softly.

"What kind of power?" Soonifer asked.

"To create rifts, to heal…even to stop reading from the Book of Infernal Knowledge…by yourself," she replied.

"But I don't know how…"

"But you do."

Soonifer nodded as he slowly pulled his hand away from hers. Edge'knol stepped back, keeping her eyes upon him. Soonifer held out his hand over the Book of Infernal Knowledge.

"Show me Kovick'kal." As he spoke, the pages of the book flipped rapidly towards the front few pages and then stopped. He was about to look into the book before Ker'es appeared behind the book. Both Soonifer and Edge'knol had looks of bewilderment on their faces with the sudden arrival.

"Soonifer, prepare yourself. You will lead an army of demons to retrieve the Hammer of Creation from the humans at Light's Reach" Ker'es prophesied "It shall be an easy task of your current caliber," Ker'es replied as Soonifer gave a nod, obeying the Tormentor's order before he vanished, leaving a slight dark cloud.

Ker'es walked over, closing the Book of Infernal Knowledge before picking it up with both hands.

"What do you plan on using the book for, Tormentor?" Edge'knol asked, shyly hiding her hands behind her back.

"Tipping the scales to our advantage," Ker'es whispered before disappearing with the book in his arms.

Chapter 18

<u>Claudius</u>

Merriment. Claudius placed his arm on Allister.
"Congratulations, Allister," he smiled.

"Thank you," Allister replied, looking at him.

"Three months?" Lance blurted out with a question.

"Something like that, why? Are you surprised?" Allister
returned with a sly smile.

"Corn doesn't even grow that fast!" Lance replied in jest
as all three paladins laughed.

"Have you heard any word?" Allister's laughter quickly
shifted into a serious tone.

"None. I sent so many scouts that even the captain of the guard was getting irritated. 'He felt it was chasing after a ghost.' His words not mine," Claudius replied.

"Yeah, well, it's not his sister who's lost."

"I understand, we will find her Allister, rest assured."

A guard ran into the room towards Claudius. "Claudius, an elf is seeking you, she goes by the name of Lunnah."

"Why? What has happened?" Claudius asked with a concerned look.

"She said it's urgent and she is waiting at the capital gates!" the guard replied. Claudius took off running, letting out a sharp whistle to summon Sundra who appeared in the sky and flew down.

"Capital gates!" Claudius cried as he quickly hopped on Sundra who immediately took off flying towards the gates.

"Are you ready for your first mission?" Lance asked Allister.

"Where is he going?"

"Don't know, but let's go!" Lance replied as they both started to chase after Claudius.

"Have you received your griffon yet?" Lance asked.

"No."

"Okay, just hop on mine," Lance offered as he let out a sharp whistle to which Surina let out a loud squawk and descended towards them. Surina landed in front of them as Lance hopped on her back.

"Woah, they are beautiful," Allister admired.

"Yes, she is magnificent. Now hop on!" Lance ordered as Allister obeyed. They quickly caught up to Claudius at the capital gates.

Claudius spotted a treant and a golem at the front of the gates. "There!" Claudius pointed as Sundra descended towards the gates.

"Claudius!" Lunnah yelled.

"Lunnah!" Claudius yelled back as he dismounted his griffon. The two embraced each other in a hug for a moment before they broke off. "What is the matter?" Claudius asked.

"I need your help! We must go to the Silpine forest! Someone has attacked the elves and destroyed our home!" Lunnah exclaimed with a mixture of sadness and anger in her eyes.

"Let's go!" Claudius cried out as he climbed on top of his griffon and urged Lunnah to hop on too. She climbed onto the griffon and placed her arms around Claudius' waist.

"Rockstead, Oakheart! Meet us at the Silpine forest!" Lunnah yelled as both of the beings started to walk away from the capital.

"He ah!" Claudius yelled as Sundra took to the skies. "Tell me where to go," Claudius asked.

"The main elven encampment in the middle of the Silpine forest!" Lunnah replied.

"Understood," Claudius remarked as Sundra's wings beat heavily, cutting through the sky.

"Follow them!" Lance yelled, pointing at Claudius' griffon, Surina let out a loud squawk in reply, beating her wings faster, trying to catch up.

They flew across the massive sea of lush green tree tops until Lunnah pointed towards some holes that exposed the floor of the forest. They descended, landing on the soft grass as both Claudius and Lunnah leaped off the griffon but were soon surrounded by elves with drawn bows.

"Hold your arrows, he is with me!" Lunnah yelled out as the elves slowly lowered their bows. An elf sentinel briskly walked towards her.

"Why do you bring a human to our home?" the sentinel demanded in an angry tone.

"He is going to help us, Roarick!" Lunnah replied in the same tone.

"How can a human help us?"

"Shut up, we have the injured to attend to," Lunnah remarked. The sentinel reluctantly accepted that Lunnah wasn't going to take any attitude. At that moment, another griffon landed next to them with Lance and Allister dismounting. The elves re-aimed their bows at the two paladins while Lance remarked.

"Bad time?"

"There's more of them?" Roarick barked.

"Calm down! They are with me and we are here to help, take us to the injured" Claudius ordered as the elves lowered their bows once again.

"Follow me, humans." the sentinel called as he walked away. Claudius started to follow the elf as Lance and Allister caught up to him.

"What happened?" Lance asked Claudius.

"Well, judging by a few fallen trees and half their village being destroyed… something bad happened here," Allister suggested.

"Yeah, we'll find out soon, I guess," Claudius replied.

The elf sentinel brought the group to a crowd of elves who were injured in several different ways. Some were wounded by claw marks, others had broken bones and a few had survived a spear thrown at them.

"Lance, Allister, spread out and help those in dire need first," Claudius ordered as the two paladins took quick action. Claudius knelt down to an elf sentinel who had a large black spear stuck in his chest. Lunnah stood next to Claudius, watching him as he questioned the elf.

"Who did this?"

"Some… man with red eyes…" the sentinel managed to say as he groaned in pain.

"This is going to hurt, but I need to remove the spear," Claudius told the sentinel as he stood up and placed both hands on the spear. His hands instantly became cold as he quickly pulled them back. Claudius' eyes immediately became bright blue as giant ethereal blue wings erupted from his back with a faint shimmer of light surrounding his entire body. All of the surrounding elves quietly gasped and whispered to one another. Claudius grabbed the spear and pulled it out – tossing it to the side as the spear instantly crumbled into black dust. Claudius knelt down once more next to the elf and placed his hand on the wound. A bright light emitted from his hand as the wound healed completely. Claudius' blue eyes and wings faded as he returned normal. "Better?" Claudius asked the elf. The elf placed his hand over the wound and felt it healed completely and looked at Claudius in disbelief.

"Much better, who are you?" the elf asked with a face of bewilderment.

"Claudius, I am a paladin," Claudius replied and at that moment the elves all were quiet and amazed, witnessing what just happened.

"Thank you, Claudius," the elf spoke as he got up.

"Hurry, we have to help the others!" Claudius ordered as all the elves circled around them quickly, moving to aid him in any way. Claudius turned his face to Lunnah and spoke. "Everything is going to be okay," he assured her as he quickly made his way to the other injured elves. Lunnah revealed a heartfelt smile before seeing the sentinel watching her and quickly changing his facial expression. "Stop standing around and help!" Lunnah barked at the sentinel who turned around and ran to help the others.

Lance knelt down next to an elven child who was crying horrifically. The elf's mother was sitting next to her, trying to console her child.

"How can I help?" Lance asked the mother who was nervous to answer. "Your child is crying! How can I help?!" Lance demanded in a louder tone as she finally got the courage to answer.

"My daughter… she was in the tree hut when it crashed into the ground," she replied as she grabbed the blanket off her daughter's legs, revealing that they were badly broken. Lance looked at the child's mangled legs and showed a frown.

"That's not good… okay… okay I got this," Lance spoke to himself. Lance closed his eyes for a moment, clenching his teeth, trying to focus, but nothing happened. "Dammit!" he muttered to himself under his breath. He opened his eyes and looked around, seeing both Claudius and Allister healing the injured in their ascended forms. "The stupid pitchfork can do it on command but why can't I?" Lance looked around on the ground and saw a broken arrow. He quickly grabbed it and held it for a moment.

"This better work…" he muttered to himself as the elf mother frantically looked on, trying to make sense of what he was doing. Lance slammed the sharp arrowhead into the palm of his hand as he let out a muffled groan, clenching his teeth in pain. At that moment, light blue light exploded from his eyes and giant blue glowing wings emerged from his back sending the mother backwards in surprise. He dropped the arrow on the ground, then he placed a hand on each of the child's legs and bright light emitted from his hands. Lance moved the girl's legs in a straight position as the child quickly stopped crying. The light faded from Lance as he returned back to normal, and the little girl sat up and moved her legs in disbelief. She then stood up as her mother quickly scrambled towards her and wrapped her arms around her daughter, tears coming to her eyes. Lance looked at his slightly injured left hand before looking at the two with a smile.

"Thank you," the mother spoke as she held her child.

"Humans aren't so bad," the elf child spoke, smiling at Lance.

"Yeah, something like that," Lance replied as he got up to go help more of the injured.

"There was a...lycan with the man with red eyes as well. I don't recall ever seeing one, let alone attacking elves in ages." The elf who was sitting next to the fire spoke while holding a wooden cup of water.

"It's a different age now," Allister commented.

"Demons are being more brazen and aggressive as of late, we are not sure why," Claudius stated while sitting on a log as Lunnah sat by his side. At that moment, a large group of elves arrived near the camp fire.

"What are humans doing in our home?" a stern but calm voice asked. The group of elves and paladins turned their heads to see an elf wearing the traditional elven clothing, along with a giant stag horn crown. Lunnah was the first elf to leap up and defend the paladins.

"They were here to help us."

"Yes, they healed the injured!" another elf shouted.

"What caused this horrific damage to our beloved home?" the elven king questioned.

"Demons!" an elven woman shouted as the crowd of elves agreed.

"Demons?" the elven king replied.

"No, it was a demon and a lycan, just two," an elven man corrected.

"Two beings did this?" the elven king asked, holding out his hand to the fallen trees. The paladins stood up and walked towards the king.

"Humans still causing trouble, I see" the elven king sneered at the three paladins.

"Demons are the ones causing trouble and it seems that the humans are the only ones who care enough to try and fix the mess," Allister challenged.

"It is a different time now, it seems that demons are becoming stronger," Claudius added.

"A demon I can comprehend but a lycan attacking us, I cannot. We elves have settled our differences with those dogs a long time ago," the elven king replied.

"We must be going, but if you need any help – the capital is right there." Claudius pointed in the direction of the city. The elven king let out a gentle sneer as the elves watched the paladins walk towards their griffons.

"Claudius," Lunnah let out as she chased after him. Claudius turned around as Lunnah embraced him with a hug.

"Thank you," she whispered into his ear as they parted from their hug but held hands for a bit longer.

"You know where to find me, be safe," Claudius whispered back as he mounted his griffon. The griffons took to the skies and Lunnah could see them become smaller and smaller until they completely disappeared from sight.

"Your father would be disgusted," Roarick roared out.

"No, your father – who fought alongside humans a hundred years ago – would be of you," Lunnah returned as she walked away into the forest. Roarick tried to hide his anger but his eyes gave it away as he stomped off in the other direction.

"We shall rebuild this anew," the elven king declared. A little elven girl walked towards the king and tugged on his robes. The elven king knelt down to match the little girl's eyes. "How are you, little one?" he asked in a much kinder voice.

"Humans are kind," she said with a giant smile as her mother ran towards her.

"There are some things you will learn someday," the king replied.

"One of them fixed my legs."

"Oh, did they?"

The little girl nodded as her mother came and scooped her up in her arms. "I'm sorry" her mother whispered.

"Oh, it's no trouble at all," the king answered. "She mentioned something about her legs?" he questioned.

"Yes, she was in one of the tree huts when the encampment was attacked. The tree fell and the entire hut collapsed, crushing her legs... I feared she would never walk again until one of the paladins healed her legs," she explained as the king raised an eyebrow. "I saw it with my own eyes! His eyes glowed bright blue and he had wings when he healed her legs!" the mother exclaimed as the little girl kicked her legs. The mother could see that the king didn't show any facial expression but his eyes showed something else.

"It's probably not my place, but perhaps we should go to the capital – at least to say thank you to the humans," she added as the king gave a nod in reply. She turned around and walked away as the elven king turned to a few of the elders who had arrived with him.

"They weren't just humans, paladins." the elven king spoke.

"Perhaps there is a real threat looming?" an elder spoke.

"Perhaps, we shall depart shortly with a group of sentinels, the rest will start rebuilding," the king ordered as the group of elders nodded.

***

The three paladins arrived at the capital. Dismounting their griffons Claudius with urgency "I will speak to my father about the incident in the forest"

"I will go to the inn and grab a few drinks then," Lance replied with a smile.

"Don't get too drunk!" Claudius replied as he let out a clicking noise with his mouth which sent Sundra off to the skies. Allister leaped off of Surina and started to walk away.

"Hey! You don't want to go to the inn?" Lance questioned.

"I'm not much of a drinker," Allister replied as he continued to walk away.

"Where are you going...?!" Lance shouted.

"I need to find someone!" Allister shouted over his shoulder.

"Suit yourself," Lance muttered to himself. "Hey, you ready for some food?" Lance asked Surina who let out a sharp squawk in excitement and took off into the sky.

Claudius didn't mentioned it but he feared the man with red eyes that the elf spoke about was Soonifer. *What have you done brother? Have you become mad?* Claudius thought to himself as he entered the castle.

A few hours later, a party of elves arrived at the capital gates just as the sun had begun its descent.

"We seek entry to your city," Roarick informed the gate guards.

"What are elves doing here?" a guard replied in a stern tone.

"Due to some recent events, I would like to speak with your king, Claudius," the elven king replied. The gate guards thought for a moment but finally came to an agreement with each other.

"You may enter but your weapons stay here," the gate guard told them.

"Take them," Roarick replied, pulling his dark green cloak aside, exposing his elven dagger attached to his belt. The gate guard reached for the dagger but Roarick quickly grabbed the guard's wrist and snapped it as the guard yelled in pain. At that moment, the gate guards unsheathed their swords and the guards standing above on the wall drew their bows, and the party of elves

drew their bows as well. There was a small moment of silence as

the tension between the two races grew. The massive wooden gate

doors opened as king Renner walked towards the party of elves

with a group of knights walking behind him, while the younger

Claudius and Nara walked beside him.

"Lower your weapons!" King Renner ordered as all of the

gate guards lowered their bows and sheathed their swords. The

elves looked towards their king who nodded and they did the same.

"He broke my wrist, your highness!" the gate guard

angrily complained to the king. The king glanced to the elf before

looking back to the guard.

"Never try to disarm an elf sentinel, they will fight to the

very end – Instead just prepare for a fight. Take him to the medical

ward," the king commanded as the gate guard nodded before being

escorted by a knight into the city. King Falyour, I don't think

coming to the capital and hurting my men makes a good first

impression"

"…and leaving hundreds of elves being chased by

vampires gives a good impression too?" Falyour replied.

"That was not my choice, regardless the alliance won the godless war."

"Is that what you humans teach to your young?"

"No, we teach that each race – Lycans, Humans and Elves all sacrificed brave people to stop evil. But I will save you the history lesson because you are one of the few elves who was there, correct?"

The elven king nodded slowly as everyone remained silent while the two kings talked.

"After decades of seclusion, what brings you here?" King Renner questioned.

"He does" Falyour softly replied, pointing to the paladin standing beside him as everyone shifted their gaze to young Claudius.

"My son has told me there was some sort of incident in the Silpine forest and he went there, along with two other paladins, to aid the elves."

"Your son is not doing princely things, like lounging around in silken clothes or riding horses across the countryside but instead he is a paladin."

"When he told me he wanted to become a paladin, I, too was surprised as well." Renner spoke proudly.

"Heh, you humans still surprise me to this day," Falyour said with a very faint smile. "I came to talk about what happened in our forest and from what my people are describing about the demon who came, I fear that demons have grown much stronger."

King Renner nodded to Falyour's words. "Please come inside, we can speak there in much length and you can keep your weapons."

"I accept" Falyour responded.

The group of knights behind the king moved, forming a line on each side as the group of elves walked past them. The two kings sat next to each other at a large marble table which contained a map of the known world. Claudius and Nara stood close, listening intently as the elves did the same.

"A demon and a black lycan came to our forest and destroyed our encampment, unprovoked. We elves keep to ourselves and attract no demons" Falyour broke the silence

"Perhaps they were after something?" King Renner added

"What could we possibly possess that demons would want?"

"The Blade of Life" King Renner answered as everyone's attention became fully alert

"A fairytale!? Are you suggesting demons attacked my people and destroyed my forest over a fairytale?!" Falyour's voice rose

"You know the story as well as I do, the dagger exists." Falyour rolled his eyes. "Look at yourself. You haven't aged in over a hundred years, you – yourself witnessed the godless war. How can that be?!" King Renner exclaimed "You elves cannot live forever but that dagger gave life to that tree which emitted its powers to you elves, enabling you to live for a very long time."

Falyour stopped rolling his eyes and looked at the palm of his hand before slowly curling it into a fist. His eyes became more stern and serious as he looked at King Renner.

"If what you say is true, then we are doomed" Falyour lamented.

"Your reasoning?" King Renner asked.

"The demons must have all three tools by now?"

"No. We possess the Hammer of Creation" Young Claudius interrupted. Falyour turned his head to look at the young paladin before turning his gaze to the king.

"Is that how your paladins are so strong? Because you are drawing power from the hammer?" Falyour asked.

"No. My father would not allow the hammer to become tainted like that. All paladins follow the old tradition of becoming one," King Renner replied.

Falyour nodded, thinking for a moment "I have to ask, why do you have a lycan among your ranks? Wearing human armor?"

"Nara is an extraordinary paladin" King Renner replied as Falyour tried to hide his surprise, however none of the other elves could hide it so easily.

"Lycans cannot become paladins, it's a human thing" Falyour stated

"No, I am a paladin!" Nara said with a slight smile

"I don't believe any of this" Falyour insisted

"Observe!" Nara curled her paws into a fist, closing her eyes for a moment. Everyone in the room quietly watched on as Claudius smiled. Nara opened her eyes as bright blue light poured from her eyes and a giant pair of ethereal blue wings formed behind her. A faint light emitted from her entire body for a moment before it disappeared. "See?" Nara spoke with a big smile. The room erupted into gasps as the elves whispered amongst each other. Roarick even had his mouth open at the sight.

"She is the first lycan to become a paladin" King Renner stated, a thought crossed his mind "Possibly an old alliance can be rekindled anew?"

"Perhaps it's time," Falyour spoke, nodding his head. "What about the lycans?" Falyour added.

"Nara and I will go to the Lycanian Kingdom and petition," said Claudius. King Renner stood up as a servant walked up to him.

"Prepare a feast to celebrate a new alliance."

"At once," the servant replied before running off.

Roarick walked towards the lycan, puttering around before finally skittishly asking, "So, can anyone become a paladin?"

"Yeah! I think so! Although, I hope more people with tails become one because getting a custom leg plate with a tail hole from a blacksmith was interesting..." Nara replied as Claudius let out a laugh and Roarick revealed a faint smile.

Chapter 19

<u>Allister</u>

Troubled. Allister arrived back in his small wooden home. He leaped off his horse and tied the reins to the wooden post. He hurried towards the house with a small glimmer of hope that his sister had managed to find on her way back. Pushing the wooden door open to a dark, untouched room quickly erased all hope from his mind. He unsheathed his lightblade and held it out in front of him. A soft glow emitted from the sword, allowing him to find his way around the small house, trying to find any sort of indication that his sister had returned. He found no such sign and quickly left the house, sheathing his lightblade and climbing on top of his horse. He snapped the reins and the horse started to gallop out of town as he headed towards the countryside.

He rode to the outskirts of the town, dismounting his horse and tying the reins to a tree. Allister walked across a short meadow towards thicker brush and vegetation when instantly a figure appeared before him. He quickly grabbed the hilt of his lightblade and pulled the sword from the sheath, steadying the blade in front of him. In a quick moment of examination, he noticed the figure clutched a giant book with both hands and was wearing a strange black armor that he had never seen before.

"Allister," the figure whispered.

Allister examined the figure more carefully, noticing that it did not have a human head but instead a barn owl's upon a human body. It stared at him with hollow black eyes as deep as the abysmal depths of the nether itself.

"You do not share the likeness of any divine, so you are a demon," Allister challenged, pointing his sword towards the figure.

"Indeed, you are correct, however I come here as temporary friend not foe," the figure whispered.

"You have nothing to offer me!"

"On the contrary, your sister." The word seared into his mind. Finally, someone who knew something about his sister! He lowered his sword and tilted his head in curiosity.

"Speak!" Allister ordered the figure.

"This book contains all knowledge of demons, surely one would know the whereabouts of your cherished blood?" the figure replied in a sly whisper.

"In exchange for what?" Allister asked, narrowing his eyes.

"Nothing."

"Nothing? Surely you would want something in exchange?"

"I too, have lost a dear loved one, I would wish it for no one to feel the same pain," the figure whispered again as it opened the giant book, revealing the ashen pages as it glowed blood red. Allister sheathed his sword and walked towards the book and with each step more doubt left his mind. He stared deep into the pages, the foreign symbols and letters quickly turned into shapes and from the shapes into pictures. He could see his sister walking alone on the hillside. He stared more intensely into the book as he felt a sharp pain in his eyes. The image of his sister started to become smaller and smaller until everything went black. He yelled out in pain as blood streamed from his eyes. The figure stepped back and disappeared as Allister clutched his face to feel that he was still alive. He drew his lightblade and swung it around in rage but quickly realized that the figure had long left his presence. He stopped for a moment and turned his head, looking around. He could see nothing but blackness but could feel the soft breeze touch his skin, even hearing the leaves rustle against the wind. "Arrrraaaaggghhh!" Allister yelled with all of his might as he slammed his fists into the ground.

Chapter 20

<u>Claudius</u>

Revelation. A knight busted through the giant hall doors. "Claudius!" the knight yelled as everyone quickly fell silent.

"Yes?" Claudius stood up from the dinner table in the morning and looked in the knight's direction. The knight caught sight of Claudius and ran towards him.

"There you are!" the knight exclaimed as he breathed heavily to catch his breath.

"What is it?" Claudius asked with much concern.

"Demons! An army's worth!"

"Where?"

"Just north-east of here, I came here as fast as I could on horse!"

"Why are they there?"

"I couldn't tell you. They attacked the town suddenly, only a small group of paladins were fighting the horde as I left."

"Alert the king, I'll go immediately!" Claudius ordered as he ran out of the hall, running into Lance. "By the divine!" Claudius uttered. "A demonic army has risen just north-east of here. Where is Allister?"

"He mentioned he had to go find someone," answered Lance.

"Shit. Alright, let's go!" Claudius exclaimed as they exited the castle and climbed on their griffons and quickly took flight. As they flew, Claudius turned his head, looking back at the capital, seeing a mass of armored knights upon horses leaving the city and following in their general direction. "We need you, Allister," Claudius whispered underneath his breath.

The two paladins could see just over the horizon a mass of blackness that covered the lands.

"There!" Claudius yelled as he pointed towards a group of paladins fighting demons, their ascended form emitting a bright blue light which could easily be seen from above. Lance looked to where Claudius was pointing and nodded his head.

"Looks like a fun time!" Lance shouted back as he took one of his hands and rubbed Surina's neck. As they drew closer to the raging battle, Claudius could see two giant purple rifts, with a demon on each side holding it open, as hundreds of demons poured out of it.

They landed in the middle of the fight as both paladins leaped off their griffons and hurried to join the fight. Claudius ripped his lightblade from his sheath and slashed a charging demon into pieces.

"Thank the divines! You received word from our knight?!" Alorah yelled as she parried an incoming attack and forcefully thrust her sword into the torso of a demon.

"Yes, we did!" Claudius managed to reply as he swung his sword sideways, slicing demons in half as they let out a demonic roar.

"They sent just the two of you? Did the knight not stress there was an entire demonic army?" Alorah mentioned as she let out a grunt, swinging her sword in various directions – killing demons left and right.

"Five legions of knights are coming on horse," Claudius replied back as he leaped towards a demon, vertically slicing the demon in half, his sword covered in thick black blood so that the sword no longer emitted a soft light.

"Just five?! Send the entire army for divine's sakes!" Alorah yelled back over the sounds of metal clanging and roars of the demons.

"The rest are preparing the capital to defend against any demonic attack!" Claudius replied back as Sundra leaped in front of him, knocking several demons to the ground while swinging her massive claws and ripping the flesh off of the demons.

"Why? There is nothing the demons want from there!" Alorah yelled back.

"The Hammer!" Claudius shouted in a moment of clarity, rearing his sword back before slamming the blade between a demon's eyes.

Lance

Lance grunted as he swung his hammer colliding the hammerhead with a demon's head, killing it instantly. "Where the heck are all these demons coming from?" he shouted as he lifted his hammer into the air and slammed it into the chest of a demon.

"I'm not sure! But I don't think we can last much longer!" a knight shouted over the echoes of metal clanging.

"Yeah, you might not, but paladins can last much longer in bed!" Lance replied with a laugh, swinging his hammer into the incoming waves of demons. His laughter was cut short as a demon caught him by surprise, knocking him backwards. Surina leaped at the attacking demon and head-butted it to the ground. She swung her massive claws, killing wave after wave of demons. Lance steadied his ground and leaped back into the fight with increased vigour. "Yeah!" He shouted, swinging his hammer and killing any demon who managed to catch the end of his hammerhead.

"Lance!" A familiar voice shouted his name as he looked around, scanning the battlefield until he saw another paladin. Her long blonde hair was stained with demon blood and her blue eyes stared directly at him.

"Alorah?!" he shouted as he swung his hammer with all of his might, the hammerhead slamming into the chest of a demon, knocking it backwards several feet.

"Over here!" she shouted while slashing several attacking demons.

"These demons never stop!" Lance yelled as he swung his hammer once more. In the brief moment of rest Lance saw that the demonic army had lessened. "Where is Claudius?" Lance wondered aloud, gathering his strength as he clutched his hammer with both hands.

"I'm not sure, I was speaking to him earlier but was overrun by demons!" Alorah replied as she combed her hair which was stuck in place with demonic blood.

A giant volley of arrows flew through the sky as they rained upon the ocean of demons, killing entire waves. Lance, Alorah and the remaining knights turned their heads to see a large group of elves behind them with bows and Lance noticed one among the crowd.

"Lunnah!" Lance shouted as he ran towards her. Another wave of demons charged towards them, however they were quickly cut down by a rain of arrows. "Thank the divine you have arrived to help!" Lance spoke to Lunnah.

"Repayment for helping us in our time of need, Lance," she replied as she looked at Lance with concern. "Where is Claudius?" she continued as Lance widened his eyes.

"We aren't winning…" Lance voice trailed off.

"What do you mean?" Lunnah questioned.

"It's Claudius!" he exclaimed as he turned around and ran towards the sea of blackness. "Surina!" Lance shouted as Surina let out a sharp squawk and flew to him. Lance quickly hopped on her back. "Fly!" Lance ordered and pointed towards the army of demons. They flew over the waves of demons, the waves less and less filled with demons. He looked forward and could see a bright light in the distance. As he flew closer he could see a mass of dead demon corpses, so many that he could no longer see the ground. He could see Claudius swinging a halberd, slicing tens of demons in half in a single swing, a streak of light following his every swing cut the demons further. Lance leaped off of Surina as he landed on the dead bodies of demons with a squash.

"Claudius!" Lance yelled as he ran towards him. He had to squint his eyes as the light became ever so bright. Claudius continued to kill groups of demons with each swing of his halberd, his giant ethereal blue wings beating in such a way as to give him extra momentum with each swing. "Claudius!" Lance yelled with all of his might as he reached him. The waves of demons paused momentarily, some even backing up as they realized they were running towards certain death.

Lance grabbed Claudius' shoulder as he turned around, his eyes widening in surprise, all while trying to cover his eyes with his left hand. He had never seen any amount of light as bright as

Claudius' eyes and he could see cracks in his skin emitting light, surrounding his eyes. Upon quick examination, he saw Claudius' armor was lined with dents. The careful silver decorations were no longer there but instead, vicious cuts and indentations of attacks. Both of his arms and a shoulder were wounded badly but instead of blood pouring from them, light flowed out. Lance looked back and tried his best to look into Claudius' eyes.

"You fool..." Lance's voice trailed off as he couldn't think of anything else to say.

"We have won," Claudius replied back in an almost unrecognizable voice. In a divine tone, as if there were multiple Claudius' speaking in unison, and every word trailed with an echo.

The horde of demons tried to retreat back into the purple rift, however they were quickly stopped by a giant demon who stood at the height of three regular demons who grabbed the fleeing demons, and hurled them into the sky.

"Why are you running?!" the giant demon yelled in a demonic tone.

The light in Claudius' eyes started to fade away as his regular blue eyes returned. The giant ethereal blue wings disappeared and light was no longer pouring from his wounds but instead red blood. Claudius, unable to stand, collapsed as Lance caught him and slowly placed him on the ground. Lance looked at his broken brother with much concern, seeing that Claudius tried moving his mouth to say something but closed his eyes instead.

"Noooo!" Lance cried as he clutched Claudius' lifeless arm.

"Lance!" a voice yelled out to him as he turned his head slowly to see the legion of knights and the group of elves running towards him. He turned his head in the other direction to see the once scared and retreating demonic army now fulling charging upon him. Caught in between, he knew he had but one choice.

Chapter 21

<u>Claudius</u>

Bliss. Claudius opened his eyes and found himself in an endless meadow. He looked around and could see no one was here except himself. The meadow stretched for miles meeting the sky at the horizon. He turned his head forward and saw a man standing there in front of him. The man seemed to wear traditional paladin garments that were worn decades ago. He had long, dark brown hair and a small strain of his hair was in a braid in the front.

"Where am I?" Claudius asked the man.

"The Higher," the man replied in a stern but calm voice. Claudius looked around once more before looking back at the man.

"What is to become of the world below?"

"Do you really want to know?" the man inquired.

"Yes," Claudius replied, awaiting some thoughtful answer or solace. The man turned around and moved his hands with his words.

"The paladins, knights and all who take up arms against the demons will fight a noble battle… but they will all eventually parish. Demons will destroy and devour all and little of humanity will be left."

"Liar!" Claudius interrupted the man. The man abruptly turned around to face Claudius, this time with bright glowing blue eyes.

"What would a divine gain from lying to you?" Claudius' eyes widened with surprise at this but it quickly turned to anger.

"Why would a divine hide from war?"

"Not hide, it is none of mine or your concern anymore; that burden was lifted when you died," the divine remarked.

"…and you aren't going to help?"

"Why? Mortals always run and tuck tail in the end."

"Not all."

"My grandfather, the bravest man that I have ever put in such regard, was in turn a coward."

"What happened, if I could ask?"

258

"He fought in the first godless war, helped build the paladin's doctrine – the very words you spoke when you said the oath – he wrote. He volunteered to become the first Light Warden and suddenly he disappeared."

"Could he have died?" Claudius inquired.

"I even believed that death feared him – perhaps I was wrong."

"You wish to return back to the realm of the living, mortal?"

"Absolutely!"

The man smirked, revealing a sly smile as if he were looking upon a fool "Come, I wouldn't want you to return without being properly equipped" Hysolin said, raising his right hand which he closed into a fist. Claudius walked towards the man as a bright light emitted from the man's fist. "Give me your hand," the man ordered as Claudius obeyed, lifting his right hand to the man. The divine placed the light into Claudius' hand as he narrowed his eyes to the extreme brightness. Claudius closed his hand into a fist and instantly felt a jet of intense pain shoot through his entire right arm. He grimaced at the discomfort, opening his hand to reveal a magnificent silver bow. Upon a quick examination he could see delicate carvings of lines that wrapped around the entire bow.

"Is this your gift?" Claudius asked, turning his attention to the divine.

"Try using it," the divine replied.

"Without any arrows?"

"You won't need any."

"If you believe that Hysolin is the weakest divine, then surely you are misinformed."

Claudius turned around and held the bow in front of him while pulling the string with his left hand. He let the string go and a light arrow shot from the bow, however, instead of the arrow going straight, it curved rapidly to the right. He was confused at the sight and drew the string again, this time pulling it back further. Releasing the bow string, a light arrow immediately fired from the bow, this time the arrow spun rapidly to the left before eventually disappearing. Claudius turned his head to the divine, opening his mouth to question before the divine interrupted.

"Gently tap the string as if you are playing a harp." Claudius turned his head back around and this time gently tapped the bow string as a light arrow shot directly in a straight line.

Claudius revealed a smile at the small victory of learning how to use the bow before everything around him started to become bright. "A single arrow only holds a fraction of my vengeance. Shower the world in it," the divine spoke.

"That's good to know...but what is happening? Why is everything getting brighter?" Claudius questioned as the sky started to become so bright that Claudius had to cover his eyes to avoid becoming blind. The meadow started to become just as bright before he closed his eyes completely.

"Try not to throw away your life again, mortal."

Lance

A few demons were hurled from the purple rift as a giant demon with four arms stepped through. "Why are you running?!" The demon yelled at the fleeing demons, grabbed a few by the waist and hurled them away from the rift.

"Kill them!" the giant demon ordered as he pointed his muscular hand at the paladin. The multitude of demons stopped fleeing and obeyed the demon as they all shifted, and like an ocean's wave, they rushed towards Lance. The group of elves and knights led by Lunnah ran towards Lance to meet the demons but they were quite a distance away.

Lance knelt down beside Claudius, holding out his fists as his eyes turned bright blue. Surina nudged Lance's back, trying to get his attention as the horde of demons ran towards them. Lance remained still, unmoving towards Surina's warning. Light erupted from his fists as a faint light surrounded Claudius' dead body. Several demons attacked Lance, thrusting their crude swords into his body, light pouring out through his wounds as Surina quickly head-butted a demon away. She then swung her powerful claws at the other demons, killing them. Surina nudged Lance more forcibly, trying to get him to move but to no avail. The giant demon rushed towards Lance as he pulled out his massive sword, readying it for a strike. Surina quickly took flight and clawed at the giant demon who roared out in pain. He turned around and swung his massive sword at the attacking griffon but Surina flew just out of reach. Surina dove back down to the demon and fiercely clawed at him, sending chunks of flesh flying into the air. The giant demon let out a hellish roar as he quickly grabbed Surina's leg and slammed her into the ground before swinging her around in the air and hurling her off into the distance. Surina's body landed on the ground with a hard thud. One of her hind legs was horribly injured as she tried steadying herself before taking flight towards the giant demon once again.

Claudius opened his eyes to see Lance at his side fully ascended as beams of light poured from his wounds. Lance revealed a giant smile, seeing his once dead brother had come back to life but his smile soon faded when he saw a frightened expression on Claudius' face. A giant blade erupted through Lance's chest as small droplets of light flew through the air. The giant demon pulled the sword back out and sprinted towards the brunt of the battle. Lance released his ascended form as the light surrounding his body suddenly faded away, leaving the burden of mortality to set in. He fell forward, unable to muster the strength to keep himself up. Claudius quickly caught him and gently laid Lance on the ground. He placed his hands over the chest wound to try and slow the bleeding as blood quickly drenched Lance's armor.

"You're a fool, brother," Claudius spoke, trying to hold back a stern tone.

"Just the price of victory," Lance managed to muster before coughing up blood.

"Don't die yet, we have to drink for this impending victory."

"You forget, you don't drink, remember?" Lance weakly spoke, struggling to keep his eyes open and focused on Claudius while taking in a deep raspy breath. "Don't try to save me, save Lunnah and the others who are here." Lance tried his best to show a smile as his eyes closed for the last time. His lifeless body slumps over as Claudius slows his fall and gently sets him on the ground.

Claudius' hand on Lance's chest quickly turned into a fist as he slowly got up. He drew in a long breath and felt as if time had slowed down. The yelling and shouts of men and demons, the clashing of metal and steel were all drowned out by an uncomfortable silence. Light quickly flooded Claudius' eyes as he raised his left hand in front of him. A bright light formed in his left hand as a beautiful silver bow appeared in his grasp. He reached for the bow string with his right hand and barely touched the string as a light arrow shot from the bow. The arrow danced through the air as the head of the arrow slammed into the forehead of a demon, instantly killing it. The demon fell backwards as his body quickly became trampled by the ocean of incoming demons. Claudius then rapidly plucked the bow string with his fingers as hundreds of light arrows erupted from his bow. The arrows quickly found their targets as waves of demons fell to the ground.

The thousands of demons witnessing the event quickly turned around and retreated towards the rift, not wanting to share the same fate; however, the light arrows were merciless as they struck the backs of the fleeing demons. Claudius continued swiftly plucking the bowstring as scores of demons fell victim to the barrage of light arrows. The entire ocean of demons soon retreated back into the purple rift as Claudius caught sight of the giant demon who was also retreating. He moved his arm in the general direction of the giant demon and hastily plucked the bow string, releasing a barrage of light arrows that took flight. Several light arrows struck the giant demon's shoulders and a single arrow pierced its throat. The giant demon let out a horrific demonic groan as he grabbed his throat and quickened his pace towards the rift. Claudius unleashed another volley of arrows, killing scores of demons however, the giant demon narrowly escaped into the rift. The two rift guardians released their grasp on the portal and leaped into the rift as it started to close. Claudius shot another barrage of arrows into the rift until the rift ceased to exist.

"Claudius!" a familiar voice shouted as he turned around to see a welcoming face. Lunnah sprinted towards him and wrapped her arms around him as the light faded from his eyes, he

265

wrapped his arms around her and gave a gentle squeeze. "The look on Lance's face...I was afraid something had happened to you," Lunnah softly said.

"Shit!" Claudius blurted out as he broke away from Lunnah's embrace and ran towards Lance's body with Lunnah quickly following behind. Claudius stopped a few feet away at the sight of Surina lying beside Lance, softly nudging his body. "Surina?" Claudius called out as he slowly walked towards her. However, the griffon ignored the paladin's words and kept trying to wake up Lance. "Surina?" Claudius spoke again while placing his hand on Surina's back. She instantly turned her head and let out a defensive squawk, nearly snapping her beak at him before turning her attention back to Lance.

"What...what happened?" Lunnah asked as she looked upon Lance's bloodied corpse.

"It's my fault," Claudius whispered as he stared at the corpse.

"Help!" A loud yell echoed in the air. The two looked around but did not see anyone yelling. "Help!" The voice cried again louder as the two looked up to see a paladin mounted upon a griffon fly closer to them. The griffon landed on the ground near them and walked towards the two.

"By the divine! Claudius, I have found you!" the paladin exclaimed with a troubled look on his face. "Demons attacking the Citadel of Light!"

"Now?!" Claudius replied with worry.

"Yes! An ocean of blackness is at the gates! I was the sole messenger to give word to the capital to send help!"

"What do we do?" Lunnah asked, looking at Claudius for direction.

"Captain!" Claudius yelled as the group of knights rushed towards Claudius.

"Yes, Claudius?" the captain of the knights answered.

"Attend to the wounded, ensure every last paladin's body is removed from here."

"Of course," the captain replied as he started giving the other knights orders.

"What is your name?" Claudius asked the paladin.

"Tonedan," the paladin replied.

"Send word to the capital with haste."

"And you?" Tonedan asked.

"I must go to Light's Reach at once!" Claudius replied as he whistled for his griffon. Sundra let out a loud squawk as she flew over to let Claudius leap on her back.

"I'm going with you" Lunnah pleaded as she climbed on the griffon. Claudius knew that she wouldn't accept 'no' for an answer and remained quiet instead. Lunnah held her bow in her left hand as she wrapped her right arm around Claudius' waist.

"May the divines help us all!" Tonedan spoke as Claudius let out a 'heeyaah!' and Sundra took flight.

Sundra beat her wings heavily as the two approached Light's Reach. The Citadel of Light sat upon a small mountain surrounded by five smaller stone forts almost forming an outline of a hand. The entire backside of the area was blocked by bigger mountains, the only way into the area was through the front which was completely flooded by a black ocean of demons. They flew closer and could see paladins upon the tops of the forts, hurling boulders from catapults along with archers firing arrows upon the army of demons. The demons had their own nefarious contraptions of giant ballistas that would fire massive arrows into the sides of the fort, nearly destroying portions of the wall. Claudius scanned the massive ocean of blackness and could see one demon in particular who stood a giant among the others. He leaned forward and pointed in that direction.

"Take me there!" he shouted as Sundra let out a squawk and started to fly in that direction.

"Claudius, you can't be serious?" Lunnah was incredulous.

"Sundra will take you to the Citadel, ensure no demon takes the hammer!" Claudius replied.

"You will fall to your death!" Lunnah shouted.

"That's the least thing I am worrying about. Be safe, my moon," Claudius replied back as he slid sideways off of Sundra and descended rapidly towards the ground.

"Claudius!" Lunnah shouted as she peered over to see Claudius falling through the air. Sundra quickly beat her wings towards the Citadel of Light while Lunnah kept her sight on the falling paladin.

Claudius descended rapidly towards the ground as he kept his eyes fixed upon the giant demon who was barking orders. The face of his dying brother seared in his mind and all that was left was revenge. He narrowed his eyes, gritting his teeth as the details of the giant demon became clearer. Light filled his eyes as giant ethereal blue wings erupted from his back. Holding out his right arm, he held his hand in a fist, light emitting from his fist. Porth's mace appeared in his hand. He could feel the wind rustling through his hair and howling against his armor. He reared his right arm for a strike as thousands of demons stopped in their tracks and looked up to see the bright light.

"For absolute justice!" Claudius yelled as the giant demon tilted his head up to see what all the other demons were looking at. Claudius slammed the mace head into the skull of the giant demon, instantly killing it as the demon's body fell forward, carrying the full force of the blow. Claudius beat his glowing wings only a single time to break his fall as he landed on his feet. All of the demons stood still for a moment, in shock of what just happened, before they readied their crude swords and clubs and ran towards the paladin. Claudius swung his mace, splitting a demon's head in two before releasing the mace which vanished into thin air. He closed his right fist which then spawned Kionta's halberd. The silver hue of the weapon shone against the sun, almost blinding all the demons who surrounded him. Heavily he swung the halberd in a circular direction as it sliced a dozen demons in half, with a ghostly trail of a second swing slicing them into smaller pieces.

The demons who fell victim to the attack died so fast they could not let out a scream from their inflicted injuries. More demons stepped towards the paladin, filling the empty space but soon fell victim to his attacks. Claudius swung the halberd in every direction and with each swing, scores of demons fell to the ground with their black blood spewing into the air. A herd of demons unaffected by the sight of his power charged towards Claudius, holding their swords, axes and clubs in the air, trampling the corpses of the fallen demons while letting out a mixture of howls and screams. Claudius swung his halberd at the group, effectively killing the entire herd with a single swing, blood spraying into the air, painting all nearby demons in thick, black blood.

A boulder landed near him, killing several demons on impact before rolling on to kill a few more. Claudius turned his attention to the tops of the forts to see that demons were scaling the sides and battles were taking place on the rooftops. He beat his wings heavily and quickly shot into the sky. As he flew over the forts, he could see the demons had reached the Citadel of Light but not with ease. Thousands of dead demon bodies lay across the ground as paladins fought vigorously to defend Light's Reach. Claudius reached out his left hand as Hysolin's bow appeared in his

271

grasp. He plucked the bowstring several times in rapid succession. A massive line of light arrows shot from the bow, peppering several demons who were standing in front of the citadel doors. Their corpses fell over as Claudius flew through the citadel doors. Claudius plucked his bow, constantly releasing a barrage of light arrows that filled the long corridors of the hall, killing handfuls of demons at a time. Light started to blind his peripheral vision which meant that he needed to end his ascended form soon or else he would die.

The giant wooden doors at the end of the hall were busted down as he flew past them, and there laid the Hammer of Creation on a marble pedestal. He reached out with his right hand and grabbed the handle of the hammer and swung it to his right side, barely missing Soonifer's face. "This ends here!" Claudius spoke with a deepened voice tone as he lifted up the hammer readying for a strike. Soonifer clenched his teeth in anger as he curled both hands into a fist, purple fire exploded from his hands revealing an obsidian black dagger in each hand. Soonifer let out a demonic roar as his entire body bent back for a leap towards the paladin but suddenly a purple rift appeared behind him. Edge'knol appeared, wrapped her arms around him and with all her might, she hurled

Soonifer into the rift. The rift quickly closed behind them as Claudius slammed the hammer into the ground where Soonifer would be standing. The entire Citadel shook for a moment as blue light emitted from the hammer. Claudius stood up as several paladins entered the room with lightblades in hand and their entire armor stained with demon blood. They laid their eyes upon Claudius in silence as he walked past them and into the corridor. His right arm was vibrating, trying to contain the hammer's power. He stood at the door of the Citadel, which oversaw the two lower forts. The once gigantic ocean of demons had dwindled into the size of a mere puddle as paladins lifted their light blades into the sky, cheering at the victory. Several paladins surrounded him and joined in the cheer. Claudius released his ascended form, as the burden of mortality of his strength and wounds set in. He dropped the hammer which let out a metallic ring hitting the ground. An incredible pain filled his body as everything started to turn into a blur before turning black. His body fell to the ground as he heard the muffled cries of "Claudius! Claudius!" by the other paladins.

Chapter 22

<u>Soonifer</u>

Vexation. "How dare you interfere!" Soonifer yelled, throwing his hand at Edge'knol's neck, grasping her throat tightly as his eyes glowed bright red with anger.

"You... would have... been obliterated!" Edge'knol managed to speak calmly without struggling.

"I would have ripped him to shreds!" Soonifer shouted, a demonic tone echoing with each word he spoke. He drew closer to Edge'knol with his hand still firmly clenched around her throat.

"I wouldn't want to lose you," she whispered, raising her slender hand and placing it on Soonifer's cheek before slowly running her fingers down his jawline. Soonifer released his grip on her throat and stormed off, disappearing into the darkness.

Soonifer walked out of the darkness as Ker'es appeared in front of him with his hollow black eyes set upon him. "Seek the Tormentress, Zary'Zadendra," Ker'es whispered as Soonifer held back his anger and nodded while remaining silent. Soonifer walked forward, as he was about to vanish, he felt Ker'es' hand upon his shoulder. He stopped instantly and heard him whisper again. "Show the Tormentress the utmost respect and give her something that caused you great sorrow." Soonifer vanished then appeared before a short stone staircase that led to an obsidian throne where he could see someone sitting. They were not sitting on it normally but instead, sitting on it with their back resting on one armrest while their legs dangled from the other. He noticed a greater demon standing on one side of the short staircase who looked at him menacingly. Instead of taking a step, Soonifer immediately knelt down on one knee as he lowered his head.

"You may rise." A soft demonic voice echoed from the throne as Soonifer stood up and tried to walk up the stone steps but was abruptly stopped by the greater demon. "Why have you come here?" Her soft demonic voice questioned, as she remained seated strangely in her seat.

"I seek your curse, Tormentress," Soonifer replied as a demonic tone echoed within his own words.

"What gift have you brought her Tormentress in exchange for such a blessing?" The greater demon spoke, as Zary'Zadendra remained silent. Soonifer searched his thoughts for anything until an idea formed in his mind.

"Give me one hour and I shall bring you a gift that weighs only a fraction of your sorrow," Soonifer replied, narrowing his eyes, awaiting an answer.

"Go," Zary replied in almost a whisper as Soonifer disappeared from sight.

***

The sun had started to fall behind the giant mountains in the west as streaks of orange filled the sky. Soonifer stood just on the outskirts of Solbris, as he walked towards the city his right hand became engulfed with purple fire and a spear appeared in his grasp. He hurled several spears at the wall diagonally, then reaching the city stone walls he simply leaped on the spears, crossing over the wall with ease. Standing upon the wall, he scanned the entire city and knew the one place where the Baron would be.

The Baron entered his chambers to retire for the night, closing the large wooden door behind him. He removed several golden necklaces from his neck, placing them upon his mahogany dresser. As he placed the last necklace on the dresser, he took a step closer to examine himself in the mirror. "Time has been most kind to me," he whispered to himself while noticing a red glowing object. Thinking it was a discolored light from a lamp, he turned around to face what he thought he would never see again.

"Guar…" Hallowmis tried to yell as Soonifer threw his right hand at the Baron, gripping his neck tightly. Rage instantly filled Soonifer as his red glowing eyes shined brighter. He slammed Hallowmis against the dresser where he fell to the ground. Soonifer picked him back up as Hallowmis tried to scramble to the door. Gripping his right hand around his throat again, while picking up a lit candle in his left hand, he held it in front of Hallowmis' face.

"Do you know how much rage is inside of me, just looking at you?" Soonifer questioned as the Baron shook his head from side to side. Soonifer then proceeded to press the lit candle end into the nose of the Baron who tried to yell in pain but could not as Soonifer squeezed his throat. "You don't understand true suffering, do you?" Soonifer questioned as his right hand became engulfed in purple fire. Hallowmis shook his head violently as the sound of searing flesh filled the silent room. The Baron grabbed the demon's right wrists with both hands, trying to free himself but he could not. The purple fire vanished instantly as small puffs of smoke seeped from Soonifer's hand. "Come now, I have someone for you to meet," Soonifer told the Baron who tried to move his mouth but could not speak.

Soonifer appeared before Zary'Zadendra and tossed the Baron in front of himself as he kneeled before her. "Tormentress," Soonifer spoke as the Baron yelled, "Please! Spare me!" The greater demon ripped his sword from its sheath and in a single swing, sliced the Baron's right knee causing the Baron to collapse onto his knee.

"All shall kneel before her!" the greater demon ordered as he sheathed his sword. Zary'Zadendra pulled herself off her throne and walked down the short flight of stairs.

"Rise," she softly spoke as Soonifer stood up but the Baron remained kneeling while whimpering. Soonifer looked upon her and felt a bizarre feeling. The Tormentress wore a mixture of a black gown with armor exposing much of her ashen skin. She wore no gloves nor boots but her hands and feet were blackened as if she suffered from frostbite. Long, raven black hair flowed from her head as her glowing red eyes held upon the Baron. "Who is this weak... pathetic... human?" she questioned, not moving her gaze from the Baron.

"Do you dare insult the Tormentress with such a lowly gift?" her greater demon abruptly spoke.

"He is the person responsible for my dismal existence," Soonifer spoke as a flash of rage fired inside of him. "He murdered me!" An angry demonic yell trailed from his voice. Soonifer bit down on his tongue, trying his best to gather his composure as Zary'Zadendra shifted her gaze upon him with a wide grin. She extended her slender, ashen gray hand to him.

"Take it," she offered as Soonifer raised his hand to hers. He instantly felt his entire right arm go cold before becoming completely numb. She pulled back her hand, turning around, and slowly walked back up to her throne.

"You may leave," the greater demon ordered as Soonifer looked at his right hand before vanishing into the darkness.

***

Soonifer mumbled a few words as he struggled in his restless sleep. After a few more moments of jerking his head, he stopped and opened his eyes to see Edge'knol beside him. He sat up in his chair in a more alert posture as he turned his head to her.

"Who is Alorah?" Edge'knol asked as she gazed into Soonifer's red eyes. There was a slight pause before his reply as he shifted into a more serious facial expression.

"How do you know that name?" Soonifer questioned.

"I heard that name uttered a few times in your sleep," she replied.

"No one," Soonifer quickly replied.

"But she was someone at one time?" Edge'knol pressed on.

"Yes."

"Do you remember anything about her?"

"Bits and pieces…it's all foggy." Edge'knol frowned, she could see Soonifer's eyes shift, trying to recall memories. "I can barely remember her face…it seems like a lifetime has passed since I've seen her…" His voice trailed off as his red eyes widened. "The book!" Soonifer exclaimed as he stood up. "She's a paladin; surely a demon could have seen her," Soonifer continued as he started to walk away. Edge'knol grabbed his arm and pulled him back.

"Don't!" Edge'knol shouted as he turned his head to match her gaze. Soonifer opened his mouth to reply as she spoke in a much quieter tone. "Please don't." Soonifer turned around and drew closer towards her.

"Why?" Soonifer asked as he stared intently at her. Edge'knol closed her eyes and remained holding onto his arm. "Why?!" Soonifer shouted, as his eyes grew bright red with rage.

"She's dead," Edge'knol whispered as she tried her best to hold her tears back, but a single tear escaped and trailed down her cheek. Suddenly, a pit of darkness opened somewhere inside of Soonifer. He could feel it devouring him, slowly destroying every shred of his humanity that was left. He searched in his memories, trying to find any piece of her. Any picture, any thought, any scent or smell or even touch, but it was all blank. When he came back to reality, only one question remained.

"Who?" he asked in an angry, demonic tone.

"Airoth'Kal, but he's already dead," Edge'knol pleaded as she tried to compose herself. Soonifer narrowed his eyes and stormed off into the darkness.

Soonifer appeared in front of Ker'es obsidian throne, stacks upon stacks of ancient books stood on each other. Books of every size and kind lay scattered around the steps that led to the throne, a small glimpse inside the mind of the Tormentor. Soonifer stomped the ground so hard that a small crack appeared upon the flooring. A lesser demon of slender and meek build appeared in front of him. Its small, gray eyes looked up to match Soonifer's infernal red eyes as it awaited instruction.

"Bring me Urrick'Kal!" Soonifer bellowed as the lesser demon quickly disappeared into the darkness. A few moments later, the lesser demon reappeared in front of Soonifer. He turned his head to the lesser demon which kept violently shaking its head from side to side. "Where is he?!" Soonifer roared at the demon which kept shaking its head, indicating 'no'. Soonifer's right hand exploded into purple flame as a spear spawned in his grasp. He reared his arm back, hurling the spear at full force into the skull of the lesser demon, killing it instantly.

Soonifer angrily stomped his foot into the ground again as another lesser demon appeared. Soonifer spawned another spear and gripped it tightly in his hand. "Bring me Urrick'Kal!" Soonifer ordered the new lessor demon which glanced at the dead lesser demon on the ground before looking back at Soonifer. The lesser demon vanished into the darkness. Soonifer lowered one side of the spear to the ground as he paced, the sound of metal dragging across the hard stone screeched. He felt he had been waiting for hours until the lesser demon finally reappeared. "Well?!" Soonifer yelled. The lesser demon took a few steps back as a giant figure appeared in the distance. With each step it took, the ground seemed to slightly shake in its wake. When Soonifer could see the features of Urrick'Kal, notably the three arms of the greater demon, he revealed a crazed smile.

"Why have you summoned me?" Urrick'kal spoke in a deep demonic voice.

"I wanted to congratulate your brother, Airoth, for killing paladins, but sadly he is not here so instead I'm passing it on to you!" Soonifer spoke as he quickly hurled his spear at the greater demon. Urrick grabbed the spear just before impact and threw it to the ground.

"What is the meaning of this?! You dare attack me? We may share the same title but you are far weaker than I!" the greater demon bellowed. Soonifer spawned another spear and threw it at Urrick which the greater demon slashed at, ricocheting it wildly in the air. Soonifer's right hand exploded into a purple flame as he disappeared into the darkness and reappeared in front of Urrick holding Gor'eck's hammer and with full force slammed the hammer into the chest of the greater demon. Urrick stumbled backwards and quickly steadying himself while gritting his teeth angrily.

Urrick charged at Soonifer, clenching all three of his hands into a fist. Soonifer ran towards the greater demon, rearing back the hammer for another strike. Soonifer hurled the hammerhead towards Urrick, however the greater demon caught the hammerhead with his two right hands and using his third fist, he threw a powerful punch that impacted Soonifer's head directly, sending him falling backwards. Urrick let out a demonic laugh as he tossed the hammer aside which disappeared into nothing.

"You're just a puny little demon!" Urrick taunted as Soonifer managed to get up with his infernal eyes redder than ever. Soonifer's hands were swallowed by purple flame as Ker'es' dagger appeared in his grasp. He then disappeared into the darkness, reappearing directly behind the greater demon and slashing at his back. Urrick roared in pain as thick black blood started to seep from the wound. He quickly turned around to confront Soonifer, but Soonifer tumbled to the greater demon's side and stabbed both daggers into Urrick's muscular thigh. The greater demon let out another hellish cry as he swung his massive fists, trying to hit the elusive demon. Soonifer somersaulted in between the greater demon's legs before leaping into the air and slamming the two daggers into Urrick's back. The greater demon let out another cry of pain as he tried reaching behind him. Soonifer lifted his legs, placing his feet on the back of the demon and leaped off of the demon, vanishing into darkness. Urrick became overwhelmed with anger as he swung his three arms wildly around, trying to get a lucky hit on Soonifer. Soonifer leaped out of the shadows towards the greater demon, however Urrick saw the attack from the corner of his eye and grabbed Soonifer's arm and leg with his two right hands and with all of his might slammed him to the ground. Soonifer felt a few bones in his body shatter on impact as he let out a rough cough. Urrick lifted Soonifer off the ground and held him in front of him.

"Without your tricks, you aren't so tough now," Urrick spoke as he punched Soonifer's chest with his left fist. Soonifer let out dry heaves as blood flew from his mouth. Soonifer's eyes beamed bright red as he spawned Zary's crescent blade and with

285

one quick swing, he sliced one of Urrick's right arms completely off. Urrick let out a hellish scream as he dropped Soonifer to the ground with a thud.

Thick black blood gushed from the severed limb. Soonifer struggled as he got up and looked upon the demon, revealing a wicked smile. "There…Now you aren't a freak anymore!" Soonifer boasted as he tried to laugh but instead coughed up blood.

"I will crush you!" Urrick yelled as he raised his massive arms into the air and slammed them down, but Soonifer slipped away into the shadows as Urrick's fists crushed the ground. Soonifer reappeared in the distance and spawned a spear before hurling it at the greater demon. The spear slammed into the torso of Urrick as he let out a loud groan. Soonifer walked towards the greater demon and spawned another spear, lifted his arm and hurled the spear at the wounded greater demon. This time the spear crashed into the greater demon's throat. Urrick fell backwards with a massive thud that shook the entire ground. Urrick grabbed the spear from his chest, with all of his might pulled it out, and tossed it aside. The spear let out a metallic ring as it hit the ground. Urrick pulled the spear from his neck and flung it to the side, as he grabbed his neck to try and stop the bleeding. Soonifer spawned

Gor'eck's hammer and let the hammerhead drag against the ground. The metallic grinding continued with each step Soonifer took until he stopped at Urrick's head. The greater demon tried to talk but only the gurgling sounds of blood came out. Soonifer stood there in silence with his red burning eyes fixated upon the dying greater demon.

"You destroyed the only thing I ever loved," Soonifer accused Urrick as he turned around and mustered his entire strength to walk off into the darkness.

Chapter 23

<u>Nox</u>

Silence. Curled into a ball, Nox slept in the corner of the infernal library. "Nox…" A voice whispered as the lycan's ear perked up but soon fell back down to a resting position. "Nox…" The voice whispered again as Nox opened his red glowing eyes and looked around for the body of the voice. Finding no one, Nox laid his head back down but the voice called again. "Nox…come to me." The voice whispered again. Nox recalled the voice, standing up he stretched his limbs and walked out of the library.

Nox laid eyes upon Ker'es who was standing before the Book of Infernal Knowledge.

"Nox, do you know how much power lies within the Tongs of Death?" Ker'es whispered as he stepped to the side, turning to face the lycan. Nox shook his head from side to side. Ker'es pointed towards the book, indicating Nox to look. Nox walked forward and looked deep into the ashen grey pages that were filled with crimson glowing symbols and figures. The symbols began to move and form a picture as everything started to fade to black.

A pale-skinned vampire stood before thousands of dead human and lycan bodies. His armor was pristine, free from dents and scratches. Intricate designs of swirling lines decorated his breastplate as a black half cape swayed from his back. His bright pearl eyes filled with pride as he held the Tongs of Death in his right hand – knowing that none could defeat him. Yet thousands of humans and lycans clad in battle-worn armor dared to challenge him. With a single swing, hundreds of humans died as their shadows erupted from their bodies.

Nox looked around in slight confusion as he caught sight of Ker'es hollow black eyes. He held his left paw flat and using his right paw, he pointed at the Book of Infernal Knowledge.

"That was a memory of a demon who witnessed such an event," Ker'es whispered. Nox pointed at himself and moved his paws around. "That is the end of the memory, the last demon there died," Ker'es replied. "I need you to find the whereabouts of the

Tongs of Death." Nox held his paws together then abruptly pointed at himself.

"Soonifer is currently unable to do such a task." Nox tapped his right paw with his left paw.

"Do you know Alorah?" Nox revealed a slight smile as his ears perked up while nodding. "She perished not so long ago, Soonifer mourns her death." Nox's smile instantly faded as his eyes narrowed. He clenched his right paw into a fist and punched his left palm. "Worry not, Soonifer has avenged her death. What he needs now is your help in finding the location of the Tongs. You do want to help him, right?"

Nox grit his teeth and after a moment of thought, he nodded excitedly. Nox cupped his paws together and then pointed to himself.

"I shall create a portal that will take you near the Lycanian Kingdom. There is where you shall begin your search," Ker'es whispered as he turned around and signaled Nox to follow. The lycan excitedly wagged his tail as he followed Ker'es into the darkness.

Nox found himself in the middle of a meadow where the grass covered his knees. He looked around to see if anywhere seemed familiar. The Silpine forest lined up to his left and continued far into the horizon. Turning his head to the right, he could see vast mountains into the distance and near those, he could see the tops of towers. Thinking that was his best shot to start looking, he got down on all four limbs and sprinted towards the tower.

Nox arrived just on the outskirts of the Lycanian Kingdom, stood up on his hind legs and walked towards the gate. There was a giant, light stone-grey wall which wrapped around the entire city; most of the trees in front of the city were cut down while a giant mountain stood behind.

"Halt!" a light silver lycan gate guard ordered so Nox remained where he stood.

"Let him pass, he's a lycan," the other silver-furred gate guard informed the first guard.

"Yeah, but I've never seen a lycan with red eyes before," the first guard continued as he eyed the strange lycan carefully. Nox raised his right paw and waved with a slightly silly smile.

"Same, but you know those dark lycans...still practicing the old ways..." the other guard replied.

"Look! He's not even wearing anything, just a leather loin cloth," the first guard pointed out. The second guard nodded as the first guard signaled the strange lycan to come forward. Nox walked towards the two lycan gate guards and could see they were clad in heavy iron armor. The breastplate held no detailed decorations but instead were filled with dents and scratches.

"Don't cause any trouble, got it?" the guard ordered as Nox shook his head.

"Okay, open the gates!" the first gate guard shouted as the heavy stone gates moved into action. Just as Nox was about to enter the city, he felt something grab his shoulder. Nox quickly turned around in a defensive stance, holding his claws to strike.

"Whoa, whoa! Here, take this." The second guard pulled out a multitude of golden triangles that were held together by a small length of rope that went through a hole in the middle of each triangle. Nox relaxed as he watched the guard untie and pull out a golden triangle and give it to him. He examined the golden triangle in his paw and looked at the guard.

"Do you know what it is?" the guard asked as Nox shook his head from side to side. "It's a Fangral, lycan currency. Go buy yourself some clothing and maybe something to eat." The guard spoke as Nox clutched the Fangral and smiled before walking through the gate.

"What was that all about?" the first guard asked the other.

"I feel sorry for those dark lycans, it's not their choice," the second guard replied.

"Yeah, it's not like none of the shops here will accept their rocks or twigs," the first guard added as they both let out a hardy laugh.

Nox stood still for a moment and looked around in awe, having never seen so many lycans walking in one place. He started to walk around and saw a few wooden signs, one which had the word 'Tailoring' on it. He decided to check out the shop and entered the small stone building.

"Hello there!" A sweet voice spoke as Nox set his eyes upon a light grey furred lycan who had bright yellow eyes. She wore a deep crimson dress and leaned against the wooden counter eyeing him back. Nox waved at her and looked around the shop, seeing all the various bright colors of clothes from woven to silk goods. Nox grabbed a black silk tunic and brought it up to her. "I don't think I've seen you around these parts," she spoke with curiosity. Nox pointed at himself before cupping his left paw and

293

using his right paw, tapping on the top of his cupped paw. "Oh? First time here?" Nox shook his head up and down.

"Well, I hope you find it close to home. My name is Rukan, what is yours?" Nox held both of his paws in the air and let his right paw fall.

"Night?" she guessed as the lycan shook his head from side to side. Nox repeated the hand motion but this time more slowly. "Nox?" Rukan guessed as he nodded with a smile.

"Well, that's a beautiful name, Nox! Do you plan on just buying this tunic?" Nox nodded and using his right paw, he poked at the tunic.

"You don't want anything to cover up your loin cloth there?" Rukan spoke with a sly smile as Nox looked down at himself and scratched one of his ears. "Here hold on, I'll get you something." Rukan tried to hold a giggle and walked off. Nox noticed she had a crimson ribbon that was tied to the end of her tail and watched her walk into the back room. She came back a moment later holding a set of fancy clothes. She placed them on the counter and took the first set, a dark blue tunic with silver trim. She helped Nox put on the clothes, piece by piece. Nox could smell that she wore a flowery scent as he raised one leg to put on the lower

294

garments. Rukan grabbed Nox's tail, placed it through the pants' tail hole, and gave his tail an extra tug. Nox revealed a grin as she walked playfully back behind the counter. Nox placed his Fangral on the counter to which Rukan placed her paw on the Fangral and pushed it back towards him. "Free for you darling, just make sure you come back and say goodbye," she said with a wink. Nox smiled back as he took the Fangral and placed it in his pocket, pushed against the wooden door of the building and walked out.

Nox ventured a little further to a large meat stand. "Hey there, you interested in any of these?" The butcher spoke in a rough voice as he pointed to his selected meats. Nox scanned the selection and pointed to two giant turkey legs and an entire chicken. The butcher placed the turkey legs and chicken into the basket. "That'll be one Fangral," the butcher said as Nox placed his Fangral on the table. "Come back anytime," the butcher spoke again in a rough sounding voice as he pushed the basket towards the lycan. Nox grabbed the basket and walked off.

Nox found himself at the center of the Lycanian Kingdom, where two giant statues of lycans stood. One was made out of lighter stone and holding a staff which water poured from into a small pool. The lycan statue's facial expression seemed to be of a

295

gentle and kind nature. She stood on her hind legs while holding

the staff with both paws. The other lycan statue was made out of

darker stone, which stood beside the other statue on hind legs as

well but held no weapons in his paws, instead one arm pointed

outwards. Nox examined the darker statue's features and could see

that it held anger in the stone's eyes. He looked down at the feet of

the statue and could see two flaming swords, the blades stuck into

the ground. Nox pondered how such swords could exist, but if the

Blade of Life and Tongs of Death existed, then the idea of flaming

swords wasn't that much far off. He sat at the edge of the pool,

placing the basket of meats beside him. He looked around again,

seeing the various stone buildings and noticed the difference

between human and lycan architecture.

Nox reached in his basket and grabbed the turkey leg,

raising it up to his mouth, he took a bite into it. He had noticed it

was lukewarm and wasn't roasting hot as he liked. He stood up,

jumped at the base of the statue, and eyed the two flaming swords.

He reached out with his left paw and batted at the sword, testing

the heat of the fire. When he didn't feel the flame's heat he touched

the sword and immediately looked at his paw. Nox was puzzled

when he saw no burn marks on his paw. He grabbed the hilt of the sword, pulling the entire blade out of the ground and examined it carefully. The sword seemed to be very ancient, the hilt seemed to form a lycan's paw as a blade protruded from the palm. The blade itself didn't seem to be so worn with time, however the moving flame didn't help one to see the scratches on the blade. Still confused why the fire did not hurt him, Nox took a step towards the pool and thrust the sword into the water. A hot jet of steam shot into the air as he quickly pulled the flaming sword from the pool. He hopped onto the edge of the pool where he set down his basket and sat down while he steadily roasted the turkey leg against the searing flame of the sword. Nox took a bite of the turkey and was satisfied, as he chewed vigorously, he noticed a large crowd of lycans looking at him. Nox took another bite out of his turkey leg and was confused why a large crowd had drawn attention to him. He waved his turkey leg at them as a group of lycan guards approached him.

"You need to come with us immediately," one of the lycan guards ordered in a rough sounding voice.

Nox followed several lycan guards into the Lycanian castle as a series of lycan honor guards stood in the halls. Their bodies were like statues as their heads followed the group's movement down the hall. A large wooden door was the entrance to the inner chamber. One of the honor guards pulled it open, the group entered and they stopped at the center of the room. He could see more lycan honor guards standing still in front of the twelve pillars that supported the room. He directed his attention towards the throne where he laid eyes upon a snow white furred lycan who had icy blue eyes. She held a silver staff that resembled the statue in the center of the kingdom. On her left side was a lycan with a light grey coat; however, his paws were covered with a strange piece of cloth. On her right stood a lycan who resembled an honor guard.

"Hello," greeted the white lycan whose gentle but commanding voice captured Nox's full attention. He lifted his left paw, waved at the white lycan, and revealed a slight smile. "My name is Azhmay, what is your name?" Nox placed his turkey leg on the ground as he lifted his paws in the air and slowly lowered his right paw down.

"Why doesn't he talk?" the lycan on her right spoke out in a hoarse voice.

"Because he is perhaps mute?" the lycan on her left replied.

"Nox is it?" Azhmay spoke softly as Nox shook his head excitedly up and down.

"Why don't you speak?" Azhmay questioned as she slightly tilted her head, awaiting an answer. Nox held two digits of his left paw up as he kicked the air with his right leg then immediately pointing at his throat. "Humans did such a thing to you?" Azhmay questioned as she looked on intently.

"Humans are scum," the lycan on her right spoke out.

"Silence, Kargun," Azhmay ordered, as she glanced at him he crossed his arms and shut his mouth. She turned her attention to Nox and looked on. Nox turned his left paw upside down. "A bad human?" Azhmay questioned as Nox shook his head up and down. "That is unfortunate to hear. What brings you here? Dark lycans are welcome here but I have never seen one with glowing red eyes like yours." Nox pointed at his eyes with both paws before cupping his paws together. He then lifted his right paw, clenching it into a fist while his left paw was making a grabbing gesture.

"He seeks a powerful weapon," The light gray furred lycan surmised.

"I have it right here!" Kargun joked as he grabbed his crotch; a few other lycans let out a slight howl but tried their best to hide it.

"That's not a weapon, that's a pup's toy," the light grey furred lycan replied as the chamber erupted in howls of laugher before quickly silencing down.

"The twin flaming swords?" Azhmay questioned. Nox shook his head from side to side, as he held out his right paw in front of him and gestured a striking motion.

"The Tongs of Death." The light grey furred lycan spoke as Nox excitedly shook his head up and down.

"Does such a weapon exist, Urdel?" Azhmay questioned as the light grey furred lycan tilted his head for a moment in thought.

"Yes, but not in lycan lore, this particular weapon is of demonic origins," Urdel replied in an erudite manner. "Why do you seek such a weapon, friend?" Urdel questioned Nox. Nox grabbed his right wrist with his left paw and pointed upwards.

"…his master/friend?" Urdel questioned. Azhmay leaned towards Urdel and whispered into his ear.

"This is confusing but do you know what he speaks of?" Urdel nodded his head.

"I can help him find what he needs if you wish it," Urdel whispered back.

"Nox, look on the ground, do you know who those two lycans are?" Azhmay softly spoke as she sat up in her throne. Nox looked on the ground and could see a beautifully painted mosaic of two lycans. One lycan was white with icy blue eyes, holding a silver staff; the other was a black lycan with fiery red eyes, holding two flaming swords. Nox looked back up at Azhmay and shook his head from side to side.

"You do not know the lycan lore?" Azhmay questioned. Nox again shook his head from side to side.

"The white one is Glaishell and the black one is Volcanius." Nox stared at Azhmay blankly but could not understand the relevance and lifted his shoulders in reply.

"Only direct descendants of Volcanius can withstand the flame and wield the twin swords; Cynder and Crysp." Nox knelt down, placing his right paw on the mosaic of Volcanius, and gently followed the outline of his body. He looked up at Azhmay and with his left paw, he pointed at himself in disbelief.

"Welcome home, Nox," Azhmay gently spoke as the entire chamber of lycans howled in excitement.

Chapter 24

<u>Claudius</u>

Solace. Claudius stood in front of a crowd of knights and paladins; all of them stood still and remained silent, waiting for the paladin to speak. Claudius wore his traditional paladin's armor, which was concealing all of his bandaged wounds, for he wouldn't want to speak at his brother's funeral in silken robes but attire fit for battle. He looked directly in front of him and could see thirty-three marble caskets, Lance's Warhammer laid upon his casket. Claudius took a deep breath and slowly let the air out.

"I would like to thank you all for coming, for in these trying times we must remember those who have sacrificed everything in order to protect that which is good. Lance was a paladin, my friend and brother. I have shared many battles and laughs with him and if the Higher has any ale, they are probably out by now." The crowd let out a soft laugh as they looked on. "Let these fallen brothers and sisters live on in our hearts and let their kind words echo forever in our ears; let them be a soft rain to quell the fiery doubts that may plague us." Claudius paused for a moment, the silence interrupted by high-pitched squawks. Surina flapped her wings as she scratched Lance's casket. A woman moved through the crowd towards the distressed griffon.

"Calm down, Surina," Cathevne spoke as she grabbed the griffon's neck feathers, leading the griffon out.

Claudius looked upon the stone statue of Lance; the statue was extremely realistic as it captured every single physical detail. "It's beautiful," Claudius spoke as the master artisan nodded.

"Twenty-five years of experience," the artisan replied. The statue of Lance stood tall, holding the Warhammer in his right hand, the hammerhead rested upon his right shoulder, his left hand held a tankard. "Is there a particular reason why you wanted a hammer instead of a sword for the statue?" the artisan questioned.

"Paladins use their lightblades," Claudius replied as he pointed around the mausoleum where all the statues of the fallen paladins held swords in their right hand. "Lance never used his, he preferred the Warhammer – it was his grandfathers."

"I see and by the tankard, I like to think he enjoyed a drink?" the artisan questioned.

"Many," Claudius replied as he let out a sigh.

"I'm sorry to hear, he sounds like a great warrior."

"He was," Claudius answered as the artisan nodded before walking out of the mausoleum. A steady line of people walked past the stone caskets as Claudius caught sight of someone who did not fit in the crowd. He could see a young elven girl standing in front of Lance's casket. She placed something on top of the casket as she moved her hand across her eyes trying to wipe away tears before she ran off.

"Excuse me, are you the person who crafted the statue?" Cathevne asked.

"What gave that away?" the man replied.

"Well, the apron for one…perhaps the belt of tools as well?"

The man let out a laugh as he nodded. "Yes, I suppose that is a dead give-a-way."

"Your statues are well made, if they had color I could have been fooled for a real person."

"Why, thank you, it takes quite some time to make such things out of stone."

"Could I purchase a statue?" Cathevne questioned.

"Of course, what did you have in mind?" the artisan asked curiously.

A few hours had passed as everyone said their goodbyes and left the mausoleum. Claudius was the only one who remained. He walked towards Lance's casket and stood still for a moment. He noticed there was a small woven bracelet that sat on top of the casket. He reached over and placed his hand on the casket, trying his best to hold back tears. He moved his hand, feeling the scratches that Surina had left behind.

"I'm sorry, Lance," Claudius whispered as he walked away and walked around the mausoleum, seeing all the statues of the previous paladins. He noticed that one statue in particular was not holding a sword but instead a large tower shield. He walked up to the statue and could see that the statue had been there for quite some time. He could not make out the name, as there was too much dust upon the nameplate. Claudius wiped the gold nameplate to read "Zeraph." He could not remember where he had seen the name but it was strangely familiar. Claudius was deep in thought and let out a long sigh.

"What troubles you, son of light?" a masculine yet soft and calm voice questioned. Claudius turned his head to the voice and widened his eyes, seeing a man who resembled the statue.

"Zeraph?" Claudius questioned in disbelief as the divine slowly nodded with a reassuring smile.

"I ask again, what troubles you, son of light?" Zeraph asked, his glowing blue eyes pierced his own.

"How am I to continue?"

"Your heart was filled with courage; you fight demons without fear – what changed?"

"To fight the demons of darkness by myself?" Claudius replied with harsh doubt in his voice.

"But you aren't by yourself."

"Lance, my greatest friend and ally, has perished before me. Allister, a person who I trusted, has turned his back against me and look, here I am alone."

"Paladin, ask yourself – is Lance truly gone?"

Claudius searched his mind for a moment before shaking his head repeatedly from side to side "I…I honestly am not sure about anything anymore."

"Would you search the ends of the world for your loved ones too?"

Claudius was hesitant to answer but finally nodded in agreement.

"Seek out Allister. I know you are suffering in pain but there are others in need, all of whom require just a helping hand and an open heart. Take this and show the world that kindness still exists." Zeraph spoke as he extended his arm, opening his hand to reveal a bright light emitting from his hand.

Claudius reached with his right hand and grabbed the light as it dissipated in his grasp. He could feel a soft warm glow enter his hand before slowly travelling up to his arm. "Thank you, Zeraph," Claudius spoke as the divine acknowledged with a reassuring nod.

Claudius blinked for a moment as Zeraph disappeared completely from sight. He looked around and found himself to be alone again. Looking up to the statue of Zeraph, he could see him holding the enormous tower shield with his right hand while holding a delicate lily flower in his left. Claudius took in a deep breath and narrowed his eyes before exiting the mausoleum. He whistled for Sundra and took to the skies.

The sun was at its highest with a large group of clouds scattered across the sky. A gentle breeze brushed through his hair as Sundra beat her wings heavily. "There!" Claudius spoke as he pointed to the town in the distance. Sundra acknowledged, letting out a loud squawk. He soon arrived in the town of Kolloth and after an hour of searching and questioning where Allister's residence was, he finally found the small wooden house that sat at the edge of town.

"Allister?!" Claudius called as he knocked on the wooden door. He received no answer and knocked on the door again. After waiting a few minutes, he opened the door and stepped inside. The main room was dim, even with the cloud covering the sun's rays. The sparse furniture in the room was either destroyed or seemed to have been thrown around. "Allister?" Claudius called out again, but this time he heard a weak reply.

"Claudius?" a familiar voice replied from another room. Claudius quickly navigated through the disheveled room and stood in front of an old worn out door. Claudius pressed his palm against the door and slowly pushed it open. He held his gasp as he laid eyes upon a person he almost did not recognize.

"Yes, it's me – Claudius," Claudius spoke with a gentle voice

Allister turned his head to Claudius and shook his head while trying his best not to cry "I have failed everyone," Allister lamented solemnly.

Claudius could see that there was a thin piece of cloth that wrapped around Allister's eyes "What happened, brother?" Claudius asked with concern as he could see pieces of his armor scattered around the room. He picked up a chair and sat it in front of the bed where Allister was sitting. Claudius sat down and remained silent, waiting for an answer.

"I tried finding my sister… I ran into a demon who used some book to blind me," Allister spoke with sadness in his words.

"I am here now, I can help you," Claudius assured as he reached over and placed his hand on Allister's shoulder.

"Look at me! How can I fight demons when I am blind? I bet Lance would laugh at me if he saw me right now!" Allister blurted out.

"Uh… Lance died a few days ago…we had the funeral today," Claudius spoke quietly as Allister instantly fell silent.

"I'm sorry, Claudius, I didn't mean that," Allister broke the silence as he reached out to give Claudius a hug. Claudius embraced Allister and patted his back.

"It's okay, I understand," Claudius replied as they broke from the hug. "I need your help as well."

"What do you mean?"

"The demons are getting stronger and after the attack on the Citadel of Light, left us with fewer paladins."

"I cannot fight, I can't see, Claudius."

"I may have an idea if you are willing." The room fell silent for a moment as Allister searched his mind before giving a nod.

"Let's give it a shot," Allister spoke in a more uplifting tone as he stood up. Claudius helped Allister navigate his way through his wrecked house and onto Sundra's back.

With a long, reassuring flight, the two paladins arrived in the courtyard at the Citadel of Light. Claudius leaped off the griffon as Allister carefully slide off her side, testing where the ground was first. Claudius extended his arm to Allister. "Here, take

311

my arm." Allister reached out and grabbed his arm. It felt like they were walking for miles when Allister finally asked a question.

"Where are we going?"

"The inner chamber of the Citadel where the Hammer of Creation is stored."

"And this might work?"

"I'm not sure, we'll see."

Claudius opened the inner chamber doors and guided Allister towards the pedestal. Ten other paladins in the room guarded the hammer. Claudius let go of Allister's arm as he grabbed the hammer.

"Here goes nothing," Claudius whispered as he handed the hammer to Allister. The hammer instantly glowed bright blue as Allister changed to his ascended form. Giant ethereal blue wings erupted from his back as his body filled with light, his entire right arm glowing blue as the energy of the hammer syphoned into his body. Bright blue glowing eyes pierced behind the piece of cloth that wrapped around his eyes. Allister handed Claudius the hammer back as his ascended form quickly faded away. However, the bright blue glowing eyes remained. "Did it work?" Claudius asked as he waited anxiously for an answer. Allister reached for the cloth with

312

both hands, pulled it off and looked directly at Claudius with glowing blue eyes. He blinked and then turned his head, looking around the room.

"How many people are in this room?" Allister whispered.

"Twelve, including me and you," Claudius replied, a little puzzled. Allister turned his head again, looking around the room in disbelief.

"That's strange… because I count twenty," Allister replied.

Chapter 25

Nox

Tranquility. The sun had just begun its descent from the sapphire sky towards the granite gray mountains. Nox sat in a large mahogany chair facing Urdel who was also sitting in a large mahogany chair. Nox held out his left paw, revealing his palm face up, pointing in the middle of it with his right paw. Urdel closed his eyes for a moment and searched his thoughts. Nox waited anxiously for an answer as he placed both of his paws on the round marble table.

"The last known whereabouts of the Tongs was in the possession of a vampire," Urdel stated. Nox lifted his right paw and curled two fingers while holding his left paw cupped underneath it. "Yes, vampires." Nox punched his own paw as he frowned.

"Nox, if I could make a recommendation?" Nox nodded his head. "Don't go out and search for it, the Tongs will only bring destruction and its vampire territory." Nox held out his left palm and hit it with his fist. "Well, if you must. You have been warned." Urdel spoke as two lycan guards arrived at the table.

"The queen summons you." As one of the guards spoke, Nox looked up with a face filled with confusion but nodded in agreement. Nox stood up from his chair and followed the guards through several halls and up two staircases.

One of the guards knocked on a beautifully carved mahogany door that had several lycans carved in it. The door slowly opened as Azhmay stood in front of Nox.

"Leave us," Azhmay ordered; the two guards nodded and followed her order. She turned around and signaled for Nox to follow. She sat down in a large mahogany chair with her tail curled around her. A small marble table stood between the two chairs and upon it were silver plates that held various foods and fruits. Nox's eyes widened at a particular bowl of fruits as he quickly sat down and grabbed a pomegranate. He bit down into the fruit, juices squirting everywhere followed by a soft giggle that escaped Azhmay's mouth. Nox's ears perked up as he paused his chewing and matched eyes with Azhmay. He jabbed one of his fingers into the fruit and pulled a hunk out, then extended his paw over the table to her. Azhmay tilted her head in curiosity before she leaned over the table and took the piece of fruit with her mouth, afterwards quickly giving his finger a sly lick. Nox retrieved his paw back while he revealed a big smile, showing the loose fruit among his sharp teeth. She let out another giggle, closing her eyes before stopping and watching the black lycan eat. Nox slowly bit into the fruit, trying not to make a mess, while he watched Azhmay's icy blue eyes upon him. Her snow-white fur was pristine and beautiful. Something inside him felt something he had never felt before. It was warm, it was welcoming and above all, he felt happy. Nox paused for a moment as he searched his thoughts. *Was this the feeling Soonifer felt? Is it possible that he does not feel this anymore? Alorah?*

"Is something the matter, Nox?" Azhmay's soft voice asked as Nox snapped back into reality. Nox shook his head from side to side, as he finished the fruit. "Do you know the history, between Volcanous and Glaishell?" Nox once again shook his head from side to side.

"Thousands of moons ago, there existed only two lycans. Volcanous, made of fire and Glaishell, made of ice. They hated each other because the other was something they were not. They would create lycans made in their own image and wage war upon each other. At every battle they would see only a glimpse of each other – who knows what they felt. Many thought it was anger because more and more battles would be fought until at the last battle they stood in front of each other. They were mere arms apart when Volcanous' fire started melting the ice. Glaishell's ice let out fridge cold vapors that would choke out the fire. They looked deep into each other's eyes, knowing how they could never hold one another and that life would be pointless in living if they could not hold each other in their embrace. Therefore, they threw themselves at each other with open arms and for a single second, they held each other before they smoldered, and within the ashes and vapor there were three lycan pups. One black as the night sky, one white as winter's snow and one gray as the mountains that surround us."

Nox smiled as he clapped his paws together. Azhmay tilted her head downwards in a sly fashion. "Thank you," she spoke as Nox pointed to one of his ears, before touching his mouth and pointing at Azhmay. "You like hearing my voice that much?" She

317

spoke with her icy blue eyes piercing his. Nox could do nothing but nod his head up and down, as he got lost in her eyes. "I like your glowing red eyes," Azhmay blurted out as Nox pointed to himself. Azhmay nodded slowly. Nox stood up in his chair and looked into a nearby tall mirror. He gazed into the mirror for a while, having never noticed the red glowing eyes, and they were beautiful. Azhmay let out a loud cough to catch Nox's attention as he turned his head to see she was in bed. She held her right paw up and curled a finger at Nox, motioning him to come. Nox revealed a sly smile as he obeyed.

Nox woke up in the middle of the night; he turned his head to the right to see Azhmay fast asleep. He then turned his head to the left and could see the moonlight piercing through the balcony's glass door. He got out of bed quietly and walked over, opening the glass door. He stood outside in the warm air, a gentle breeze greeting him every few minutes. Thoughts of Soonifer ran though his mind. An imagine of Ker'es appeared in his mind followed by a faint voice.

"You do want to help him, right?" Nox shook his head, remembering what he needed to do. He turned his head, looking back into the room and saw Azhmay for the last time on the bed before he leaped off the balcony.

Chapter 26

<u>Claudius</u>

Courage. The sun had just begun its journey ascending upwards when a loud horn was blown, awaking the paladins for the start of the day. Claudius rubbed his eyes as he sat up in bed and looked over to see Allister still asleep. He grabbed his pillow and threw it as hard as he could at Allister, waking him up.

"Hey! What was that for?" Allister complained as he tossed the pillow aside.

"Didn't you hear the horn?" Claudius asked as he put on his plated leggings.

"Yes. Are we under attack?"

"No, it's the horn to wake up."

"Well, when the demons do attack, they can fight me here, in my bed." Allister spoke in a groggy tone as he buried his head further into the pillow. "Give… me fifteen minutes…" Allister mumbled as Claudius finished putting on his armor.

"Ok, if I come back here past fifteen minutes, I'm throwing something heavier on you," Claudius replied as he walked out of the room.

"Claudius!" a familiar voice shouted. He turned his head to spot a lycan wearing paladin's armor.

"Nara!" Claudius shouted back as they ran towards each other. The two embraced each other in a hug before they faced each other. "I haven't seen you in so long, how have you been?" Claudius questioned as he looked at her worn and scratched armor.

"I have been well and just returned from a campaign in the southern plains, destroying every demon that we came across. We returned when we received word that the Citadel of Light was under attack…I guess we are a little late?"

"Yes, we defended the Citadel and the demons have withdrawn – but we do not know when they will attack again."

"Where is Lance? Sleeping would be my guess?" Nara questioned with thoughtful eyes.

"Uh… "Claudius tried to speak but was quickly cut off.

"I guess I could wait and give him a giant hug when he wakes up…" Nara blurted, her grin showing a playful plan brewing in her mind.

"He perished during the attack," Claudius spoke as the shine in Nara's eyes faded away. Her heart dropped for a moment as she stared blankly at Claudius while slowly raising her paws to cover her mouth. Claudius slowly nodded his head and placed his right hand on her shoulder. "I know now is not the best time… but I need your help with something, Nara," Claudius spoke solemnly.

"Anything," Nara replied in a choked up breath.

"The elves and humans have rekindled their old alliance. I need your help with the lycans." Claudius spoke as Nara remained silent but replied with a nod. Claudius patted Nara's shoulder a few times before she turned around and walked off.

"I swear if Allister isn't up…" Claudius whispered to himself while he pulled off his gauntlet to throw at Allister. He walked into the room and saw Allister fully geared while sitting up in his bed. "Are you okay, Allister?" Claudius asked with some concern. Allister snapped out of his trance-like state and turned his head to Claudius.

"Yes, of course. What's for breakfast?" he replied as he stood up.

"Let's go find out" Claudius spoke as he revealed a gentle smile. An hour had passed after breakfast as Claudius and Allister searched the entire Citadel for Nara.

"Do you think we really need her?" Allister asked a little disgruntled.

"Yes, even though the lycans are ok with trade and such with humans… dying for humans isn't a widely accepted idea," Claudius replied with a sigh.

"What do you mean?" Allister questioned.

"Over one hundred and fifty years ago, the lycans and vampires waged war against one another. Tens of thousands of both lycan and vampire perished throughout the bloodshed. The lycans eventually blamed the war on humans for banishing vampires from their communities."

"How come this is the first I have heard of such a war?"

"Because the entirety of the war was fought between lycan and vampire. Humans blamed vampires for all sorts of things and chased them off into the Silpine forest. The elves did not want them there so they chased them off to the Urrogoth Wastes. The lycans did not want them there so they chased them off until the vampires claimed the black rock mountains and Vivian coast. Legends claim that the vampires were the first to discover the Hammer of Creation and through its use – they had become a powerful force but the lycans proved themselves well and the vampires couldn't take revenge on both elves and humans."

"How come humans didn't help in the war?"

Claudius lifted and dropped his shoulders "I don't know. Much of the remaining texts that exist today from that era suggest that since the burden was on the lycans – they were the ones to deal with it."

"But… we created the burden?"

Claudius nodded his head in agreement but said nothing. Allister bit down on his tongue.

"Sorry for the history lesson" Claudius spoke as he crossed his arms.

"I enjoyed it; perhaps Nara as a lycan would know more about it?" Allister suggested as Claudius' eyes widened.

"I know where she is!" Claudius blurted as he quickly ran towards the door with Allister following behind.

Claudius and Allister entered the mausoleum and instantly spotted Nara standing in front of a statue of Lance. She was looking up at the statue while holding both of her paws together at her belly. The two walked towards Nara as she turned her head to greet them.

"Hey," Claudius whispered as Nara replied with a solemn "Hey."

"It looks exactly like him," Nara spoke as she turned her head back to the statue.

"Yeah, yeah it does," Claudius replied.

"Although I have never seen Lance with a serious face."

"I have," Claudius admitted as he looked upon the face of the statue and held back his tears. His memories flashed back to when he slew legion after legion of demons, he turned around to see a face exactly like the one on the statue. Allister walked in-between the two and knelt down in front of the statue, placing a silver spoon on top of the stand. Claudius revealed a soft smile, seeing the spoon as Allister took a few steps back and crossed his arms.

"I don't think he loved anything more than drinking," Allister said.

"Surina," Claudius whispered as Allister nodded. Nara looked at the spoon and turned to Allister.

"What's that for and how are your eyes glowing like that?" she questioned.

"It's a long story…but I can tell it to you on our trip to the Lycanian Kingdom" Claudius promised

Nara hit her forehead with her paw "I totally forgot about that!" She quickly turned around to Claudius. "I'm sorry!"

"Its fine, trust me – I think we all needed this. Let this be more than just a memory, it's a reason why we fight this war." Claudius spoke solemnly as he turned around and walked out. Nara and Allister both nodded their heads and followed Claudius.

***

. Claudius, Allister and Nara stood in the middle of the throne room as they waited for one of the honor guards to return with the queen. Claudius was the first to notice the beautifully painted mosaic of two lycans on the floor. "Look at that," Claudius said and pointed to the mosaic which caught the attention of Allister and Nara.

"Wow, that is quite breath taking," Allister replied as he examined it closer.

"Wow!" Nara blurted out as she quickly knelt down and placed her paw over the mosaic and slowly moved her paw down, feeling the faint impressions of the artwork.

"Who are the two lycans?" Allister questioned.

"Oh, that's easy! This one is Glaishell!" Nara exclaimed as she moved her paw and pointed at the white colored lycan. "And this one is Volcanous!" she continued as she excitedly moved her paw to the red colored lycan.

"He doesn't look too friendly…" Allister added.

"No… he's kinda mean…" Nara's voice trailed off.

Azhmay

The honor guard knocked on the wooden door but heard no sound. He knocked on the door a second time but much louder and waited for a reply but received none. He took in a deep breath and opened the door slowly while peeking his head inside. "Your highness?" he spoke softly, scanning the room but no one was in sight. He opened the door further and poked more of his head into the room. He caught sight of the balcony window and could see her standing outside. The honor guard let out a loud cough to get the attention of the queen. Azhmay turned her head to see the honor guard.

"Oh, sorry. Did you need something?" Azhmay softly spoke.

"Uh…um…is there something bothering you, your highness?" the honor guard asked with a kind tone. Azhmay fell silent and turned her head to look out at the fountain where many lycans walked about, carrying on their business. "It's the black lycan, Nox, isn't it?" the honor guard asked as Azhmay quickly turned her head back to look at him.

"Any word on him?" Azhmay questioned, her icy blue eyes falling upon the honor guard.

"No. I am afraid not, your highness. We searched everywhere, nobody knows where he went and nothing was reported stolen," the honor guard replied. "Um… you have visitors in the throne room who seek your audience," he added as he shifted around.

"Very well, I shall be down shortly," Azhmay replied as the guard nodded and left the room, closing the door behind him. *But he did steal something…* Azhmay whispered, letting out a deep sigh.

Claudius

The queen finally arrived in the throne room where the entire honor guard stood at attention. Azhmay walked across the throne room as all eyes were upon her. She sat down in her tall silver throne and shifted her gaze upon the three paladins, Claudius, Nara and Allister, who stood before her. "I understand that you asked for my audience?" Azhmay softly spoke.

"Yes, that is correct," Claudius replied.

"How can I be of service?" Azhmay asked with her icy blue eyes fixed upon Claudius.

"An enormous horde of demons have attacked the Citadel of Light – we have successfully defended the Citadel but have concern that another attack will be forthcoming. I wish to have the lycan's support to join alongside humans and elves in battle."

"We have defended the world from vampire attacks for over a hundred years without asking help from others!" Kargun blurted.

"We aren't asking for much!" Nara shouted back and stepped forward while a look of surprise was plastered on many of the honor guards in the room, including Kargun and Urdel.

"Why does a lycan wear human armor?" Kargun questioned in a rough voice.

"Because what I wear means much greater than just metal! It's honor, a code! It is much more than fighting for ourselves but fighting for what is right. Many who wore this very same armor have died protecting those in need and if we don't do anything about the demons, many more will die – most who do not wear armor!" Nara shouted with her heart beating fiercely while trying to hold back tears. "There is a paladin who would fight for anyone, any elf, any lycan or human – he would be there! He didn't see stupid racial bias, but only good." Nara stopped as she bit down hard on her tongue trying to hold back all of her emotions.

"And who is this paladin that fights for such a noble cause? Him?" Azhmay accused as she pointed at Claudius. Nara shook her head as Claudius interrupted.

"No. I believe it is my brother, Lance, she is speaking about. He had given his life to become a paladin and it has been savagely taken away from him when the demons attacked the Citadel of Light." The room fell into an uncomfortable silence as everyone stared intently at one another.

"How many lycan lives would match a single human?" Urdel questioned, breaking the silence.

"One. We are all the same," Allister spoke out.

"Then one you shall have. I will join your cause," Azhmay softly replied as the room fell silent and in shock.

"Then I shall join the queen!" one honor guard yelled as more honor guards shouted the same. The three paladins looked at each other with smiles while Nara smiled the biggest.

Chapter 27

<u>Soonifer</u>

Umbrage. Soonifer slouched deeply in the seat as Ker'es appeared before him. He stared at him blankly as emotions of Alorah's death still raged inside of him. "Soonifer," Ker'es whispered. The storm had quieted itself to allow Ker'es words to be heard as clear as a calm day. "Through Nox's help, we have discovered the location of the Tongs of Death," Ker'es whispered as Nox peeked his head from behind Ker'es and looked at Soonifer. Soonifer shifted his gaze from Ker'es to Nox as the lycan sprinted towards him and lunged on top of him. Soonifer placed his left hand on Nox's side and began petting him. After a moment, Soonifer turned his head to see Ker'es.

"Where is it and why should I care?" Soonifer spoke as a demonic tone echoed with each word.

"The vampires have it and because it is one of the three tools you need to get whatever you want," Ker'es whispered.

"Whatever I want?" Soonifer replied and stopped petting Nox.

"There is a portal waiting for you," Ker'es whispered back and he disappeared into the darkness. Soonifer sneered, watching Ker'es disappear as he pushed Nox to the side.

"Let's go get the Tongs, I guess," Soonifer spoke as Nox licked his cheek.

Soonifer and Nox entered the purple portal and stood before a giant mountain. The side of the mountain was a huge flat cliff. He looked around at the base of the mountain and could see countless skeletons, rusted armor and weapons lying about. He looked up to see the side of the mountains seem to touch the sky itself. Just as the portal started to close, Soonifer stepped back in and Nox quickly followed.

"Is this a joke!?" Soonifer yelled at one of the rift guardians. The two rift guardians looked at one another and then looked at Soonifer in confusion.

"What do you mean?" one of the rift guardians asked in a stern voice.

"I'm not climbing that. Make a portal at the top of the mountain," Soonifer replied as his eyes glowed a fiery red.

"You cannot order me, we are both greater demons," the rift guardian replied, clicking his tongue at the end of his sentence. A burst of purple flame enveloped Soonifer's right hand as a spear appeared in his grasp. He quickly thrust the spear towards the rift guardian and stopped when the tip rested at the nape of his neck.

"I am asking nicely," Soonifer angrily said.

The rift guardian eyed Soonifer menacingly before gritting his teeth and then took his obsidian dagger and slashed the air in between the two rift guardians. The two rift guardians grabbed the edges of the tear and pulled heavily, creating a portal. Soonifer peered up to see the ledge of the mountains, confirming that the portal was on top of the mountains. Soonifer tossed the spear in the air, let it hit the ground with a metallic ring and then took a step into the portal.

"Gor'eck Kal will know of this!" the rift guardian yelled as Nox followed Soonifer through the portal.

"Gor'eck can eat my spear!" Soonifer replied as the portal abruptly vanished.

The sun had started to descend downward through the sky as a stream of cold breezes rushed past Soonifer and Nox. The air was cold in the high mountains; the rock they stood upon was solid black. Soonifer looked around and could see that the area seemed dead and desolate; there was not much vegetation nor any signs of life. He walked towards the other side of the mountain and could see an endless ocean that touched the sky at the horizon. He looked down, seeing a very steep drop-off and a small shoreline where the ocean started. A giant black castle stood near the top of the mountain, half of the castle seemed to be partially cut from the mountain itself. Soonifer walked towards the castle and Nox followed closely behind, zig zagging and sniffing all sorts of things.

As the two approached the black castle, the desolate picture began to fade as pieces of clothes, discarded food or other remains became more prevalent. Soonifer stopped; standing still, he noticed several extremely bright lights come out of nowhere near the stone windows of the castle. Nox looked up towards the upper level of the castle to see what Soonifer was looking at. Soonifer's hand exploded in purple flame as a spear spawned in his grasp. Rearing back, he hurled the spear at one of the stone windows. Two of the bright lights disappeared along with a strange scream. Suddenly, the stone windows became filled with bright lights but Soonifer quickly realized they were not lights at all, but the bright eyes of vampires as they flew from the window towards them. Nox readied his claws as Soonifer spawned another spear and hurled it at the incoming flock of vampires. Soonifer hurled a barrage of spears as one by one, vampires would fall towards the ground. The entire flock of vampires arrived, half of them landed, withdrawing their short swords for an attack. Nox leaped at them, swinging his powerful claws as chunks of their pale flesh ripped off. Their thin steel armor was no match for Nox's claws, sheer metal pieces of armor hit the ground, letting out a faint metal ring over the screams and howls of vampires.

The vampires who remained in the air swung their blades at Soonifer, maintaining their aerial advantage. Soonifer spawned Zary's crescent blade and hurled it at a vampire, slicing it in two as its body hit the ground with a thud. Dodging the swift slashes of the vampires, he decided to stick to a more offensive strategy. Soonifer spawned more spears and hurled them at close range at the attacking vampires, causing fatal injury. A flying vampire swung his sword at Soonifer but the demon quickly parried it with a spear. Soonifer then hurled the spear which slammed into the torso of the vampire. The vampire fell to the ground, lifeless. The horde of vampires thinned out, with only a few remaining, they retreated – flying back towards the black castle as Soonifer proceeded to throw more spears. One such spear slammed into the right wing of a fleeing vampire who fell from the sky, hitting the ground with a thud. Soonifer walked to it as it struggled to crawl towards the castle. Soonifer wrapped his hands around its thin throat as it stared scarily at Soonifer.

"Where are the Tongs of Death?" Soonifer questioned, a demonic echo ringing through each word. The vampire remained silent while grabbing the demon's wrists, trying to free itself. Soonifer walked towards the edge of the mountain, and with each step the vampire moved more frantically to free itself. Soonifer held the vampire off the mountain's edge and asked again. "The Tongs of Death, where are they?"

"Dolamar!" The vampire meekly spoke with its bright eyes fixed upon the demon's red glowing eyes.

"Dolamar?" Soonifer questioned as the vampire tried to shake its head to agree. "Then Dolamar I shall seek," he replied as he hurled the vampire off the cliff. The vampire let out a bloodcurdling scream as it flailed its limbs and tried using its tattered wings to fly but it was of no use. Nox caught sight of Soonifer walking towards the black castle and he dropped the corpse of a vampire to race after him.

Soonifer stood in front of a large black wooden door that was reinforced with darkened iron bars. Purple fire erupted from his right hand as Gor'eck's hammer appeared in his grasp. He reared back, wrenching all of his strength into the swing of the hammer. The hammerhead smashed into the door and the entire top portion of the door caved in. Soonifer swung again, this time the entire door collapsed under the sheer strength of the impact. He tossed the hammer into the air where it disappeared into nothing but black vapor. Soonifer stepped inside the main hall as Nox stood next to him. He looked around and could see wall-mounted candles dimly lighting the hall. "Dolamar!" Soonifer shouted and then waited silently for some sort of an answer. A strong gust of wind flowed through the halls while letting out a howling wail. Soonifer decided to walk into the hallway where the strong wind came from as the soft footsteps of Nox trailed behind him.

The two entered into a giant room which contained shelves upon shelves of books stacked against the stone castle walls. The room was more illuminated than the rest of the castle.

"Why are you killing my kin?" a dark voice asked. Soonifer quickly turned in the direction of the voice to see a vampire sitting in a large crimson chair. The vampire looked vastly different from the ones he'd seen earlier. This one, who wore a fancy black tunic with blood red trim, long black trousers with white frills down the sides of the pants, he saw cross-legged on the seat.

"For fun of course," Soonifer replied as he clutched his right hand into a fist, readying for anything. The vampire closed the book he was reading, and gently placed it on a nearby table and looked up. His raven black hair was parted down the middle, the lengths of his hair neatly tucked behind his ears, he was looking up at Soonifer with bright white eyes.

"Why has a demon come such great lengths to be here?" The vampire questioned as he stood up from the chair.

"The Tongs of Death, give them to me!" Soonifer demanded as an obsidian spear appeared in his grasp.

"If it's death you seek, then I shall deliver!" Dolamar shouted as he ripped the rapier from its sheath. The blade of the rapier glowed a ghastly gray as Dolamar steadied his hand for an attack. Suddenly, a group of vampires stood in front of the door with their short swords at the ready. Soonifer hurled the spear at Dolamar; however, the vampire lord sidestepped the attack and lunged at Soonifer, swinging his rapier. Soonifer spawned Ker'es twin daggers, blocking the attack with ease as Nox charged the group of vampires and began tearing them into shreds. Soonifer launched a multitude of rapid strikes with his daggers, however Dolamar held his arm still, moved his wrists in quick succession and parried each of the attacks. Soonifer spawned Gor'eck's hammer and swung it heavily at Dolamar. The vampire lord dodged the hammer's swings with various side steps and bobbing as Soonifer furiously swung the hammer.

"Is this all the tricks you can conjure, demon?" Dolamar taunted as he eluded Soonifer's attacks. The vampire lord leaped into the air, turning his body upside down in mid-air, and swung his rapier at Soonifer who blocked the attack with the hammerhead. Dolamar landed feet first on the ground as he swung his rapier at the demon. Soonifer quickly spawned Zary's crescent blade and

340

slashed in an upward motion, cutting Dolamar's hand off. The rapier hit the ground with a metal ring and the vampire lord stared at his dismembered hand in disbelief. Dolamar bit into his own bleeding wrist and began thirst fully drinking his own blood as his eyes widened with rage. His entire body exploded with muscle, ripping his tunic into shreds. Dolamar swung his left claws at Soonifer's chest, scrapping bits of metal off. Dolamar attacked with increased ferocity and strength, Soonifer hurling the crescent blade at the vampire lord who easily dodged the attack and pursued Soonifer with his own relentless attacks. Soonifer's right shoulder and torso became filled with deep cuts as black blood poured from his wounds.

Dolamar leaped at the demon but Soonifer quickly spawned a spear, and using both hands, he slammed the spear into the vampire lord's left shoulder. Dolamar staggered backwards a few steps and tried to pull out the spear but was unable to lift his arm high enough. Dolamar charged the demon again as Soonifer's eyes glowed bright red in anger. Soonifer spawned another spear and with all of his might he slammed the spear into the torso of the vampire lord and swung the spear upwards, lifting Dolamar into the air. Then Soonifer forcefully slammed the spear into the ground, pinning Dolamar to the ground. Soonifer spawned Gor'eck's hammer and struck the end of the spear, bending it into an 'L' shape, preventing the vampire lord from freeing himself. Dolamar let out deep howls as he tried to struggle free. After a moment of struggling, Dolamar stopped and reverted to his normal form.

"Where are the Tongs of Death?" Soonifer questioned angrily. Dolamar coughed up blood as he lifted his head up to eye the demon.

"I don't have it" he replied weakly "In fact, you have done me a favor, demon. I grow tired of existence"

"I don't care for you or your story, vampire." Soonifer said as he walked closer to Dolamar. The vampire lord struggled to keep his eyes open as crimson blood poured profusely from his wounds.

"…But I do curse you for slaying the third child of Lord Volten," Dolamar weakly whispered as he closed his eyes for the last time.

Soonifer spawned Gor'eck's hammer and smashed tables, chairs and shelves in frustration. Entire wooden shelves collapsed under the hammer's infernal strength. "Rrrraaaahhhh!" Soonifer shouted as he destroyed another shelf, causing books to fly in every direction.

"Demon." A powerful yet calm voice spoke as Soonifer stopped in his tracks. He quickly turned around and saw a pale-skinned woman who stood at the top of the steps in the room. She walked down the short flight of steps, taking care with each step. She wore an elaborate dark purple robe with crimson red trim going down the side. As she approached Soonifer, he could see she wore a golden amulet that hung from her neck, a large ruby hanging from the chain. She stared deep into the demon's eyes and he felt a strange feeling flow over him. "I have something you seek," she spoke. With every word she spoke, his anger slowly dissipated with his eyes glowing a soft red. He dropped the hammer and it vanished into black vapor.

"What is it that I seek?" Soonifer replied as he felt her gaze pierce his own.

"The Tongs of Death," she answered, as Soonifer's eyes became bright red with anger.

"Give it to me!" Soonifer shouted as he threw his right hand and grabbed her throat.

"No! You shall listen to me, demon!" she replied in a serious tone. He gripped her throat harder until she disappeared, leaving a small pool of blood in her place which hit the ground with a splat, some of it covering Soonifer's right hand. He looked at the puddle of blood and then his hand before hearing a voice coming from behind him.

"That is no way to treat a lady."

He quickly turned around to see her standing unharmed, revealing a sly smile with bright white eyes. Soonifer reared back his right hand but felt as if someone was holding it in place. He quickly glanced at his hand and noticed the blood seemed alive. Soonifer stopped resisting, dropping his right hand as the lady's smile grew.

"Good. Now that we are being civilized, allow me to introduce myself. I am Tiana" She spoke as she started to walk in a circle around him. "I appreciate you killing my father, he was quite controlling."

Soonifer turned his head to the left to see Dolamar lying on the floor with a large pool of blood surrounding him. She approached, holding the Tongs "But if you want the Tongs, you are going to have to give me something in return" she continued as Soonifer turned his head to the right, watching her in front of him.

"What do you want?" Soonifer inquired slowly, trying to conceal his anger as a demonic tone echoed with each word.

"Follow me" she softly instructed and began to climb the stairs to walk into another room. Soonifer could do nothing else and followed, walking up the stairs and into the room.

***

Nox returned to the library, seeing all of the furniture shattered. He scanned the room to see a pale woman and Soonifer standing there while he was holding the Tongs of Death. It was solid black but held strange symbols that glowed red wrapped around the handle. The pale woman caught sight of the approaching lycan. "Well look at this cutie!" she exclaimed as Nox put some pep in his step, a trail of blood following behind him. He glanced at Soonifer and nudged him with his head, trying to get his attention.

"We did it, Nox," Soonifer whispered, his eyes remaining fixed on the Tongs.

"Aww, you look hurt," Tiana spoke, pressing her finger gently on Nox's wounds, and following the injury with her finger, the wound healed instantly. Nox looked down at his wounds to find them completely healed; he looked up at her with a confused look. "There! Good as new," she told Nox, who leaped at her and furiously licked her face. Soonifer held the Tongs of Death firmly in his left hand as he spawned Ker'es dagger in his right. Slashing the air, a purple rift appeared. Just as he took a step inside, he heard her voice. "I am coming with you." He turned his head to see the pale woman petting Nox.

"I don't care what you do. Let's go, Nox" he ordered as he stepped into the rift. Nox's ears perked up as he followed Soonifer through the rift. The pale woman entered behind them and moments later, the rift closed.

Chapter 28

Soonifer

Ominous. The three stood in the Nether, surrounded by darkness. Suddenly, the ground shook with a tremendous force. "What is that?" Tiana questioned, looking at Soonifer.

"Leave," Soonifer ordered as he concealed the Tongs of Death behind his back, wedging it between his back and back plate.

"I will stay!" Tiana replied in a tone matching his own.

"Nox, take her to Ker'es," Soonifer ordered again as Nox obeyed immediately, scooping up Tiana with his powerful arms and carrying her off into the darkness. A giant figure stood before him, standing at almost twice the height of a regular being. "I have been looking all over for you!" Gor'eck bellowed, his red glowing eyes matching Soonifer's gaze.

"And here I stand!" Soonifer yelled back as demonic tones echoed though the voice of both demons.

"You killed my spawn! For that I shall crushed your skull into a thousand pieces!" Gor'eck roared and clenched his right hand into a fist, smashing it into the palm of his left hand while his upper two arms did the same but above his head.

"You instead should reward me for cleansing the nether of such filth!" Soonifer challenged back with his red eyes glowing brighter. He stretched his right arm up from his side and clenched it into a fist as purple fire engulfed his entire right arm.

"You are a fool to fight a Tormentor, greater demon!" Gor'eck shouted as he adjusted the shoulders of his four arms, each letting out a loud crack as he prepared to fight.

"Shut up and die already!" Soonifer howled as he spawned a spear and hurled it with full force at Gor'eck. The Tormentor grabbed the spear with his right hand, stopping it from hitting his chest only a few inches away as he took a step back, catching his balance from the sheer force of the throw. He grabbed the end of the spear with his left hand and bent the spear in half before throwing it down to the ground. Gor'eck then proceeded to sprint full speed towards the greater demon with both of his right hands raised into a fist.

Just as Gor'eck reached Soonifer, he threw both of his right fists at him; however, Soonifer slipped into darkness, evading the attack completely. Soonifer appeared behind him, leaping up, and slammed both of Ker'es' daggers into his back. Gor'eck did not even flinch at the pain but quickly twisted his body while swinging both of his right fists. The upper first slammed into Soonifer's right cheek while the lower fist struck his chest. Soonifer landed on the ground and stumbled backwards several steps before catching himself with his hands. Soonifer spit out black blood as he slammed both of his fists into the ground and leaped up. Anger seared into Soonifer's body as he clenched his bloodied teeth. Soonifer reared back his right hand, disappearing into darkness then quickly reappeared in front of the Tormentor and slammed his fist into the Tormentor's chest. It was equal to punching a stone as pain flared into his hand. Gor'eck swiftly raised both his upper two hands and dropped them on the greater demon's head. Soonifer slammed into the hard ground and blinked a few times trying to comprehend what happened. Gor'eck let out an infernal laugh as he grabbed the greater demon with both of his right hands and threw him into the air. Soonifer again landed on the hard ground with full force, pain flaring throughout his entire body.

"You are too weak, perhaps the strength equivalent of a lesser demon at best!" Gor'eck bellowed. Hearing the Tormentor's words only enraged him more as he quickly scrambled to get up. He looked at the ram-headed demon with disgust as purple fire engulfed his hand. Soonifer hurled a barrage of spears at the Tormentor. Gor'eck backhanded the spears, causing them to spin violently in the air and ricochet against the ground. He backhanded the last spear thrown at him, however he miss-anticipated the speed of the spear, causing the spearhead to rip through his hand. Gor'eck roared in pain as he pulled the spear out of his hand and hurled it back at the greater demon.

Soonifer sidestepped the attack by mere inches, spawned Gor'eck's own hammer and leaped into the air, disappearing into the darkness. He reappeared in mid-air as he tried to swing the hammer downward but Gor'eck grabbed the hammerhead with both of his upper set of hands. The Tormentor then slammed his right lower fist into the side of the greater demon. The impact alone broke several ribs and Soonifer let out a demonic roar of pain, letting go of the hammer. He dropped to the ground with his right hand clutching his side while Gor'eck reared back his right set of fists and punched downwards at the greater demon. Soonifer disappeared and reappeared a short distance away, narrowly escaping the attack. Gor'eck's fists hit the ground throwing chunks of rocks into the air. Soonifer's right hand became engulfed with purple fire as he pressed it against his side, healing his injury. Soonifer spawned Gor'eck's hammer and sprinted at full speed towards the Tormentor as Gor'eck spawned his own infernal hammer and did the same.

The two reared back their hammers and when they were just mere feet away from each other, they swung their hammers at full strength. Soonifer disappeared as Gor'eck swung his hammer in the air while Soonifer reappeared at the Tormentor's left side, slamming the hammer into his side. Gor'eck groaned in agony then swung his hammer at the elusive greater demon. Soonifer vanished, causing the Tormentor's attack to miss yet again. Soonifer appeared behind him and slammed the hammerhead into the back of the Tormentor, causing him to fall forward. Gor'eck caught himself and slammed both of his lower fists into the ground. "Enough of your tricks!" He bellowed as he stood up and sprinted towards the greater demon while raising his massive hammer for an attack.

Gor'eck swung his hammer at the greater demon but Soonifer anticipated the attack and vanished, reappearing behind the Tormentor. Gor'eck knew he would pull another trick, so instead of stopping mid-swing, he continued the motion of the swing for another 180 degrees so that the hammerhead struck the greater demon's head. Soonifer's entire body became limp as he fell backwards, hitting the solid ground. He could feel his blood gushing out of his mouth, nose and ears but he could not move to stop the bleeding. Only to stare blankly up until Gor'eck's ugly ram-headed face came into view.

"Did you expect anything different?" Gor'eck spoke, a demonic tone echoing with each word. Soonifer tried to move his hand and legs but they would not respond. His eyes glowed a bright red with anger in sheer frustration that his body would not move while more and more blood poured from his mouth.

Just as he was about to give up, he felt the blood stop flowing from his orifices followed by a loud snap in his neck. He lifted his right hand in front of his face in disbelief as Gor'eck grabbed him by the throat and lifted him up. Flailing his legs in the air, Soonifer grabbed Gor'eck giant wrist with his left hand trying to free himself, but the Tormentor's stone-like grip was no match.

"Ker'es spoke of much potential, but I see none!" Gor'eck bellowed. Soonifer quickly spawned a spear in his right hand and thrust it into Gor'eck's chest. Black blood began pouring profusely from the wound as Gor'eck let out a demonic laugh unflinched by the wound. He reared one of his lower fists and slammed it into the greater demon's chest. Soonifer let out a cough as blood spewed from his mouth. "You are nothing more than a broken soul which everyone will soon forget!" Gor'eck bellowed as he squeezed the greater demon's throat. Soonifer squirmed, trying to breathe as he spawned Ker'es dagger in his left hand, stabbing the Tormentor's hand viciously. Black blood oozed out of each stab wound as Gor'eck let out another demonic howl tightening his grasp. Soonifer's stabs became slower and his red eyes started to dim as his vision began to blur. "Oblivion awaits!" Gor'eck howled in excitement.

In the last few seconds of his life, Soonifer reached behind his back and grabbed the Tongs of Death with his right hand. He poured any of his remaining strength into a final swing which slammed the head of the Tongs into Gor'eck's face. A black shadow of the Tormentor flew out of his body as his laughter became slow and distorted. Gor'eck's grip loosened as he fell backwards. Soonifer fell to the ground and dropped the Tongs, a metallic ring echoing in the air. Grabbing his neck, he breathed intensely, gasping for air. As soon as his breathing became normal, he grabbed the Tongs and stood up to find himself surrounded by thousands of demons, all of which laid their eyes upon Soonifer and Gor'eck's lifeless corpse.

"All who dare challenge me will meet the same demise!" Soonifer yelled, his red eyes flaring. The crowd of demons stepped aside, making a small entrance as a familiar face appeared. Tern'natha stood among them in silence, looking at what just happened. Soonifer clenched the Tongs, readying for anything as he eyed the Tormentor of Pride. Tern'natha simply kneeled and like a cascading wave, the thousands of demons joined in and kneeled before Soonifer.

Chapter 29

<u>Soonifer</u>

Hate. Soonifer sat upon the obsidian throne that Gor'eck once claimed. The enormous ram skull that once hung above the throne was on the ground shattered into pieces. Both of his arms rested on the armrests of the throne, his right hand held the Tongs of Death. Nox sat quietly on his right side looking up at Soonifer, awaiting some sort of command or action while Tiana stood very close on his left.

"You know, my father would often complain that he lived in the shadows of his older brother and sister's achievements. The oldest, Vazimar became a general – leading the vamperic army against the lycans as Dacia became the first blood mage. Dolamar? He would often spend his entirety in the library filling the void with books," Tiana described softly as she leaned against the throne looking at Soonifer intently.

"He and I could have been friends in another life," Soonifer whispered, turning his head to Tiana. She leaned inward, trying for a kiss but Soonifer abruptly turned his head away and stood up. Tiana's face filled with disgust as she pushed herself off the throne and stood in front of Soonifer.

"Where are you going?" she asked as the soft tone vanished and became stern.

"Ker'es calls me," Soonifer uttered as he stepped around Tiana, but the vampiress grabbed his shoulder, turning him around.

"Not even a thank you nor a kiss for saving your pitiful life?!" Tiana yelled.

"You should have just let me die," Soonifer replied as he tried to turn around but Tiana once again pulled him back and scratched his face. Her index and middle finger dug into Soonifer's skin. Two deep scratches started from the top of his left eye down to his lower cheek, blood slowly seeping from the wound. Tiana's scornful eyes, replaced by eyes of regret and care. She raised her right hand and gently pressed it against the start of the scratch and moved her finger downward following the scratch to heal it immediately.

"I'm sorry... I just crave your love," she softy spoke, kissing where the scratch had been. Soonifer disappeared into the darkness as she turned to the lycan. Nox shrugged his shoulders while holding his paws up in the air. Soonifer stood in front of Ker'es who stared at him intently with his hollow black eyes.

"Well done, Tormentor. Now we shall devise a plan to draw out the Hammer of Creation," Ker'es whispered.

"I grow tired of waiting!" Soonifer replied, a demonic howl echoing in his words.

"If you do not wait, then everything you have worked for... Alorah will be lost," Ker'es spoke as silence fell between them. Soonifer's eyes flickered, his eyes showing a faint madness that had been brewing inside of him.

"I have already lost everything, what more could I lose?" Soonifer trailed off

"Nothing." Ker'es whispered back, revealing the Blade of Life and held it out for Soonifer to take.

<u>Claudius</u>

"Claudius!" Lunnah yelled as she ran towards the paladin. Claudius turned his head to see a familiar face.

"Lunnah!" he let out as he did the same. They embraced each other followed by a short heartfelt kiss. "Where have you been?" Claudius questioned as he looked into her soft hazel eyes.

"I gathered the elves," she told him, breaking from the embrace and pointing to the enormous group of elves who stood at the gates of Light's Reach.

"That's incredible!" Claudius exclaimed as his eyes widened, seeing the thousands of elves.

"Only a few hundred are elf sentinels, the rest are volunteers," Lunnah explained. Claudius turned to her, grabbing her hand, and held it.

"Thank you," he spoke solemnly. Lunnah smiled and replied with a nod.

"Uh… guys… you won't believe this!" Allister yelled as the two turned their heads to see a slender, lion-headed demon with bright red eyes. Allister held his sword out while Claudius drew his lightblade and Lunnah readied her bow with an arrow.

"I'm not here to fight, but to give you a message," Tern'natha spoke.

"You shall die before you say anything!" Claudius spoke as his eyes started to become bright blue.

"I sense your hostility, so I shall be quick. I am the Tormentor of Pride; I do not submit to anyone yet I do to Soonifer because he has the Tongs of Death. He has already killed one Tormentor, who knows what he will do next. His demonic army stands on the outskirts of Solbris and he intends to kill every single one of you," Tern'natha finished as a purple rift appeared. He stopped mid-step from entering the rift and turned to Claudius. "So, for my sake paladins, win." Tern'natha spoke before fully entering the rift, then disappearing.

"I will not be tricked again! It's a trap!" Allister bellowed as he turned to the two. Claudius sheathed his sword and Lunnah relaxed her bow.

"What does he gain from lying?" Lunnah questioned.

"It could be a trap, but that demon did seem to be afraid," Claudius spoke while he searched his thoughts for possible answers.

"He mentioned that Soonifer has the Tongs of Death?" Allister questioned.

"If he has all three artifacts – The Blade of Life, Tongs of Death and the Hammer of Creation – we will be doomed," Claudius replied.

"How can we protect the hammer if it was nearly taken by the last demonic assault?" Allister wondered aloud.

"We have no choice but to take it with us," Claudius replied.

"But we are bringing the last artifact to him?!" Lunnah spoke.

"I trust Claudius," Allister replied while eyeing Claudius.

"Ok, we'll do this. Allister, send two paladin scouts by griffon to confirm the demonic army, if they see it – we go. Lunnah, prepare the elves – I have to find Nara!" Claudius ordered as Allister and Lunnah nodded, and all three went their separate ways.

Azhmay

A lycan honor guard knocked repeatedly on the wooden door to the queen's chambers. He finally opened the door, scanned the room to find it empty, and slowly walked to the balcony.

"Your highness?" the guard called out as he finally heard a reply.

"Yes?" Azhmay turned around, facing the guard as he stood at attention.

"We believe there are sightings of vampires on the horizon!" the guard reported.

"Vampires?" she questioned with her icy blue eyes showing concern. "Take me to the tower, I wish to see this for myself," she ordered as the guard nodded and proceeded to escort her to the wall of the Lycanian Kingdom. The tower guard bowed before handing her the spyglass which she raised to her eye and looked outward. She could only see specks of black that lined the entire horizon with massive purple flags that seemed to be waving in the wind. "I can't really make it out; they are so far off in the distance," Azhmay said as she handed back the spyglass to the guard. "Prepare the kingdom, ensure all guards are ready," was Azhmay's order. The tower guard nodded as he sprinted away, obeying her command.

"What about the paladins?" Urdel asked.

"Our kingdom comes first," Azhmay replied.

<u>Kylar</u>

The two paladin scouts rode upon their griffons with a strong wind against their backs. The sun was at its highest in the sky with spare clouds spread throughout the sky. "I can see Solbris in the distance!" Kylar yelled as he pointed to the city that lay in the distance.

"Do you really think the demons are preparing for an attack?" the other paladin questioned.

"No, demons lie all the time," Kylar replied as he looked around, seeing the boundless landscapes that they were flying over. They flew over Solbris and headed towards the outskirts of town.

"I don't see any demons, do you?" Kylar asked as he scanned the various landscapes. "Paulin?" Kylar asked as he turned around to see the other paladin's griffon dive bomb downwards. He looked down to see Paulin's corpse fall from the sky, an obsidian spear protruding from his chest while drops of blood followed behind his body. "Paulin!" Kylar shouted as he looked for the attacker. He could see hundreds of thousands of demons who stood on top of the plateau of the cliff with three individuals standing in the front. "By the divine!" Kylar shouted as he heeded his griffon to retreat.

Chapter 30

Claudius

Dismal. Claudius stood silently looking upon the massive cliff where hundreds of thousands of demons stared back, standing on the edge of the cliff. He could see three figures standing in the middle and in the center; he knew it was him by the two bright red glowing eyes in the distance. Allister stood to the left of Claudius while Lunnah stood to his right and beside Lunnah were her two companions, Rockstead and Oakheart. Behind them was a line of paladins that counted to a few hundred. Behind the paladins were a few thousand knights, elven archers and armed soldiers; behind those were tens of thousands of humans who volunteered to give everything they had to try to tip the scales.

"Where are the lycans?" Allister questioned as two men approached them.

"I don't know, but everything we have is here," Claudius responded sternly as he placed his left hand at his side, gently touching the Hammer of Creation which hung from his leather belt tied in a knot.

"Our knights are ready and at your command, but I advise that you lead into battle with them." The general spoke as he crossed his arms.

"No, we should attack with unrelenting force with paladins!" Andros urged as he slammed his right fist into his left palm.

"Whatever we decide, we have small groups of eleven sentinels scattered around to provide help," Lunnah added.

"How will your knights attack the demons when they are so high above?" Andros questioned the general as the general rebutted.

"We wait for them to come on level ground, of course!"

Claudius searched his thoughts as all four people looked upon him for direction. "Paladins will lead the battle and behind them the army of ground knights shall back them. We are hoping

364

that the demons will come face us on this very ground we stand on. The paladins will ascend and fly above several leagues of demons, allowing the grounded knights to fight head on. General, have your mounted knights ready to ride from the right side, trampling and killing all caught between our grounded knights and paladins," Claudius ordered, as both Andros and the general seemed to approve and leave.

"This is it?" Allister questioned as he looked upon his brother.

"By all means, he is not to lay hands on this Hammer," Claudius spoke sternly as both Lunnah and Allister nodded.

The entire valley was silent as they waited anxiously for the start of the battle. "You have stood too long in the dark and have lost sight!" Claudius yelled as he gripped the hilt of his lightblade. Soonifer remained silent as his half torn black cape waved gently in the air, revealing the Blade of Life stuck in his upper back while he firmly held onto the Tongs of Death is his left hand.

"…and you paladin, have stood too long in the light and have gone blind!" Tiana shouted back and at that moment, Soonifer leaped off the massive cliff. Nox followed immediately as the

365

entire demonic army followed seconds behind. Claudius kept his eyes fixed, watching Soonifer fall, the seconds seemed like hours as he fell downwards. The Tormentor crashed into the ground like a falling star hitting the earth kicking up dirt and dust into the air.

"Steady!" Andros shouted as humanity watched the ocean of demons crash into the ground and sprint towards them. "Steady!" Andros shouted again as he held out his lightblade in the air. Allister unsheathed his lightblade while Lunnah grabbed several arrows from her quiver and readied her bow.

The demonic army with raised swords, axes and clubs drew only mere yards apart of the paladins when Andros shouted, "Now!" As the entire line of paladins ascended in unison, a flash of bright blue illuminated the battlefield. They leaped into the air with a single beat of their wings and crashed down upon the demons like a giant ocean wave crashing against sand. Instantly sounds of metal, screams and demonic yells filled the air. Lunnah and her two companions ran to the right to help as she unleashed a barrage of arrows while Oakheart whipped its branches at the demons. Rockstead raised its huge stone arms and proceeded to smash any and every unfortunate demon that faced it. Allister ran to the left joining the fray of ground knights.

Soonifer

Soonifer charged Claudius, holding his right arm extended, a spear appeared in his grasp. He hurled the spear at the paladin who summoned Zeraph's tower shield. The spear slammed into the shield as faint ancient symbols glowed where the spear struck the shield. When he and the paladin were only an arm's distance apart, Soonifer summoned Zary's crescent blade and raised it up for a strike. Claudius hid behind the shield and used his entire strength to block the attack. Soonifer slashed the crescent blade at the shield causing faint symbols to glow on the face of the shield. Soonifer spun rapidly, striking the shield with such a fast tempo the entire shield started to glow. Claudius shoved the shield into Soonifer, knocking him off balance and stumbling backwards. Light flashed in Claudius' right hand as Hysolin's bow appeared in his grasp; he plucked the bow swiftly sending a barrage of light arrows flying towards the Tormentor. Soonifer spawned Ker'es' dagger in his right hand as he proceeded to block the attack, slamming the dagger's tip into the arrowheads of each light arrow, ricocheting them from their projected path. Soonifer slid backwards from the sheer force of hundreds of light arrows which flew in all directions after ricocheting.

Claudius summoned Porth's mace and smashed it against several heads of demons who interrupted the fight. Soonifer was about to charge Claudius once again but stopped as he heard a thunderous noise coming from his left. He turned his head to see legions upon legions of knights on horseback stampeding right towards him. The legions of knights swung their swords at demons, their horses trampling the bodies of countless demons. Just as they were about to trample the Tormentor, he swung the Tongs at the stream of knights, sending them airborne as horses crushed both demons and humans alike.

"Left!" a knight ordered the entire stream of knights who all turned a sharp left, avoiding the Tormentor.

The demons were slowly winning by sheer numbers. Scores of demons would be slain only to be replaced a moment after. The ocean of demons falling from the massive cliff never seemed to stop. Andros witnessed this as their numbers started to dwindle, he knew that the rifts had to be closed. Andros threw his hand in the air as light glowed brightly in his hand; seconds later, his griffon flew to him. The griffon was flying low to the ground, knocking demons to the ground. Andros leaped onto his griffon and shouted, "Fly!" while pointing to the cliffs. The griffon heeded his command with a loud squawk as it beat its wings heavily, ascending to the skies. Several arrows shot past the griffon, narrowly escaping injury. Andros leaped off his griffon; landing on the plateau, he began swinging his lightblade wildly, killing all demons in his path as he sprinted towards a giant purple rift. He slammed the lightblade into the torso of a rift guardian who released its grasp on the portal, falling to the ground. He leaped at the other rift guardian with his sword high in the air. The rift guardian pulled out its own sword and held it sideways with one claw on the blade, blocking the attack. Andros hit the sword repeatedly before swinging his sword sideways, cutting both of the rift guardians' hands in a single motion. The rift guardian let out a demonic howl as the purple rift started to close. A giant demon standing twice the length of a human exited the portal and slammed into the paladin, knocking him off the cliff. The light in Andros' eyes exploded into bright blue as he ascended. He flew back up onto the cliff, slamming his sword into the torso of the giant demon before hurling the corpse of that demon off the ledge.

Nox swung his massive claws at the attacking knights. His claws would shred the metal plates of the knights like butter as chunks of metal and flesh flew into the air. Nox leaped into a group of knights, trampling a few on impact before he swung his muscular arms, sending knights airborne or tumbling backwards. Soonifer caught eyes on Claudius in the battlefield, seeing the Hammer of Creation dangle from his belt drove him into madness as he charged the paladin with the Tongs of Death raised in his left hand. Claudius swung Kionta's halberd in several directions, cutting scores of demons around him into shreds. He saw a glimpse of glowing red eyes from the corner of his eye; turning around he spawned Zeraph's shield just as Soonifer swung the Tongs at him. The Tongs slammed into the shield causing the entire shield to light up in glowing symbols. Soonifer slammed the Tongs at the shield again, hoping for it to break, as Claudius could do nothing except block the attack. Allister saw that his brother needed help and ascended, flying across the battlefield while extending his right hand out, holding his lightblade.

Just as Soonifer raised his Tongs for another attack, he felt a sharp, burning pain coming from his chest. He looked down to see the tip of the lightblade protruding from his chest. His red glowing eyes grew brighter as he exploded in anger. Instead of swinging the Tongs downward he swung the Tongs sideways in a complete 180 degree motion, slamming the Tongs into the chest of Allister.

Claudius peeked out from behind his shield to witness the action. A shadowy silhouette flew out of Allister's body as he collapsed to the ground lifeless.

"No!" Claudius shouted as the tower shield disappeared. He spawned Porth's mace and swung it at the Tormentor, the mace colliding with Soonifer's head with a loud crack sending the Tormentor stumbling backwards. Claudius ascended in mid-leap towards Soonifer, swinging his mace as the mace head smashed into the jaw of the Tormentor. Several teeth along with blood flew into the air as Claudius leaped again, swinging relentlessly. Soonifer's vision became blurred from the first impact as he tried swinging the Tongs at Claudius. The enraged paladin dodged the physical blow of the Tongs but was sent tumbling backwards from the force.

***

"You cannot interfere! Let the mortals fight, they will prevail!" Porth called out as he eyed both Kionta and Hysolin.

"I will not sit idle and watch my people die!" Kionta shouted as she disappeared. Porth turned to Hysolin.

"And you?" he questioned.

"What kind of father would let his own son die?" Hysolin spoke sternly as he too disappeared.

"You fools," Porth whispered.

***

A giant streak of lighting hit the ground, sending several groups of demons airborne as Kionta appeared. The hundreds of demons that surrounded her struggled to stand, the sheer intensity of her divine presence causing their legs to buckle. She spawned her halberd and with a single swing, scores of demons were sliced into threes, their black blood flying into the air.

"Incoming!" a paladin shouted as a giant volley of black demonic arrows flew towards him. Hundreds of knights raised their shields towards the sky as thousands of volunteer fighters raised their hands in front of their faces, having no shield to protect from the attack. A giant flash of lightning struck the ground as Hysolin appeared in front of the crowd. The divine clenched his right hand into a fist as a bright light emitted from his grasp. The light was so bright that the knights and fighters alike looked away. Hysolin hurled the light from his hand towards the enormous volley of arrows. The wave of light knocked or snapped all of the incoming arrows, raining the broken pieces down from the sky. The knights and fighters looked onward with mouths open in awe to what had just transpired. Hysolin spawned his bow and began plucking furiously releasing thousands of light arrows which pierced scores of demons, killing them instantly. The humans and elves cheered and fought with increased vigor, seeing a divine had come to their aid. Hysolin caught sight of Claudius and flew to him immediately.

Claudius landed on his feet as he spawned Hysolin's bow which he plucked the bowstring of, sending a steam of light arrows towards the Tormentor. Soonifer spawned Ker'es' dagger in his right hand and tried his best to deflect the arrows. His blurred vision caused him to miss several arrows which slammed into his chest, shoulder and stomach. Hysolin appeared at Claudius' side, pointed his bow at Soonifer, and began firing a hail of light arrows. Claudius turned his head to the divine and widened his eyes in shock.

"Why are you here?" Claudius questioned. Hysolin ignored Claudius as he continued the barrage of light arrows. Soonifer had no choice but to drop the Tongs of Death and summon Ker'es' other dagger to deflect the hundreds of incoming arrows. Between the blurred vision and increased arrows, he could not deflect them all as more and more arrows slammed into his body. Suddenly, the ground to his left opened up as a purple rift appeared to his right. Ker'es slammed into Soonifer, causing him to fall into the ground rift. Soonifer's anger soared inside of him as he descended into the darkness. He grabbed the necks of the light arrows and ripped them out of his body.

Ker'es deflected the stream of light arrows with ease and perfect precision, his hollow black eyes staring at the two. Ker'es could see Kionta sprinting towards him and he knew he could not take all three in a fair fight. In between blocking the arrows, Ker'es slashed the air, creating a black rift which he leaped inside of. Kionta leaped inside the rift after Ker'es as Hysolin sprinted into the rift after her.

Hysolin

The two divines found themselves surrounded by darkness, only a small amount of light emitted from their glowing bodies. Hysolin clenched his right fist as a large amount of light emitted from his fist. He threw the light at the ground where they stood and a giant flash of light exploded, illuminating their vision of the place temporarily. At that moment, millions of demons covered their eyeless faces and turned their heads from the two divines. Hysolin caught sight of a single demon who stood still, not

374

facing away from the light. Ker'es stared at the two divines while slowly stepping backwards behind several demons, slipping away from their sight. The light began to slowly recede as darkness itself rushed towards the divines, the millions of demons started to turn their heads back at the two. Kionta readied her halberd, narrowing her eyes.

"All of you come at me at once, it won't be fair otherwise!" Hysolin yelled as he lifted his bow in front of him.

Claudius

Claudius spawned his mace, reared back his right hand and brought down the full force of the blow on the head of a demon. He swung the mace sideways, cracking the skull of another demon. He clenched his teeth while scanning the battlefield quickly to find Soonifer. He looked on until he saw a pile of dead humans with a rift closing behind them, and could see only one person standing in the middle of it. That person turned around and the fiery red glowing eyes was a dead give-a-way. Claudius spawned Kionta's halberd, and raising the head to the sky, he sprinted at full speed towards the Tormentor. Soonifer spawned Gor'eck's infernal hammer and charged towards the incoming paladin in a head-to-head fight. Claudius quickly swung his halberd at the Tormentor;

Soonifer willingly decided to accept the blow as he swung the hammer at the paladin. Two deep cuts appeared on Soonifer's chest while thick black blood poured from his wound as Claudius tumbled backwards from the blow of the hammer. When Claudius stopped tumbling he felt the entire right side of his ribs were broken, then he looked at his dented armor to see what other wounds he sustained. When he looked up he saw Soonifer's palm and within the palm was a black eye staring back at him. Claudius instantly felt his arms were so heavy he could not lift them, as though time itself seemed to have stopped. He noticed that Soonifer was no longer standing in front of him but instead there stood a cloaked figure. The cloaked figure walked slowly towards Claudius, stepping over bodies and walking through people unobstructed. Claudius tried to yell and even ascend but for some reason he could not and all he could do was watch this figure walk closer to him. The figure was only inches away before it disappeared and Soonifer reappeared back in front of him with an arrow sticking in his palm. Soonifer looked up to see Lunnah readying another arrow to fire at him. He spawned a spear, striking the ground and which opened up as he hurled himself into the abyss. Claudius ascended as he leaped towards Soonifer but the ground had already closed up. He turned his head to where Soonifer was looking and saw Lunnah.

"Lunnah!" he shouted as he beat his wings, trying to get to her. Lunnah felt the ground under her shake as she leaped backwards.

"Rockstead!" she shouted as the giant stone golem raised its massive stone arms into the air. Soonifer burst through the ground, swinging his crescent blade upward but was met with Rockstead's fists, causing him to be knocked back down into the abyss.

Claudius saw the Tormentor burst through the ground again, this time he sliced a knight in half as blood painted the sky. Claudius' eyes turned bright blue as giant wings appeared behind. He sprinted towards the Tormentor and slammed Porth's mace into the infernal demon's chest. Soonifer tumbled backwards from the force as he spewed up black blood from his mouth. Claudius grabbed the lip of Soonifer's chest plate, picking him up and with all of his force, punched the Tormentor square in his jaw, knocking him backwards yet again. Soonifer's back slammed into the wall of the cliff as he tried to recover from the relentless blows. His right hand exploded with purple fire as he tried to spawn any weapon but

Claudius shoved the entire length of his lightblade into the torso of Soonifer, pinning him to the wall. Soonifer leaned forward while he could barely stand up; his entire body was limp and weak. Claudius scanned the battlefield as both humans and demons alike were sparce, the entire landscape filled with corpses.

Soonifer

Soonifer grabbed the hilt of the lightblade that scorched his hand as if he was holding hot lava. Jets of steam was seething from his hand as he used all of his strength to slowly pull out the sword inch by inch. The Tormentor opened his mouth to yell from the pain but only blood and a distorted demonic gurgle came out. Suddenly, two flashes of light appeared in the sky and headed towards Soonifer like a comet. Soonifer released his grip on the hilt and spawned a spear in his grasp, hurling it at one of the bright lights. The light exploded, illuminating the sky while the other kept flying towards the Tormentor. Soonifer spawned another spear and tried to throw it but the light smashed into Soonifer, pushing the lightblade back into him. Soonifer dropped the spear which hit the ground with a thud, his head slammed back against the rock wall and his head drooped forward. He coughed up thick black blood once again as the burning sensation from the lightblade intensified his pain. When he finally looked up, his red glowing eyes widened to the sight.

Her blonde, golden hair fell from her head with the ends slightly curled and her ocean blue eyes stared forward. *How could I ever forget those eyes?* He thought as he tried his best to speak but the only word he could utter was "Alorah" in a half demonic, half distorted voice. She faintly smiled and she nodded her head. Tears of blood ran down his cheeks, as he could not do anything except stare at her.

"Come with me," Alorah whispered as he nodded his head up and down slowly. She gently pulled at his hand and he looked down to see a ghost-like image of his hand being pulled from his body. Just as his entire hand was out of his body, something deep inside of him made him shout in a horrific demonic tone, "No!" Using his left hand to push her aside, his right hand engulfs in purple flame and spawned another spear, hurling it straight.

Claudius

"Claudius!" Lunnah cried as she ran towards him. Claudius turned his head, hearing her voice as he heard a loud snap. He looked down and could see a giant spear protruding from his torso. Light poured profusely from the wound. "Claudius!"

Lunnah screamed as she saw the spear pierce through Claudius' body. Tears streamed from her face as she could see cracks of light surrounding Claudius' eyes.

"Lunnah, my moon. I love you," Claudius sputtered, the light escaping from his eyes as his ascended form faded. Lunnah caught his body and slowly laid him on the ground.

"No….No…please…. this can't be happening…" she softly whispered as she lowered her head with her teardrops hitting Claudius' face.

Soonifer

He felt his body slip from existence as he slid downwards into an endless black abyss. Before falling into complete blackness, he stopped, feeling his heart being pulled from his body which shot pain throughout his entire body. He looked down and could see nothing except darkness and a thin silver chain that seemed to come from his heart leading up. He looked upward to see his physical body still pinned to the wall of the cliff and that is where the chain ended. The chain length seemed to stretch for miles as he dangled from one end.

Chapter 31

A paladin walking in the hallway heard a very faint knock. He stopped in mid-walk and listened intently to see where it had come from. No noise came as he continued his walk but he heard the soft knock again, walked towards the paladin academy's wooden door, and opened it to find a young elven girl standing in front of him.

"Yes?" he questioned looking at the girl.

"Is this where people go to become paladins?" she asked in a very soft and shy voice.

"Indeed, why do you ask?" the paladin asked.

"I wish to become one," she whispered while looking at the paladin.

"Oh, you are far too young!" the paladin spoke while letting out a gentle laugh.

"Please? My friend died and I want to make a difference like him," she whispered again as tears started to fill her eyes.

"Oh, don't cry, please come in and tell me," the paladin spoke as he opened the door wider for her to come in.

Hallowmis

He kept his head facing down near the ground, hearing voiceless whispers that would taunt him until he heard a voice with words. "Look up," the voice whispered as he kept his head down and tears ran down his cheek from the pain of his right knee. Rubbing his forehead into the ground, he wished for everything to vanish and for him to be back at Solbris. "Look up," the voice spoke again. As he had nothing else to lose, he looked up to see two hollow black eyes looking upon him. An icy cold chill ran down his spine as he stared into those eyes. "How would you like to become more powerful than you can fathom?" the voice spoke as he nodded his head up and down furiously. "Follow." The voice ordered as he could do nothing except follow this demon. It felt like he had crawled for miles, his energy drained but he still crawled onward. The demon stopped at the edge of a pool. Hallowmis drew near the pool, grabbing the edges of it and pulled himself towards it, looking down, his eyes widened at the sight.

Cathevne

She opened the wooden door as the sun's bright rays shone upon her. She raised her left hand over her eyes to block the sunlight while walking forward. She could see a griffon laying in front of a statue. She knelt down and slowly stroked Surina's head. Surina kept her head down, her eyes glued upon the statue. Cathevne looked up at the statue of Lance, who instead of holding a Warhammer or tankard was holding a griffon chick in front of him with both hands. She revealed a soft smile and looked back at Surina. "You know...he loved you from the moment he picked you up," Cathevne spoke as a tear started to trail from her right eye.

The end

Made in the USA
Monee, IL
31 January 2023

26774065R00225